Mama's Boys

a novel

JEFF GEIGER JR.

Jan-Carol
Publishing, Inc
"every story needs a book"

Mama's Boys
Jeff Geiger Jr.
Published April 2023
Little Creek Books
Imprint of Jan-Carol Publishing, Inc.
All rights reserved
Copyright © 2023 Jeff Geiger Jr.

ISBN: 978-1-954978-85-0
Library of Congress Control Number: 2023936322

You may contact the publisher:
Jan-Carol Publishing, Inc.
PO Box 701
Johnson City, TN 37605
publisher@jancarolpublishing.com
www.jancarolpublishing.com

For Grayson

Author's Note

I remember the day the idea for this story hit me. I was finishing up a job at work when the antagonist and a few other characters popped into my mind. I'm not sure how or why those characters came to me when they did, but I knew I needed to keep thinking of ideas for this new story, since my debut novel, *The White Room*, was scheduled to release that December. What I had was the idea for an antagonist, mostly. The plot wasn't completely there, but enough of it was for me to begin.

At first, I had planned on *Mama's Boys* being a short story, but as I began to write I quickly realized that wouldn't be the case; there was simply too much story to tell with this one. Around halfway into writing *Mama's Boys*, I knew two things: I really liked where the story was going, and that I had absolutely no idea how it would end, which is how this writer likes it. If I don't know how it'll end, the reader probably won't know either, right?

When I finally did reach the end of the story, the ending nearly fell into my lap. I saw it all laid out in front of me, sitting there as if it were waiting to be discovered. Writers love when that happens, because the alternative is ruminating on it until that light bulb in your head flicks on with the right ending. And believe me, sometimes that can take a while.

The fictional town in this story is something else I wanted to touch on; it's based on the town I live in, but in this story, I call it Abbott for a reason. If you look up the history of Zephyrhills, you'll learn that over a hundred years ago the town used to be known as Abbott Station. Some of the places in the story do exist in the town and some do not. Hole in the Woods *is* one of those places; however, we had a different name for those woods when I was younger.

I suppose the only other thing I'd like to tell you, reader, before you begin to read this book, is this: Thank you for being here.

– Jeff Geiger Jr.

Chapter 1

Barry Kendall was seventeen years old in the summer of 2006 when his dad, Carl Kendall, paid him fifty dollars to help clean out one of his rental properties on Spring Street. It sounded like easy money to Barry at the time, who had just bought his first car and needed gas money. *How bad could it be*, he thought.

He sat in the passenger seat of his dad's Silverado. Behind them, connected to the truck, was a single-axle trailer. A few garbage cans lay in it for any trash the tenant had left behind; there was always some trash and a few holes in the walls to patch.

As Carl pulled into the single-wide trailer's driveway, Barry's eyes widened with the realization that this job wasn't anything like he expected it to be. He looked around at the waist-high grass as they drove through it. The yard needed mowed desperately, but before anyone could do that, the acre of trash and random junk would need to be picked up first.

"Cripes, Dad, what happened to this place?" Barry asked.

Carl put the truck in park and shut it off. "The lady just took off. It happens." He sighed.

"Let's just hope the inside doesn't look as bad as the outside."

Carl lifted the front door key from the truck's cupholder and slid out of the driver's seat.

When he opened the front door, a pungent odor of something dead permeated out and into their nostrils.

"Oh, just lovely!" Carl said with a grimace of disgust.

"What is that?" Barry asked.

Carl let out a heavy sigh. "I don't know, Barry. My hope is that it's just rotten food."

They walked in, each of them pinching their noses with their thumb and forefinger. They saw lots and lots of garbage. It was as if the woman had hoarded pizza boxes and two-liter soda bottles as a hobby.

"Dad, I don't know if—"

"You already agreed to help," Carl said. "I'll open all the windows. You grab one of those trash cans. It's looking like it's going to take more trips to the dump than I had thought."

Barry went outside and grabbed some gloves out of the truck before reaching in the single-axle trailer for a garbage can. From everything he saw inside of the single-wide, he would undoubtedly need the gloves.

He began placing pizza boxes and obvious trash in the garbage can, filling it up and putting the can back in the bed of the pick-up truck. He grabbed another one after that one was full, then another. He was glad that the electric was still on because the Florida heat in the middle of summer would be absolute hell without a little central heat and air to cool the place down.

After every garbage can was full, Carl and Barry removed the furniture and loaded it in the single-axle trailer. After loading the couch and end tables in the trailer, they started to lift the woman's dresser. When they did, they found the reason for the dead smell.

"You've got to be kidding me," Barry said, turning his face away from the dead kitten.

"Go on, Barry," his dad said, "I'll get this cat out of here. You go see if you can get that mattress out of the spare bedroom."

Barry walked to the other side of the trailer, listening as the floor creaked beneath him, wishing he were with his girlfriend instead of cleaning out this smelly single-wide. When he reached the spare room, several rats scattered and hid underneath a few piles of clothes next to the mattress.

"How long has this lady been gone?" he said to himself. "How did she live like this?"

He gripped the mattress with his gloved hands and pulled it out of the room as quick as he could. As he was loading it in the trailer, his dad came out of the single-wide holding a cardboard box full of books. Barry saw the one on top and said, "Wait, don't throw those away."

"Why not? Do you want to donate them or something?"

The book on top was *Harry Potter and the Half-Blood Prince*. Barry's girlfriend, Holly Chandler, loved the series.

"We can donate the others, but I want to give that one to Holly," Barry said, grabbing the book.

He held it out in front of him and examined the book's dust jacket. Not a crease or rip to be found. If the lady read it, she must've taken the dust jacket off and placed it somewhere for safe keeping.

Carl smiled. "Smitten with that girl, aren't you?"

Barry blushed. "I just know she likes this series. She's into witches and things like that."

"Okay, well, put that in the front seat. We need to load a few more pieces of furniture in the trailer."

Barry placed the book in the passenger seat and went back inside of the single-wide.

After loading a TV stand and another mattress, the little trailer was as full as it was going to get.

While Carl was strapping the trailer down, he threw a set of keys to Barry.

"What do these go to?" Barry asked.

"They're to the shed out back. Go take a peek inside while I'm strapping all this down.

I'm scared to even look. Just let me know how much junk is in there," his dad said.

Barry ambled around the single-wide and up to the shed, hoping like hell it wasn't packed full of miscellaneous junk. The shed was mid-sized. Its gray paint was faded from years of sun exposure. The roof appeared to have several rust spots in the metal, but none of the spots were rusted all the way through yet. He stuck the key in the lock and twisted it. At first, the door wouldn't open. He wiggled the handle while pushing on the door with his shoulder. It took a few tries before it finally swung inward on its unoiled hinges. He discovered that it wasn't nearly as bad as the single-wide trailer, as far as trash goes. Spider webs covered milk crates with records by Elvis, KISS, and Jethro Tull. Then, to his right, on a metal table was perhaps a dozen candles next to a dozen hardcover books. He saw some that he had never seen before, with authors he had never heard of, but one in particular stood out from the others. It lay there, leather bound, secured with a strap and lock. There were boxes, tools, and other items scattered around the shed, but the one thing Barry couldn't help but see was that leather bound book with the little silver lock.

Barry stepped into the shed. His eyes fixated on the book. He stood just inches away from the metal table now, not remembering the steps he took as he walked up to it. There were no lights in the shed, however there was just enough light to make out one word engraved above a star with a circle around it: *witchcraft.*

"Whoa," Barry said as a thought flared in his mind.

Holly would love this.

"Come on, Barry, we have plenty more to do today!" his dad shouted from the front yard.

Barry lifted the book and stuck it under his arm. After he closed the door to the shed, he jogged over to the front yard. His dad was sitting in the driver's seat of the Silverado, motioning him to hurry up. Barry slid in next to his dad, the book still under the meat of his arm and rib cage.

"How bad is it?" his dad asked.

"Not too bad, if you're comparing it to what's in the trailer."

"This lady is going to cost me a fortune in dump fees," his dad said, then eyed the book between Barry's arm and rib cage. "What do you have there?"

4

"Another book for Holly."

Carl Kendall grinned and put the truck in drive. "I guess we better get a move on. I'm sure you want to spend time with her later."

Barry's complexion reddened. "Yeah, I'd like to. What time do you think we'll be done?"

"Maybe two or three o' clock. Let's get one more load today. We'll get some more tomorrow after you get out of school."

Carl and Barry came back and mostly focused on getting everything out of the trailer. Holes would need patched, walls would need repainted, and Carl knew the shed could wait until last, since the house would need many more repairs. After a solid hour and a half, Carl and Barry were drenched in sweat, but they were also done for the day.

Once home, Barry picked up the two books he kept for Holly and went inside. He tossed the books on the edge of his bed and texted Holly to meet him at *their spot* in Hole in the Woods. The place they first met a year ago at a bonfire.

A year ago, at the bonfire, Barry was with his group of friends and Holly was with hers. They were all sitting around a small fire and Barry kept looking over at her every so often, trying to build up the courage to start a conversation. Her natural beauty made him nervous. More nervous than he had ever been with a girl.

"Dude, just go talk to her," Eddie, his best friend, had told him.

"I can't," Barry said. "I'll make a fool of myself."

Eddie grinned and placed a hand on Barry's shoulder. "Only one way to find out."

Barry watched with wide eyes as Eddie walked around the fire to talk to Holly. He saw his friend point in his direction, and that was when Holly's eyes and Barry's met for the very first time. The rest, as they say, is history.

After Barry finished showering, he made his way to the edge of the bed, where the books were, and checked his cell phone. He had one unread message from Holly, saying that she'd be there. Barry got dressed, snagged the books up, and texted her that he was on his way.

Abbott was still somewhat of a small town in 2006; it was growing, like everywhere else in the world, but still rather small compared to cities like Tampa or Orlando. Being thirty or so miles north of Tampa, the little town had a few places in it that remained undeveloped and surrounded by woods. One of these areas, perhaps the most well-known, the locals called Hole in the Woods.

Barry piloted his scratched-up Toyota Celica around the curve that led to the entrance of Hole in the Woods. The entrance was narrow and easy to miss if you weren't looking for it, but Barry and many other high-school kids had the narrow opening memorized.

At the apex of the curve, Barry slowed and turned off the hard road. To his right was a narrow dirt path leading into the woods. Thin branches screeched on either side of the car as he went through the opening. They were the same thin branches that had been scratching the sides of teenagers' cars for years and years. He traveled roughly two hundred yards until he reached the big oak tree next to the small lake that Barry and Holly called *their spot*.

Holly was his first real love. She was the first girl he'd made love with, the first girl he felt he couldn't live without, and he was dead set on marrying her one day. He had already begun saving money for a ring in an old shoebox he kept hidden in his closet.

Barry felt his phone vibrate as he drove down the dirt road. He took it out of the cupholder and raised it up, seeing that Holly had texted him:

I'm here.

He didn't need the text to know that, though, because he could see her standing next to her car by the big oak tree; the one he had carved his and her initials in with a Case pocketknife that Holly had given him as a birthday present.

Barry pulled his Toyota in next to Holly's car and turned the engine off. He got out, almost forgetting the books he wanted to give her, and walked over to where she was standing.

"Hey, Hols," Barry said, holding the books behind his back.

"For what do I owe the pleasure, Mr. Kendall?" Holly said, dropping him a wink.

"I come bearing gifts, Mrs. Chandler."

"Okay, ha-ha, now give up the goods," Holly said, reaching behind Barry.

"Wait just a second now," Barry said, backing away. "Kiss first, gifts second."

Barry leaned in for a kiss, the books still concealed behind him, and Holly leaned in too.

Although, when Barry closed his eyes, Holly shot around and grabbed the books.

"Wow, where did you get these from?" she asked, observing the covers.

"Top secret. Also, that was a dirty trick, Hols."

"You're so cute when you're indignant."

"I'm not indignant. I just wanted to surprise you."

"Well, I am surprised. Except, I have already read the *Harry Potter* book. I got it as soon as it hit the shelves."

"Darn. I thought you still needed that one."

"It's okay. It's the thought that counts, right? That's the phrase, I think, anyway."

"What about the other one?"

Holly ran her hand over the black leather cover of the book on witchcraft. "This one I definitely don't have. It feels so old and the leather is incredible, like it was handmade or something." Holly's eyes hovered over the lock. "Do you have the key to open it?"

Barry didn't have the key, but he had a way to open it.

He dug his Case pocketknife out of his front pocket and rested its blade against the leather strap. As he began to apply pressure, Holly jerked the book away from him.

"No! What are you doing?"

"I was trying to open it—"

"Well, how about we try picking the lock first instead of damaging the book?" Holly said, removing a bobby pin from her hair.

She stuck the bobby pin inside of the lock, twisting and turning it. After fifteen or twenty seconds, Barry said, "Are you sure you don't want me to—"

The lock made a *click* sound as the bobby pin hit the right spot. The u-shaped shackle popped up and, for a few seconds, Holly and Barry just stood there looking at the book.

"I can't believe that worked," Barry said.

She gave Barry a smile that made his entire body go warm. "Let's see what it says."

She removed the lock and gave it to Barry, then flipped the book open to the first page and read aloud, "Elaine Henley, the mother of three."

"Spooky," Barry said with a grin.

Holly flipped through the book, riffling the pages. "Looks like a lot of old incantations.

Where did you find this?"

"Believe it or not, in a shed behind one of my dad's rentals."

"The tenant must have been practicing witchcraft. Or maybe he or she just thought the book was cool."

"I don't know, but she definitely wasn't reading any *Good Housekeeping* magazines."

"Why do you say that?"

"The house was just a mess, is all."

"Yikes. Well, at least it wasn't all bad. This book is pretty interesting," Holly said, moving closer to Barry.

Barry knew what was coming. He could see it in those big hazel eyes. When her lips touched his, he wrapped his arms around her, holding her there close to him. To Barry, the feeling he felt right at that very second was worth cleaning that messy trailer out a hundred more times, if that's what it took to kiss Holly all over again. He was in a state of bliss, a state that only she—his teenage mind thought—was capable of putting him in.

While kissing, Holly dropped the book and it landed in the dirt next to her feet. The book opened to a page with several symbols and some words written in both English and Latin. Holly lifted it up and read the words above the Latin that were handwritten in English.

"Elaine, the mother of three," Holly said. Then, she began to read the Latin as best she could. None of the words made much sense to either of them, but as soon as she finished reading them aloud, the book flew out of her hands, landing next to the oak tree with their initials carved in it.

Holly and Barry exchanged a look, then rested their eyes on the book still lying on the ground. Even though it flew out of her hands, flipping in the air, it remained opened on the exact same page Holly had been reading.

"How did that happen?" Barry asked, his eyes wide and scared.

"I don't know," she said, placing a shaking hand over her mouth. "It just did it on its own."

"Maybe we should just get rid of it. I'll throw it in the lake."

Holly looked back at Barry, nodding in assent.

Barry took a few steps toward the book. As he bent down to pick it up, a brilliant white light shot out of its pages, knocking him over. In his disoriented state, he couldn't even see his hands in front of him. He could hear, though. And what he heard was Holly screaming at the top of her lungs. At first, he thought she was screaming because she was worried about him. He told her over and over again that he was okay, but she continued to scream.

He rubbed his eyes, hoping his vision would come back. It did, a little, but he still couldn't see why she was screaming.

"It's coming out of the lake, Barry. We have to go now!"

"What's coming out of the—"

"Let's go!" she yelled, grabbing Barry, shuffling over to her car. As she turned to open the car door, a hand grabbed her by her hair. She fell to the ground and Barry fell right next to her. His vision was becoming clearer. He saw Holly being dragged across the ground by a woman with long white hair. A pale woman that was barefooted, drenched in water, in a long dark-colored dress. Her hair hung in her face. Barry thought for a second that the lady might be homeless, but that second passed as soon as he met her misty gray eyes. They were the eyes of something else; something that couldn't possibly be human. When he saw Holly being dragged away, he jolted after her. He grabbed Holly by the hand, pulling her with all the strength he had, and then the lady with the long white hair said something he didn't quite understand. Even if he hadn't been disoriented, the words wouldn't have made any sense to him. Then something else happened that didn't make sense to him; his vision worsened, and he felt the strength leave his body. He felt Holly's hand slip from his, and he heard the water as she went under. And then . . . he heard nothing.

* * *

On that summer day in 2006, Barry told the police what he saw. They, of course, didn't believe him, and at first, they thought he might have been the one who murdered Holly Chandler; the victim's boyfriend or girlfriend is almost always the first person they suspect, but after being questioned for hours, the significant lack of evidence and the fact that Barry had told them the same story over and over for hours led to the police deducing that he couldn't have done it. Barry had always been a good kid, conscientious, always wishing to do what was right. In the end, the local police convinced Barry that what he saw wasn't what it had seemed. They told him it was the shock of tragedy working its wonder, as it so often does. As if a witch from a book drowning his girlfriend in a lake would be easier for him to cope with than some random person killing his high-school sweetheart in front of him.

A major flaw in Barry's story for the police was the book: they never found a book out there. They even checked the lake, sending half a dozen divers down to search for Holly's body. They couldn't find anything.

No book, no body, no evidence that anyone had taken her. Not a single strand of hair. Just her car sitting next to the oak tree by Barry's Toyota.

After the police had pretty much given up on the case, Barry spent years thinking about it, seeing therapists, going out to Hole in the Woods, just to find himself leaning against the same tree that their initials were carved in, staring off at the lake. As time went on, Barry guessed that maybe he did imagine the whole thing about the book and the witch. That the incident was so tragic that his over-stressed brain just made up some loopy story, but deep down, Barry knew what he saw. He saw the book fly out of Holly's hands as she read the handwritten text aloud, knowing that the book he had given her as a gift ultimately ended her life. Eventually, he turned to alcohol to make the thoughts go away, to mitigate the pain, but he knew by the morning it would be back. It always came back.

After high school was over, Barry worked with Eddie at Gene's Tire, the local tire shop on Abbott's Main Street. Eddie had an aptitude for the job; he caught on quick. However, tires didn't interest Barry in the slightest. Barry wanted to make a difference in the world. He wanted to keep good people safe from terrible people. He wanted to protect those who couldn't protect themselves. He wanted to atone for the one thing he could never forgive himself for: Holly's death.

Chapter 2

Thirteen years had passed since that horrid day all those years ago in Hole in the Woods. Barry still thought about Holly from time to time, but not as much as he used to. He kept his mind busy, immersing himself in each case he worked as a detective for the Abbott Police Department. He enjoyed being a police officer, but when the detective position came up a year ago, Barry didn't hesitate to apply. Part of him only wanted to solve crimes and get the truth out of people; the other part, the part that kept him awake some nights, wanted to know what happened to the witch who killed Holly. None of it made any sense to him, even now after so many years.

The night's shift had just ended, and Barry opened the front door to his home on the south side of Abbott. He lived alone in a red brick house on approximately two and a half acres. After he took his shoes off at the door, he walked into the kitchen and grabbed a glass out of the cabinet, filling it with four ice cubes before pouring in the whiskey. The smell of the alcohol was one he was familiar with, a scent he often craved, and his nightly routine before bed.

Barry heard his cell phone ring. It was his dad.

Barry leaned against the countertop, putting the phone to his ear. "What's up, Dad?"

"How was work?" Carl Kendall asked.

"Eh, you know. Same shit, different day."

"Well, listen. Your mom is still feeling weak from chemo, but she told me to tell you that she'd like to see you this weekend. Maybe get some lunch or dinner."

"I work . . . but I'll be there. I should be able to get away for an hour or two. Can I talk to her?"

"She's asleep. Resting after everything she's been through today."

"Okay. Tell her I love her when she wakes up."

"Of course . . . take care of yourself, Barry."

"I will."

"I mean it."

Barry ended the call, staring at the glass of whiskey in his other hand. He thought of his mom getting thinner as each month went by. He thought about the new case he was working. A single, middle-aged woman went missing a couple days ago, a lady named Nancy McIntyre.

Just like Holly's death, they couldn't find any evidence whatsoever. And then that made him think of Holly as she went under the water. As the thought entered his mind, he raised the glass to his mouth and drank. He downed the entire glass, relishing the burning sensation inside of him that he had grown so accustomed to. Then, he set the glass down and poured himself another drink. This one he sipped.

He began to feel the effect of the alcohol as the night went on. Feeling warm and able to think more pleasant thoughts than he had earlier, he stumbled to his bedroom. Right before he fell asleep, which didn't take long, he glanced at his phone. The screen displayed a picture of him and his mom from a year ago, right before she was diagnosed with stage two lung cancer.

He looked at the time, checked to make sure he set his alarm, and thought about how his mom had never smoked a day in her life.

Life isn't fair—but hell, Barry knew that. Actually, he knew it better than most.

* * *

A few minutes after four in the morning, Barry's cell phone began to ring. He snapped awake at the sound and looked at the screen. It was Rick Donaldson, his sergeant.

"Sarge?" Barry answered.

"Barry, can you come down to the station? We found something that might lead us to the lady that went missing two days ago."

"Seriously? What'd you find?"

"Come down here and I'll fill you in. We need to work fast."

"Why do you say that?"

"We have another missing person, Barry. As of about an hour ago. It's worse this time, though."

"How's it worse?" Barry asked, sitting up in his bed now.

"It's a boy. A twelve-year-old boy named Denny Molasky."

A deep breath on Barry's end of the line. "I'll be there in ten minutes."

Barry ended the call and rolled out of bed, throwing on his uniform as fast as he could.

He slid in behind the wheel of his police-issued black Dodge Charger and took off down the road, chirping his tires on the asphalt as he hurried to the police department.

When he walked in, he saw Donaldson waiting for him to arrive. Donaldson held a manila envelope in one hand and a cup of coffee in the other, with a look that said, *I know you're tired, but you're not alone, kid.*

"Okay, so what in the hell is going on, Sarge?" Barry asked.

Donaldson handed the manila envelope to Barry, and said, "Open it."

Barry unclasped the envelope and pulled out an 8x10 photograph of an early 2000's Chevy Suburban.

"Notice anything familiar about that vehicle?"

"This is same white Suburban the lady that went missing owns," Barry said, meeting Donaldson's eyes. "I remember seeing it in her driveway when we discovered she was missing. It even has the same Nancy's Mobile Dog Grooming decal with her phone number underneath on the back window."

"Bingo. And it was taken from a street-light camera a quarter mile from the house the boy was taken from."

"So, what are you saying? That Nancy McIntyre abducted the Molasky kid? Why would she do that?"

"That's why I called you, Barry. You're the best detective I have at this department. I need you to figure that out. Then, I need you to find the kid and bring him back here."

Barry glanced back down at the photograph. "Which intersection was this taken at?"

"Third Street and Sixth Ave."

"I'll let you know what I find out."

Barry walked out of the police department and back to his car. When he sat in the front seat, he turned the dome light on and stared at the photograph of the white Suburban again. A woman who recently went missing abducting a twelve-year-old kid in the middle of the night. It didn't sit right with Barry. Nancy had no known criminal record. No obvious motive, either. She probably knew that if you're already missing, the police wouldn't suspect you to be the one who committed the kidnapping, which would have been the case if they didn't already have photographic evidence that she did it. And why in the hell would you use your own vehicle? Criminals could be unbelievably stupid sometimes, sure, but something wasn't right here.

Barry drove to the intersection the picture was taken at and parked on the shoulder of the road. He got out and looked around, scanning the area for perhaps twenty minutes. After he found nothing more than a few empty soda bottles and a candy wrapper, he realized he wasn't going to find anything useful.

He turned the car on and saw a small piece of paper in the grass just twenty feet or so ahead of him. *Probably just more trash*, he thought as he put it in drive. He began to drive away but stopped as he came abreast of the small piece of paper. He wasn't sure why he stopped. Maybe it was instinct, maybe it was curiosity. Either way, what he read on the paper made his stomach churn.

Don't try to follow me. Soon enough, you'll end up like her.

It was handwritten—badly—but it was legible enough to read.

Barry raised the paper up to his eyes to examine it, to make sure it said what he read the first time. He cocked his head to one side as he tried to figure out if this person was referring to Holly's death. Who else would *her* be?

Barry folded the piece of paper and stuck it in his front pocket. He looked at the asphalt and imagined the white Suburban cruising on it the way he had just come. He didn't have much to go on. He looked around some more, hoping to find something that might lead him to the missing woman.

But nothing was found. Nothing but the disconcerting note.

* * *

Denny Molasky had been sitting in bed. The lights were off. He was under his covers, reading a *Goosebumps* book with a flashlight. He felt reading it that way made it spookier somehow. He got to a part in the book that really made him feel like he was right there in the story with all the characters. His eyes were glued to the page, reading the words as fast as he could. When he was near the end of the chapter, the sheet was ripped off him and a dark figure stood at the side of his bed. He dropped the book and aimed the flashlight's beam at it.

"Mom, you scared me to death," Denny said.

"Well, it's nine-thirty on a school night. It's past your bedtime," his mother said.

"I'm sorry. I was just reading and couldn't stop until I found out what happened."

"Well, you'll just have to wait until tomorrow. A boy needs his sleep."

She grabbed his book and placed it on the nightstand by his bed.

"You know, Denny," she said, "I really wish you would read something a little less scary. You'll have nightmares."

"I like those books. And it's been a long time since I had any night-mares, Mom."

"Okay. Just get some sleep, sweetie. You have school tomorrow," she said, and kissed him on his forehead.

Before she walked out of the room, Denny said, "Night, Mom."

"Night, Denny. Sweet dreams."

She closed the door. Within a few minutes, Denny Molasky fell asleep.

He didn't have any nightmares. He was telling his mom the truth about that. But hours later, he did wake up to a nightmare.

A *real* nightmare.

He woke to a tapping sound coming from the window next to his bed. He remembered his curtains being closed before he went to sleep. He remembered the window blinds being down behind them too. So, how were the curtains open? How were the blinds up now? And better yet, why was there a woman standing outside of the window? Why was she smiling at him and tapping on the glass?

He threw the covers off his body and swung his legs out of bed. The floor felt cold on his bare feet. He met the woman's eyes. They were a misty gray, and once he met her gaze, he had a hard time looking away. He noticed her hair was golden and curly. She seemed like a nice lady, but something was different about the way she looked. Something differ-ent from other people.

Her stare looked as if she wasn't all there, like she had just escaped an insane asylum. But, at the same time, she appeared to be kind and amiable. Denny was confused by her stare. He was confused why she was outside his window in the middle of the night. And he was confused as to why he was taking off his pajamas, especially when he was in front of a stranger. He was in his boxers now, and he was opening his dresser drawer. In his hands were a shirt, a pair of denim jeans, and a pair of socks. He flipped the light on. Then, without even realizing he was doing it, he put the clothes on that he grabbed out of his dresser.

He did all this as the woman watched from the window, still smiling that profoundly odd smile.

Lastly, he put on his shoes, a pair of red Converses he'd gotten for his birthday. As he tied his shoelaces, he felt her eyes on him. He felt her making him do the things he was doing. He didn't know how she was doing it. He tried to stop tying the laces. He tried as hard as he could possibly try. Whatever she was doing to him was too strong for his pliable mind. Kids were easily influenced, especially at his age.

The woman outside the window said, "Come on, child. Be the little boy I used to have. Be my middle-child. Be my William."

Denny found himself opening the window. The woman had already removed the screen. As she helped Denny out of the window, he kicked the nightstand and it fell over, smacking hard against the tile floor. In another room in the house, Denny's mom heard the loud noise. The light in her room turned on and she walked quickly down the hall to Denny's room. When she opened the door, she saw that Denny wasn't in his bed.

"Denny?" she said.

She looked around and saw that his dresser drawers had been left open. She saw the nightstand on the ground next to his *Goosebumps* book. Her eyes shifted up to the window and realized it was open. When she looked outside, she saw taillights going down the road.

Then, she screamed.

Chapter 3

Barry sat down behind the wheel of his Dodge. He knew he had to go searching for the vehicle in the photograph. It was dark. It was the middle of the night. That didn't stop him from checking nearly every cult-de-sac in town, though.

Barry was the best detective in the police department for a reason. He was thorough. And the job was his life. Other than Eddie and his parents, it was all he had.

After two and a half hours of searching for the white suburban, and coming up with nothing, he finally took a break. It was a little past seven in the morning. He hadn't slept much, and he sure as hell knew it. He had trouble keeping his eyes open as he walked in through the front door of the police department. He asked one of the police officers where Donaldson was, and they told him that his sergeant had gone home to get some rest.

Barry thought that was a good idea. He could use a good eight hours of sleep too. Hell, even five or six would do. He sat once more in the front seat of his car, blinking slowly, just wanting to go home and close his eyes for a while. He pulled out of the police department's parking lot and headed to his house. Halfway there, he came upon a stop sign. He looked to the left, to ascertain that no one was coming. When he checked his right, he did a double take. His eyes narrowed on what he saw parked next to an old, abandoned house.

A white suburban.

His eyes went from barely staying open to being unable to close them. He slammed the transmission in reverse as if worried the Suburban wasn't going to be there much longer. Barry drove in reverse and cut the wheel to the right, backing into the house's driveway. He parked his car right behind the Suburban and removed his Glock from its holster. Barry knew the house had been vacant for years. He drove by it all the time. Everyone in town knew that no one lived there.

Barry walked past the Suburban. The one with the Nancy's Mobile Dog Grooming decal on the back window. He checked in the vehicle to see if anyone was in there, but all he saw was a dog crate in the very back, along with a bag of dog-grooming equipment.

He continued up the front porch to the front door, forgetting to contact dispatch. Forgetting to tell them what he was doing and where he was. Barry was in what he referred to as "the zone." And when Barry gets in "the zone," he is only focused on one thing: getting to the bottom of it all.

Barry gripped the doorknob and twisted it. All in one quick motion, he raised his nine-millimeter, pushed the door open and took a step back. A woman stood there as if she had been expecting him to visit. A woman with golden curly hair and misty gray eyes. The missing woman. She didn't try to hide, either. She stood there, slightly smiling. Then she simply looked at him, her eyes cheerful in a way that made him feel immensely uncomfortable, and said, "Did I do something wrong?"

"Where's the boy?" Barry asked without preamble.

She remained unsettlingly cheerful when she said, "What do you mean? There's no boy here."

"You're a bad actor, Nancy. We know you took Denny Molasky," Barry said, his Glock aimed at her chest.

Her eyes flicked to the gun. "Are you going to shoot me?"

With one hand, Barry snapped open a pouch and procured a pair of handcuffs. "I'd rather not. Here's what is going to happen. I'm going to place these handcuffs on you, and we're going to have a chat after I search this house."

The woman grinned. Barry looked in her strangely cheerful eyes again.

"Turn around and place your hands behind your back. Whatever you do, don't move," Barry said.

To his surprise, she did exactly what he told her to do. Without letting his guard down, he locked the manacles around Nancy's wrists and walked her over to his car. After putting her in the back seat and locking her in, he kept an eye on her as he called dispatch and apprised them of what was going on.

Barry knew she was trapped. This would be the end of whatever she had planned. He hit the lock button on his key fob. The headlights and taillights illuminated as the horn chirped twice. Then, to make sure for himself, Barry grabbed the door handle and tried to open it. The car was locked.

He made his way back up to the house and went inside. The electric hadn't been on in years. Light shined in through only a few windows; most of them had been boarded up. He pulled out his flashlight and saw cobwebs just about everywhere.

"This is Detective Barry Kendall with the Abbott Police Department," he said loudly.

"If you can hear me, Denny, follow the sound of my voice, and I'll get you back home."

No answer.

Barry walked down the hallway and into what was once a living room. All the furniture had been removed a long time ago, back when the people that lived there moved out. As he walked through the house, he thought about the rental he helped his dad clean out. He thought about the dead cat behind the dresser. He thought about the book. He thought about Holly and the woman who killed her.

He heard a child's voice from upstairs.

"Who's there? You're not going to hurt me, are you?"

Barry shook his head, getting rid of the images in his mind. "No, I'm here to help get you back home to your parents. Where are you?"

"I'm up here. In the bedroom. She locked me in here."

"I'm coming, buddy. Just sit tight," Barry said, and ran up the stairs, taking them two at a time. When he reached the top, he saw three doors. "Which room are you in, Denny?"

"The one in the middle," he said. "Please, hurry."

Barry grabbed the knob and twisted it, realizing immediately that it was locked. He rammed the door a few times with his shoulder, but the door still wouldn't open. Barry kicked the doorknob from the side, and it started to loosen a little after every kick. After the third or fourth kick, the knob broke completely and fell to the ground. Barry opened the door and couldn't believe his eyes. The missing woman's arm held Denny from going anywhere. She sat on the ledge in the open second-story window.

Barry raised his Glock and aimed it at her, right above Denny's head, but he couldn't get a clear enough shot.

"You don't remember me, do you?" the woman asked, holding Denny in front of her body.

"How'd you get out of the car?"

"I know you got the note I left you," she said with a bright smile that sent a shiver down his spine.

That stopped him for a second. Barry thought about the note in the grass by the traffic light. "What do you mean I'll end up like *her*? Who the hell are you?"

The woman in the window mussed Denny's hair, still smiling. "Someone that has been waiting a long time to see you again, Barry."

Barry didn't break eye contact with her as he thought it over. He thought of the woman who killed Holly, but she didn't quite look like her, not in the face anyway. She looked as normal as any woman you'd find grocery shopping at your local supermarket.

Except for . . . her eyes. Barry remembered those gray misty eyes looking at him as he tried to save Holly from the witch who drowned her in the lake. Barry tried to think of the witch's name in the book he had given Holly. After a couple of seconds, he had it.

"Elaine," he said, still aiming the Glock at her.

"You *do* remember me," she said, gripping Denny even tighter. "Look a little different now, don't I?"

"But why? Why are you doing this?"

"You'll find out sooner or later. Or maybe you won't. Your family has always been full of people that are wrong. Why should you be any different?"

"You don't know my family. Get out of that window and release the kid."

"Help me, please!" Denny shouted at Barry.

"Sleep, boy," Elaine said, gesturing her hand in front of his face.

Denny fell asleep almost instantly.

Barry's eyes went wide behind the Glock's iron sights.

Elaine fixed Barry with a withering glare, completely unafraid, at least on the surface. "I know more about your family than you think."

The door behind him slammed closed, causing him to lose focus. When Barry checked behind him, Elaine jumped out of the window with Denny. Barry ran over and looked down to see Elaine running to the white Suburban with Denny over her shoulder.

Barry thought about jumping out of the window, but he knew he'd break something if he tried. The fact that she was able to jump down the way she did without bodily injury terrified him.

She's gotten even stronger, he thought. *Of course she has. It's been thirteen years.*

He felt hot. Much hotter than he was a second ago. He cast his eyes away from Elaine after she tossed Denny in the Suburban and saw flames surrounding him.

He knew she did it. He knew she wanted him dead, but he didn't know why exactly. Right now, the thing he knew most was that he had to get out of this house before it burned down with him inside of it.

Barry looked outside of the window again. The Suburban's headlights were on now. She was pulling up to back around his car and out of the driveway. He glanced at the door that had been slammed shut and remembered that he had broken the doorknob. He rushed and ripped the door open easily, swatting at the flames as they grew larger. He ran down the stairs, taking them three at a time, and tripped on the bottom step. Barry rolled to the floor and saw the ceiling above him was falling in certain areas. While on the floor, a large piece of flaming wood from the floor upstairs landed six inches from his head. Sparks flew all around and a few landed on the skin of his face. After brushing them off, he worked on getting to his feet.

The smoke inside the house was increasing by the second. Barry ran to the front door, only to find it locked. He knew she did it somehow. He knew she had this all planned out. Barry went to the closest window that wasn't boarded up and put his foot through it. The window shattered and smoke plumed out from the inside of the house. Barry saw the broken shards of glass still connected to the edges of the window, but he jumped out of it anyway. He couldn't stay in that house a moment longer. His lungs were nearly full of smoke.

Barry landed outside of the window on his shoulder. He felt pain, but that's not what worried him. He was having a hard time breathing. All he could taste was smoke. And all he could think about was Elaine getting away again. He lay there, struggling to breathe, wondering how in the hell she had taken control of some other woman's body. He thought she must have been planning all of this for years. Then he realized that if he died here on the grass in front of a burning house, he wouldn't make that lunch date he told his mom and dad he would be at. His head began to ache. It went from ache to pounding by the time he heard the fire rescue sirens getting closer to him.

Someone must've seen the smoke and called nine-one-one, he thought.

Barry got to his feet and walked back to his car. His chest hurt worse than he could ever remember it hurting. He thought that this must be what it feels like when you're having a heart attack. Then he thought, *Maybe I am having a heart attack.*

He wasn't.

Barry looked down the road and saw flashing lights coming his way. As fire rescue pulled into the driveway, he felt dizzy. He saw the truck become blurry. The people inside of it were blurry too.

Then he collapsed and lost consciousness.

Chapter 4

Barry's eyes opened slowly. He blinked a few times, looking around. He was in a white room, lying down on a bed. A machine of some sort was beeping, and a man was standing next to him. He was bald and wearing a white lab coat.

"You're lucky to still be with us, Detective," the man said.

"Where am I?" Barry asked.

"You're in a hospital. The carbon monoxide from the house fire nearly killed you. It's a good thing you got out when you did, and that fire rescue took immediate action."

Barry glanced down at the IV in his arm and the O2 monitor on his index finger. "What day is it?"

"Friday. Ten o' clock in the morning," the doctor told him.

"I need to leave," Barry said, trying to get up.

The doctor put his hands up to stop him. "Oh, I'm afraid you can't go anywhere just yet."

"Why not? I feel fine."

"We just need to do a chest radiograph to make sure you're *fine*."

"A what?"

"A chest X-ray."

Barry sighed. "How long do you think that'll take?"

"If everything goes as planned, as early as tomorrow afternoon," the doctor said with a smile. "Now, I'll leave you with the nurse.

She'll take your vitals periodically. I'll see you tomorrow morning. Any questions?"

"Did they find her?"

"Did they find whom, Detective?"

"The woman that took the boy."

"Not that I'm aware of. All I know is that they found you on the ground in front of a burning house, and that you had inhaled a fair amount of carbon monoxide."

Barry shook his head. "Can I have my cell phone?"

"The nurse can bring it to you. She'll be in presently. As for me, I'll see you tomorrow, bright and early."

As soon as the doctor left the room, a blonde-haired woman walked in pushing some sort of medical cart with a laptop attached to the base. She walked the cart over to Barry and introduced herself before taking his vitals.

"Can I have my cell phone, please? I need to make a call," Barry said.

"Yes, of course. As soon as I finish taking your vitals, I'll go get it." A minute or two later, she finished up by typing something on her laptop that Barry couldn't see. "Okay, Mr. Kendall, I'll be right back with your cell phone."

Barry watched her leave, and then looked at the analog clock on the wall. "It's going to be a long day," he said aloud.

"You can say that again."

Barry shifted his gaze to the sound of the voice and saw Sergeant Donaldson standing at the door's threshold.

"Hey, Sarge."

"How are you feeling, Barry?"

"Like I jumped out of burning house a couple of hours ago."

"I think maybe it's time you finally take a week off. I'm sure you could use the break."

"No," Barry said, his eyes locking on Donaldson's. "I need to find that woman. I saw her take the Molasky kid, Sarge. I tried to stop her, but she was too fast. And she set the house on fire while I was in it."

"You're sure she kidnapped Denny Molasky?"

"I *saw* her take him." He didn't mention the fact that she jumped out of the second-story window with the boy.

"Shit. Okay, but how the hell did she set the house on fire?"

With a spell, of course, Barry thought.

"I don't know," Barry said, his eyes shifting away from Donaldson's. "It was like the flames came out of nowhere."

"The fire marshal can't figure it out either. He ruled out it being an electrical fire, being that the electric has been off for years. He couldn't find any evidence that the place had been doused in gasoline or any other flammable liquid either. I was told that it's as if the fire started from thin air. Sounds to me like the dumbass just couldn't figure it out."

"Yeah, that's what it sounds like," Barry agreed.

Barry didn't want to sound crazy. He knew he couldn't tell Donaldson what he really thought. Not unless he had substantial evidence. Evidence that even a skeptic couldn't deny.

"Listen, Barry," Donaldson said. "I know you won't take a week off. You haven't had a week off since you started here at twenty-one years old. But I really think you should at least take a few days off. You need a break, kid."

Even at twenty-nine, Barry was still considered a *kid* to Donaldson, who was pushing fifty. Barry looked down at himself in the hospital bed, not knowing what he would do if he took a week off. He had no hobbies, no wife, and hardly any friends; the results of being completely engrossed in a career like his. He narrowed his eyes at Donaldson and said, "I'll be back Monday at the latest."

Sergeant Donaldson sighed and placed at hand on the foot of the hospital bed. "If the doctor clears you, then that'll be fine, I guess."

Donaldson got up to leave. Before he made it out of the room, Barry said, "Sarge, if you find anything out about Nancy McIn—"

"You'll be the first to know, Barry. Now try to get some rest."

Barry watched Donaldson walk out of the room. About a minute later, the nurse came back in with Barry's cell phone.

He scrolled through his contacts until he found his dad's number and hit CALL.

"Hello?" Carl Kendall answered.

"Hey," Barry said. "I don't know if I'll make lunch tomorrow. I'm in the hospital."

"In the hospital for what?"

"Carbon monoxide poisoning. Don't worry. I'm okay."

"What the hell happened?"

"Long story."

"We're coming up there to see you."

"Dad, I'm fine. Seriously. We'll get together as soon as I get out of here. I don't want to worry Mom."

Silence on the other end of the line. And then, "Okay. But tell me what happened. I got time. And apparently so do you."

Barry thought it over in his head. He didn't feel like he could tell his dad how he really felt, what he really believed. So, he told him what he felt he could. He told him how a woman and kid went missing. He told him how he found her and how she escaped with the kid and how she set the house on fire with him in it.

"Goodness, Barry. You could have been killed," his dad said.

"Yeah, I know." Barry said. "Look, Dad. I promise to let you know when I get out of here. We'll grab a bite to eat somewhere. I just had to let you know what was going on, in case I missed our lunch plans tomorrow."

"That's fine. I'm glad you're okay."

"Talk to you later."

"Keep us informed, Barry."

"I will."

Barry ended the call and picked up the TV remote. He flipped it on and surfed through the channels, stopping when he came across the local news station. The reporter was standing in front of the house the Molasky boy had been kidnapped from, informing the citizens of Abbott what transpired in the middle of the night. Next, the picture changed from the Molasky kid's house to the house that had been burned to the ground. The house that Barry had nearly died in hours ago.

Barry's eyes were glued to the screen.

A different reporter stood in front of the house. It was covered in soot. Black, badly-charred wooden 2x4s jutted out in every which direction. Then, two images appeared on the screen: one of Nancy McIntyre and one of Denny Molasky. The police department's phone number was placed under the images for anyone who had any information of their whereabouts.

Barry turned the TV off, tilted his head back, and placed his hand on his forehead as if he was checking for a fever. There wasn't a fever, but an awful ache was working its way into Barry's head.

He wanted a drink.

He checked the clock again. Only an hour had gone by since the doctor left that morning.

He began to rub his temples in hopes of mitigating the aching. He rubbed and he thought about Elaine jumping out of the window with Denny. The headache worsened. He felt like a failure not having saved the boy. He almost felt the way he did all those years ago when he couldn't save Holly. The headache started to throb. He wondered where she was, where she took Denny.

Then, he heard something ringing. It was his cell phone.

He tilted his head back, resting it on his pillow, and put the phone to his ear.

"Hello," he said.

"Glad to hear your voice, man," Eddie said. "I heard you jumped out of a burning building last night."

"Burning house."

"Tomato, tomahto. What went down at the house?"

Barry looked around the room to make sure he was alone. He was hesitant to tell Eddie the truth. When he told Eddie about the witch thirteen years ago, Eddie looked at Barry as if he were crazy. He told Barry that he believed him. He told him he believed every word, but when Barry looked at him, he didn't truly think that Eddie was being truthful. He thought his best friend was just trying to be nice, especially after Barry's girlfriend had been murdered.

"I don't think you'd believe me if I told you. I'm not even sure if what I saw was actually real."

"Barry, I'd believe you if tolld me you shot JFK back in 1963, long before you were even born. Just tell me. I'll be honest with you like I always have been."

"Okay," Barry said, sitting up in his hospital bed. "Do you remember when Holly was killed?"

"Yeah. Of course I do. Where are you going with this?"

"Do you remember how they didn't find any evidence? How they didn't find a single strand of hair from Holly or the witch that killed her?"

"Yeah, I remember, Barry."

"Do you still believe me when I tell you that she was killed by a witch? One that came out of the lake in Hole in the Woods when Holly read that book aloud?"

"Yes."

"I saw her again, Eddie. Thirteen damn years later."

Silence on Eddie's end of the line.

"Eddie?" Barry asked. "Still there?"

"Sorry. I'm just trying to wrap my head around this."

"The only thing is," Barry paused. "She doesn't look the same."

"Then, how do you know it's her?"

"Her eyes."

"What about her eyes?"

"The way they look at me. They're the same eyes I saw thirteen years ago."

"You're sure?"

"There isn't a doubt in my mind, Eddie. She set that house on fire with some kind of spell or something. From what I was told this morning, the fire marshal can't figure out how it started. There's a reason for that. I don't understand it, but I saw what I saw."

"I'll be back in town in a day or two. I'll come by your place when I get back."

"For what?"

"To lend a helping hand. We can't let her get away again."

Barry smiled despite being stuck in a hospital bed. Eddie believed him. He knew no one else would. Not even his own parents.

"I thought you were out on the road?"

"I am. Long-haul truckers get vacation time too, Barry," Eddie said, and chuckled. "Best thing I ever did was quit Gene's Tire shop and get my CDL a few years ago."

"Thanks, Eddie."

"Of course, man. Look, I have one more load to run. After that, I'm headed back to Florida. Rest up, Barry. I'll see you when I see you."

"See you when I see you."

Barry put his cell phone by his side and laid his head back down on his pillow. He noticed that his headache had subsided after talking with Eddie. He felt better after he divulged what he really saw to his best friend. He felt like he wasn't alone anymore. Eddie was coming to help, but he was also worried that Eddie would get hurt. Barry was tired of worrying. He was tired of thinking about Elaine and the boy he didn't save. He looked at the clock again before he closed his eyes. Before he knew it, he had fallen asleep.

* * *

Elaine piloted Nancy McIntyre's white Suburban down a long dirt road on the outskirts of Abbott. Over the years, she had been planning for this very moment. She knew where she would go next if something with this new location were to go awry. Except, she knew the place would be empty. An elderly couple owned the cabin out in the woods. She knew the snowbirds wouldn't be back until the winter months. She had plenty of time to do what she planned on doing.

As she pulled into the driveway, Denny woke up. He smelled a strong odor from inside the vehicle. He went to sit up and smacked his head against metal. She had put him in a dog crate.

Elaine heard the noise and said, "William, are you awake back there?"

Denny didn't respond. He quietly worked on opening the dog crate.

"William?" she asked again.

No response.

Elaine turned off the Suburban and stepped out of the vehicle. Before she walked up to the cabin, she said, "William?"

When she received no response this time, she closed the car door and hit the lock button.

As soon as Denny heard the car door shut, he slid the latch on the dog crate, pushed the door open and jumped in the backseat. Denny frantically pulled at the door handle, but it wouldn't open. The vehicle's child lock was on. Then, from behind him, he heard a knock; Elaine was knocking on the cabin's front door. She had her ear up to the door to listen for movement inside of the cabin. When she didn't hear footsteps, she twisted the doorknob. It was locked, but she knew a way to fix that. She hovered her hand over the doorknob for a few seconds before a quick twist of the wrist. She heard a click as the door unlocked, and then she went to open it. Except, when she pulled on the doorknob, the door only moved an inch or so. Elaine realized a silver chain lock was keeping the door from opening the rest of the way. There was a stained-glass oval window on the front door. Next to the door was a heavy wooden rocking chair. That gave her an idea. Elaine lifted the rocker and slung the bottom of the chair into the window, shattering the glass. She set the rocking chair aside and reached through the broken window to remove the door's chain lock. Then, as she opened the door, she heard glass shatter again; however, this time it was glass from the Suburban.

Denny had kicked out the back window on the driver's side. She saw him frantically crawling out. Elaine raised her hand in his direction, and he stopped moving away from her. It was as if someone was holding the back of his shirt. Denny couldn't break loose of the witch's hold. He looked behind him.

No one was there.

Elaine kept her hand raised, still standing by the door, forty feet away from Denny. She curled her fingers. Denny no longer had the strength to fight Elaine. He caught himself as he fell to the ground.

"What are you doing to me?" Denny asked, his voice sounding weak even to his own ears.

"Soon enough, William, you'll see. Now, stop fooling around and come to Mama."

Denny laboriously got to his feet. He felt exhausted. As he turned to meet her eyes, something happened inside of him. He didn't understand why he felt the way he did all of a sudden. He *wanted* to go to her.

"I'm coming, Mama," Denny said under his breath.

Denny looked down at his feet as he walked to the cabin's front door. Before he realized it, he was standing next to Elaine. She smiled as she held the door open for him, gently guiding him in. She put her hand on his shoulder and closed the door.

"We'll be staying here for a little while, William," she said. "We have something to take care of tonight, you and I."

"Not . . . William," Denny mumbled.

"You see, what I have to do tonight is going to make your mama tired," she said, ignoring his mumbles.

Denny walked over to the leather sofa in the living room and collapsed onto it, feeling as if he was going to pass out. He noticed he was sweating all over and couldn't remember how he even got in the cabin in the first place. She did something to him in the cabin's front yard, that much he knew. He could still think for himself, but his mind was nebulous. He fought to search through the haze of his thoughts, trying to focus on a way to get away from her. As soon as he thought he almost had something, that something slipped his mind and didn't come back.

He armed sweat off his forehead and watched her sit down on the recliner next to him.

She pulled out a book and placed it in her lap. To Denny, it materialized as if she produced it from thin air. Before she placed it on her lap, he noticed the cover had a star with a circle around it. He thought the book looked old, and he didn't like the way she flipped through the pages. She flipped through the book with the intensity of a teenager looking for their lost cell phone. She flipped back and forth until she found the page she had been searching for. Then, she relaxed and leaned back in the recliner.

"We must wait for sun to go down. Then, we can begin. In the meantime, my sweet William, we will sit here and enjoy each other's company."

Denny sat up, feeling nauseated but noticing that he had a little more energy now, and said, "Stop calling me William. My name is Denny."

Elaine dog-eared the page she was on. A second later, she closed the book and struck him across the face with it. Denny slid back down on the sofa. He saw her hovering over him with that insane smile.

"Perhaps you should rest until it is time, my child."

"I'm not your child. I'll never be your—"

"Shh, sleep, my child," Elaine said, waving her hand inches from his face.

With all the strength Denny had left, he swatted her hand away before she could make him go to sleep like she had before.

Her insane smile went away. An insane frown took its place. Her misty gray eyes darkened to black. She gripped the book in her lap with both hands and struck Denny in the face again. And again. And again.

After the third or fourth time, the boy blacked out.

* * *

Barry woke to the blonde-haired nurse taking his vitals.

"What time is it?" Barry asked, forgetting that there was a clock on the wall.

She glanced down at the watch on her wrist before saying, "Five-eighteen."

Barry sighed. Then he saw a wheelchair next to her medical cart.

She saw him eyeing the wheelchair. "They want me to take you back for a chest X-ray. I'll wheel you back and you'll be in and out before you know it."

"I can breathe just fine."

"Seems like it. They have to be sure before they release you, though."

Barry sighed again.

"I know being in the hospital isn't the ideal vacation. For what it's worth, your vitals have been nearly perfect."

"So, you think I'll be out of here tomorrow?"

The nurse looked back at the room's open door as if checking to see if anyone was listening, then said, "As long as the chest X-ray looks good, I don't see why they'd keep you any longer than tomorrow morning."

"Well, that's good to hear," Barry said. "Thanks."

The nurse smiled and said, "Do you need help getting in the chair?"

Barry sat up. "I think I can manage."

The nurse wheeled Barry out of the room and into one with a large machine on the far wall. They took an X-ray of his lungs from two different angles, and the nurse took him back to his room; just as she said, he was in and out before he knew it.

When they returned to his room, Barry slid back on the hospital bed. The nurse typed away on her laptop for a minute. Then she retrieved a piece of paper from a cabinet and scribbled on it quickly with a pen, folding it as she walked back toward Barry.

"So, my shift is almost over. The nurse starting her shift will assist you with whatever you may need. She'll also check your vitals periodically."

The blond-haired nurse smiled as she handed Barry the folded piece of paper and said, "Open this after you've been discharged, okay? They have rules in this place."

Bewildered, Barry held the paper in his right hand as he watched her leave. When she closed the door behind her, Barry looked down at the note, wondering why she wanted him to wait until after he had been discharged. He couldn't resist; he opened the piece of paper and saw her phone number written across it.

Barry knew he wasn't ugly. He didn't think of himself as handsome, though, either. He didn't understand why the nurse was into him. *Maybe she just likes a man in uniform*, he thought. Then he looked down at the hospital gown they had put him in and thought otherwise.

Either way, he was flattered, but he also hadn't been remotely interested in anyone since Holly. Sure, he had had several one-night stands over the years, but Barry never felt a real connection with them. Not like the one he had with Holly. The desire for an intimate relationship just wasn't there for Barry. He was too busy anyway. He didn't have time to go out on dates. To Barry, it seemed like a waste of time and energy. Time and energy he could be spending elsewhere, like working on finding Elaine, for instance.

Deep in his mind, he knew why he avoided relationships with women. Two words: emotional pain. It always came back to those two words. The emotional pain he experienced when Holly died broke him mentally. Barry was like an old car that kept running even though it had plenty of problems. Over time, he managed to get his act together, but not completely, of course. Even after you fix what is broken, it is never really the same, is it?

The alcohol had become a problem years ago. He knew it was a *real* problem when he had two glasses of whiskey before work one day. He was past "only a buzz" when he sat behind the wheel of his cruiser in the driveway. He started the car and began to back out of his driveway when he realized his problem was taking control. Barry didn't like that; Barry wanted to be the one in control. The one in the driver's seat, which he was that day. He stopped, putting the car back in park. He felt sick to his stomach doing what he almost did. All the drunk driver accident scenes he'd seen in his years as a cop popped into his head. He leaned forward, his forehead resting against the steering wheel, and called out sick. After that call, he called his mother and told her what was happening to him. They had a long conversation about the matter. She recommended he try Alcoholics Anonymous, but everyone in town knew Barry. He didn't want to be seen there. When he refused, she brought him a few books on how to kick the booze. They helped him slow down, but he still drank. And some nights—the rough ones—he drank a lot. And while Barry might not have been a full-blown alcoholic, he certainly flirted with alcoholism.

Barry sat up in his hospital bed. His bladder was full. When he pushed the covers off him and stood up, his bare feet felt cold against the tile floor. He pulled the IV stand to the bathroom with him and did his business.

While in the bathroom, the new nurse entered the room.

"Mr. Kendall, are you in there?"

Barry flushed the toilet, washed his hands, and opened the door. "You caught me."

"Yes, I did. You should have called me. I would have brought you a bed pan."

"I'll be sure to do that next time."

She began to massage her temples. "Please lie back down."

Barry sat down on the bed, and the new nurse introduced herself as Sarah. That was the only part he heard, though. He even forgot the nurse's name just a few seconds later. Barry nodded his head every now and then to keep up the pretense that he had been paying attention. His mind was focused completely on Elaine. He ruminated on how he would go about finding her after he got out of the hospital. He wondered what he could do while in here to pass the time in a productive way. Barry shifted his eyes from the wall to his cell phone. He decided that, as soon as this nurse was done jabbering away, he would do some research online.

"Did you hear what I said, Mr. Kendall?" Sarah asked, her hands on her hips.

Barry heard his name and snapped back to reality. "What?"

The nurse scoffed. "Look, I won't waste any more of each other's time. If you need something, use the button over there to call me," she said, pointing to a button on the hospital bed's remote.

"Oh, okay. Sure thing," Barry said with an awkward smile.

Without another word, she walked out of the room.

Barry picked up his cell phone and immediately began searching the internet, checking to see if there was any information about Elaine that could be useful. He spent hours reading various articles and learned quite a few things about witches. He read that there weren't any real witches in the Salem Witch Trials. Because of religious paranoia and the fact that puritans from the late 1600s believed every wild accusation made, many women were hanged, burned, and even drowned if they didn't confess to being a witch. He kept searching and found an article on the Bell Witch. A real witch from Adams, Tennessee. But Barry didn't believe Elaine was the Bell Witch. He couldn't find a single thing on Elaine; she was an enigma. A real witch that had never been recorded, as far as the internet goes. The only known recording that Barry knew of was the book he found in that shed all those years ago. That book was gone, though. The last time Barry saw it was on that tragic day in Hole in the Woods.

Barry scoured the web until nine o' clock. He went down a rabbit hole on witches and witchcraft, learning a few interesting things from his research, like how witch hunts didn't specifically target women, and how suspected witches were strip-searched to see if they had the devil's mark on their body. *What a crazy world those people had to live in back in those days*, he thought.

After hours of research, he was mentally drained. His eyes were strained from looking at his cell phone for hours, only to find nothing on Elaine. He felt sleep creeping up on him, and he didn't fight it. In fact, Barry welcomed the sleep. Like a kid on Christmas, the sooner he went to bed, the sooner he'd wake up the next morning to find a present under the tree. Except for Barry, his present under the tree was him getting out of the hospital and back to work.

Sleep took Barry, and he dreamed of something he had dreamed of perhaps a hundred times since Holly died. He was back at Hole in the Woods with Holly. She was reading the book he had given her aloud, just like she had when Elaine came out of the lake and took her under the water. He noticed something different about this dream. Something he hadn't ever noticed before: the book sank into the ground next to a tree. The tree with their initials.

Chapter 5

Denny Molasky woke up around ten o'clock at night. His face was incredibly sore, but he couldn't remember why, at first. Then he remembered that he had been struck with Elaine's book. He wasn't sure how many times she had hit him, but he recalled the insane look in Elaine's eyes right before she knocked him out. He tried to bring one of his hands up to feel his face, but he couldn't move his hands. He noticed he wasn't in the living room anymore, either. He was in what he thought to be a bedroom. He tried to move his hands again, but he still couldn't move them.

They were numb.

The only thing Denny could relate the numb feeling in his arms to was when he would fall asleep with his arms above his head. Then he thought for one harrowing second that she had cut them off, but when he glanced to his left and right, he saw that she used rope to tie them to the top bedposts. He realized he was lying down on a four-post bed and that his feet were tied to the bottom bedposts.

With his extremities restrained, he began to panic. He tried to pull his numb arms downward, and when that didn't work, he strained as he attempted to raise his legs. The twelve-year-old thrashed around until he wore himself out. Then Elaine raised up from the chaise lounge chair in the corner of the room. *I didn't see her a minute ago. Was she sitting there the whole time,* Denny thought as he watched her stand up.

Elaine placed her hand on his chest. He looked down at her long fingers as they rested on his shirt.

"What are you doing? Why did you tie me up?" Denny asked.

She patted his chest and slid her hand up to the boy's face, gripping his cheeks. Pain flowed through Denny when she made him look at her.

"My face," Denny said after a moan escaped him. "Please, let go."

She released his face, sliding her hand down to his chest again.

"In another ten minutes, you're going to feel something very painful. It'll feel like you're going to die, but never fear, child. I won't let you die. You're much too important to me," Elaine said. "More important than you could ever know."

Denny looked at her with wide eyes. Tears were beginning to trickle down his face. He didn't know how he'd escape the situation he was in. There seemed to be no way out.

"Please, just let me go!" Denny cried.

Elaine grinned as if there wasn't a boy screaming at her. "I'll be back at midnight, my dear boy. Then, I'll introduce you to your true self."

Denny met her misty gray eyes for just a second. He stopped crying and thought over what she had just said to him. He watched her leave the room and felt the numbness in his arms lessen. He could move his fingers to an extent. Immediately, he started working on a way to get his hands and legs untied, but no matter how hard he pulled, he couldn't get them free.

Then Denny saw what he needed to do.

He noticed how she had tied the rope to the bedpost. It was double-knotted, but there was slack. Enough that he could reach the rope and maybe untie it, even with his hand restrained. He reached toward the bedpost with his right hand, being that the rope had more slack on that side. His fingers just barely reached the knot on the post. The knot was tight, but he managed to work the first knot loose after a few minutes of trying. The second knot was easier for him to untie.

The rope was still tied around his wrist, but the knot around the bedpost had come undone. He felt adrenaline coursing through his veins while he worked on untying his left hand. The first knot was tighter than

42

the one on his right hand, but after another minute he had the rope untied and now both of his hands were free.

The boy frantically began working on untying the rope around both of his ankles. They were even tighter than the rope around his wrists; however, after a couple of minutes of working on the knots tied to the bottom bedposts, he had those off too.

Denny was unsure how many minutes had gone by, but he knew she would be back any minute to do whatever it was she wanted to do to him. He didn't plan on sticking around to find out. Denny ran to the bedroom's window and flipped the latches that secured it from opening. He pulled up and it squeaked loudly. He was sure she had heard it. In haste, the boy placed his leg through the open window and jumped out before she could investigate the noise coming from the room.

Denny lost his balance as he jumped from the windowsill. He fell flat on his back, nearly knocking the wind out of himself. As much pain as he was in, it still felt good to be out of the cabin and away from Elaine. That good feeling didn't last long, though. He heard the door to the cabin fly open. He could hardly breathe, but he got up anyway and started to run.

"Get back here!" Elaine shouted.

Denny's hands began to shake as fear crept into him. Fear at what Elaine would do if she caught him. But Denny was determined to get away from this crazy lady by any means necessary. He missed his parents, he missed his bedroom, and he missed his freedom. He knew this would be his only chance, and the boy didn't hesitate to dash into the woods.

Elaine saw Denny's backside as he entered the woods. Rope was still tied around his wrists and legs since the knots around the bedposts had been easier for him to untie.

Elaine dashed forward, running much faster than Denny. She burst into the woods, shouting words Denny didn't understand. Denny was running for his life when he felt something grab his leg, tripping him. He looked back at what had caused him to fall and stifled a scream. A large snake had wrapped itself around his right leg. It didn't bite him, but it squeezed his leg so hard that he thought it might break the bone under his flesh. As the snake continued to squeeze, he heard Elaine cackling close by. It was as if she knew he had been tripped. Denny took a deep breath and stood up. The snake didn't stop squeezing, but Denny wasn't going to wait for Elaine to find him. The boy ran as fast as he could with the snake around his leg. He jogged as if he had an ankle weight on one of his legs. Only the weight on his leg was continuing to squeeze. Just when he thought his leg might snap in half from the increasing pressure, the snake wrapped around his right leg exploded.

Denny stopped for a few seconds to observe what had happened. Blood and guts splattered his pants and the area around him. He vomited and remembered that he was being chased. Without wiping his mouth, he took off running again. Elaine was getting closer, but he was too focused on getting away to know that.

After another fifty yards or so, another snake wrapped itself around his leg as he ran. He didn't stop this time, though. He felt the same increasing pressure on his leg. Then, suddenly he felt that same pressure again, but this time it was on his other leg. He glanced down, afraid of what he expected to see, and saw snakes constricting each of his legs. Denny began to cry, but he didn't stop running until he felt something grab his arms.

The pressure he felt around each of his arms was much more intense than that around his legs. It was enough to easily bring down a full-grown man. After a few seconds Denny fell to the ground, screaming in agony.

The twelve-year-old had a snake wrapped around both arms and both legs. They squeezed and squeezed as the boy cried harder. He tried to get back up and couldn't. He couldn't move at all. He felt like the bones in his arms and legs would soon snap, but right before they did, all four of the snakes burst. Denny lay there on the ground, covered in snake blood. When he wiped the blood out of his eyes, he saw her hovering over him. The smirk on her face was just south of sane. Denny thought she might explode like the snakes.

"Looks like my friends found you, William," she said.

Elaine ran her index finger down his leg. The snake blood dripped from it. She brought her index up to her face, smelling it as if it were a sweet-scented candle.

Denny looked up at her in disgust as she placed her finger in her mouth, savoring the taste of the blood. Denny wanted to get up and run like hell, but he couldn't move. He was stuck.

"That spell I just used on you has been feeding me for a long, long time," Elaine said. "Soon, it will feed us both, William."

"That's not my n—"

Denny felt her hand grip his head tight. She squeezed and not long after he felt the pressure increase, everything went dark.

* * *

When Denny first woke up, he thought he was still lying on the ground in the woods. Then he realized he was on a mattress and that his arms were numb again. He was tied to the bed, and this time Elaine wasn't leaving. She sat on the edge of the bed, flipping through pages of a book.

He glanced down at his legs and saw that the snake blood had dried and that his shoes had been removed.

"Just do whatever you're going to do to me," Denny mumbled.

Elaine raised her eyes from her book and met Denny's. She snapped the book closed and placed it on the bed. Her feet thumped on the floor as she walked around the side of the bed to sit down next to his torso.

"In another three minutes, it'll be midnight. It'll be time to start your life anew, my boy," she said as she ran her fingers through his hair. "It's been so long since we were last together. I'm finally strong enough to bring you back."

Denny had absolutely no idea what Elaine meant to do to him. He knew she was powerful, though. Powerful in a way that normal people were not. He knew that she had to be some kind of witch; the snakes wrapping themselves around him convinced him of that. He also knew that she was crazy, and that in another couple of minutes, she would do something horrific to him. He looked at the analog clock on the wall.

It was eleven fifty-eight.

Elaine continued to run her fingers through Denny's hair as the seconds ticked away. This time, Denny didn't struggle. He knew it was futile to resist. He simply watched the hands on the clock.

Eleven fifty-nine.

"Oh, William, it's almost time," Elaine said, jumping up from the bed. She went to the edge of the bed again, down by Denny's feet. She opened the book and reached into her front pocket. Denny took his eyes off the clock to see what she was doing. Elaine raised up a small vial with some sort of red liquid in it. She unscrewed the cap, placed it just under her nose, and breathed in deeply through her nostrils.

"It's time," she said as she exhaled.

Denny lay there wide-eyed as Elaine read aloud from her book. He listened to her speak in some strange language that he had never heard of before. He watched as she made bizarre hand gestures while emphasizing certain words. Denny's heart rate quickened. He knew something was going to happen to him. Something life changing.

Elaine moved from the foot of the bed to the side, by Denny's face. She put the small glass vial up to Denny's mouth. The red liquid inside produced an acrid odor that stung his nostrils.

"Please, stop," Denny begged.

Elaine frowned from where she stood, the vial still next to Denny's mouth. "I'm afraid it's much too late for that."

She pressed the open end of the vial up to Denny's lips. He shook his head violently to the left and right, refusing to let the liquid go into his mouth. Elaine continued to speak in a language that Denny didn't understand as she struggled to gain control of Denny's head. She held him with her left hand, her fingers wrapped around his cheeks. Her nails dug into his skin. He tried to twist his head, but her grip was far too strong. She took the cap off the vial and placed it in her mouth with the open end sticking out. When she had the vial positioned just right, she used her free hand to clamp Denny's nose shut, cutting off his air. Denny knew that when he opened his mouth to breathe, she'd pour the liquid into his mouth. Except he thought he could outwit the old witch. He clenched his teeth together and opened his mouth, sucking in the air though his teeth. He felt the air he needed rush into his lungs, but then he felt something else.

Pain. Lots of it.

Elaine, with the vial clenched tightly between her teeth, smashed the open end of the vial into Denny's mouth, knocking in Denny's two front teeth. The liquid poured into Denny's mouth, and he tried to spit it out. His loose teeth flew out of his mouth, but the liquid didn't. It was like the liquid was clinging to the inside of his mouth and only wanted to go one way in particular: down his throat.

He tasted blood. Denny's mouth was bleeding from where his teeth had been knocked in, of course. He cried as he swallowed the red liquid, it and his own blood mixing together.

Through his tears, he looked up and saw Elaine watching him. She no longer spoke in her strange language he didn't understand. Her book was still open on the bed next to him, but she wasn't reading from it any longer. She simply looked at Denny as if he were the most precious thing in the world she had ever seen.

And then Denny blacked out.

Chapter 6

Barry woke up the next morning just as the sun found its way in from behind the window blinds. He didn't remember much of his dream, but he did remember the part about the book sinking into the ground by the tree that had his and Holly's initials on it.

He rubbed his eyes with his hands and heard the door to the room opening. The nurse from last night walked in with the doctor he had spoken to yesterday. Each of them wore a smile on their face as if they had just heard a good joke.

"Well," the doctor said, "I think you'll be able to leave soon enough. The chest X-rays look just fine." He walked up to Barry's bedside and placed the stethoscope on his chest.

"Breathe in and out for me. I don't want to let you go without making sure you're breathing normally."

Barry took long, deep breaths. He knew the routine.

After the fourth breath, the doctor said, "One more."

Barry gave him one more.

The doctor grinned. "Phenomenal. Your lungs sound great. You're a lucky one, Detective. I'll have the nurse check your vitals one more time for good measure, and I'll work on getting you discharged."

"Thank you," Barry said. "Do you think I'll be out of here before this afternoon?"

The doctor had already begun to leave the room, but he stopped by the threshold and looked back at Barry. "If they can get your paperwork done in the next hour, then yes."

Barry nodded.

The nurse checked his vitals once more. Everything was near perfect. "Bet you'll be glad to get out of here," Sarah said.

"Very much so," Barry said, and began to shudder.

For a second, the nurse's face turned into Nancy McIntyre's. She looked like her, except for the eyes. Her eyes didn't turn misty gray, and that was the only thing that kept Barry from completely freaking out.

"Are you okay?" the nurse asked, putting her hand on his shoulder.

Barry jerked away when she touched him. He shook his head and looked at Sarah again.

She no longer looked like Nancy McIntyre. "Yeah, I'm fine. I just had a chill."

"I'd say. You looked like you had seen a ghost there for a second."

Barry grinned despite how terrified he was only a few seconds ago. "I've seen a lot of scary things over the years, but I've yet to see a ghost."

The nurse tilted her head and furrowed her brow as if she hadn't understood him correctly. Then without saying anything, she turned around and left the room.

As soon as the door closed behind her, Barry's mind went back to the part of the dream he remembered. The part about the book sinking into the ground next to the tree. Suddenly, he needed to go there. He needed to dig next to the tree to see if he could find anything.

After a couple hours had passed, the nurse came into the room pushing a wheelchair.

"I have your one-way ticket out of here," she said, placing it next to the bed.

Barry got up and stood next to the wheelchair. "The wheelchair isn't necessary. I can walk just fine, you know?"

Sarah didn't smile. "It's protocol, Mr. Macho."

Barry wanted the hell out of there, so he conformed. He grabbed his belongings and let her wheel him out of the room. Sergeant Donaldson was waiting outside for him, leaning on his car. When he saw Barry being wheeled out, he pushed off the car and made his way over.

"I'll take it from here, ma'am," Donaldson said to her.

Still not smiling. "He's all yours."

Barry was glad to be out of the hospital and even happier to see the nurse walk away.

Donaldson rested his eyes on Barry. "I figured you would need a ride home. Come on, hop on out of that chair."

Barry pushed himself up and stood next to Donaldson. "Let's get the hell out of here," he said.

Before Donaldson even made it out of the hospital's parking lot, from the passenger seat, Barry said, "Any leads on Nancy McIntyre yet?"

Donaldson sighed as he pulled out on the main road. "Not yet. I have Deaver looking into it."

"Elliot Deaver? He isn't going to find anything, Sarge. I went to the academy with him and—"

"Save it. I know you went to the academy with him. I know you two butt heads with each other. Fact is, you were in the hospital, and I needed someone else to find more information on this case. One of my detectives is still working a homicide case that I can't take him off of, and the other is out sick with the flu."

"Well, now I'm out of there."

"Yeah, you are. And I've been thinking."

"About?"

"You taking a week off."

Barry narrowed his eyes at his sergeant, but Donaldson kept his eyes on the road. "I'm not taking a week off. If anyone is going to find that woman and kid, it's me. You know I'm right, Sarge."

"Fine. I'm not going to argue with you, but you are taking today and tomorrow off. You can come back on Monday."

Barry looked out of the passenger-side window, thinking it over. He knew he had things he needed to do that weren't work related. He promised to eat lunch with his parents, and what was really on his mind was that dream. That book sinking into the ground.

Barry shifted his gaze back over to Donaldson and nodded his head. "Deal."

A few minutes later, they were nearing Barry's house. Donaldson piloted the car down the concrete driveway leading up to the red brick house and put it in park.

Before Barry reached for the door handle, he said, "Thanks for the ride, Sarge."

"Not a problem. Rest up, Barry."

As Barry started walking away from the car, he heard the buzz of an electric motor. He glanced behind him to see the car's driver-side window down. Donaldson waved him back over.

"What's up?" Barry asked.

"Don't go hunting that woman down until Monday."

"Sure."

"I mean it, Barry. Give Deaver a chance and give yourself a break. You can worry your ass off over the case come Monday."

Barry nodded as Donaldson put the car in reverse. Barry watched him back out, knowing that Officer Deaver wouldn't be able to find anything on Elaine or Denny Molasky. He began to think what Elaine would do to Elliot if he did manage to find her and the boy. He didn't care for Elliot Deaver much, but he surely didn't want to see him killed.

Barry's cell phone began to vibrate in his front pocket, getting him out of his own head and back to reality. He squinted at the screen, trying to read the name displayed across it. The Florida sun was making it difficult, so he shaded the screen with his hand. It was his mom.

"Hey, Mom," Barry answered.

"Why didn't you tell me you were in the hospital? I had to practically interrogate your father to find out," Martha Kendall said.

"I didn't want you to worry."

"Well, we are coming up there right now."

"If you do, I won't be there."

"Why not?"

"Because I'm home. I just got out of the hospital."

"Carl, turn around," Barry heard his mom say to his dad. "Barry got out of the hospital this morning. He's home." Then back to Barry. "We'll be there in a few minutes. Do you feel well enough to get some lunch?"

"Yes, but I need to—"

"Wonderful! We'll see you shortly."

Barry heard her hang up. He put his phone back in his pocket and went inside to make himself a drink before going out to lunch. The past day and a half had been a long one for Barry.

He had a craving that kept tapping at his mind. He knew he shouldn't, but he gave in. Within a minute, Barry was inside downing a small glass of Kentucky bourbon. He didn't even bother chilling it with a few ice cubes.

He sat down on the sofa and immediately thought about the book sinking in the ground next to the tree again. He decided that after lunch with his parents, he would drive up there and take a look around.

My car, he thought just then. *I forgot all about it.*

The last time he remembered seeing his police-issued Charger was at the house that went up in flames. He didn't think to ask Donaldson what happened to it. Barry wondered if it might have burned up with the house.

Feeling the buzz in his head now, he walked to the front door to go outside. He still had his old Toyota Celica parked under the carport on the side of his house. It had been a year or so since he had started it up. He kept it legal because the insurance was cheap, and it never hurt to have a back-up car. He was sure the battery would be dead, though.

And he was right.

The door hinges of the old Toyota creaked as Barry opened the driver-side door. As he sat behind the wheel, looking around inside at the dusty interior, a multitude of memories ran through his mind; Holly leaning her head on his shoulder at the local Drive-In movie theater, he and Holly holding hands as they cruised around town, he and Holly kissing in the front seat before he dropped her off at her house. He supposed that was the real reason why he could never get rid of the damn thing.

Barry put the key in the ignition, pushed the clutch down, and twisted the key.

Nothing. The battery was toast.

Barry figured that would be the case. He got out of the Toyota and popped the hood. He saw a few spiderwebs in the engine bay, which didn't surprise him on account of how long it had been sitting. Barry then located the car's battery to see what he would need to remove it.

Although, before he got a chance to go inside to find the tools, he saw his parents' Lincoln in his driveway. He knew his dad wouldn't mind stopping at the auto parts store to pick up a new battery for his car. It was a dad thing to do. Except, when Barry saw what was pulling in behind his parents' car, he realized he wouldn't need the tools or that battery after all; a tow truck was backing in, and on the back of it was his police-issued Dodge Charger.

Barry walked up to the driver-side window of his parents' car and his dad, who was driving, rolled down the window. "Hey," his dad said, "looks like your ride just got delivered."

"Yeah, I thought I was going to have buy a battery for my other car."

"You look like you need a good meal. Hop in. Our treat, right, Carl?" said Barry's mom.

"That's very kind of you guys, but I have something I need to do after lunch. I'll just drive myself. Looks like this guy is about to block you guys in with my car anyway."

The tow-truck driver stopped behind his parents' car with just enough room to unload the Charger. Barry knew the driver of the tow truck. He had had many conversations with him in the past when Barry was still an officer working traffic accidents.

The driver of the tow truck stepped down from the driver's seat and met Barry's gaze.

"Hey there, Barry, I didn't realize this was your car," he said.

"Yeah, I found a suspect in an abandoned house. It ended up catching on fire somehow, and I inhaled in a little too much carbon monoxide. Just got out of the hospital. How have you been, Ernie?"

"I'm doin' all right, I reckon. Glad to see you ain't stuck in the hospital. I don't know about you, but I hate needles."

"I'm not a huge fan of them, but my fear of needles left around the time I was old enough to stay home without a sitter." Barry glanced back at his parents waiting inside their Lincoln.

"Hey, I'm supposed to go eat lunch with my parents real soon, and my old man isn't what you would call a patient person."

"Say no more, my friend." Ernie walked to the side of the truck and took hold of the levers that controlled the bed of the tow truck. "I'll have this off here in a jiffy."

Barry stood back and watched Ernie perform the task he had hundreds—probably more like thousands—of times. The old man in his fifties had it down to a science, and Barry's Charger was back on the ground in less than a minute.

"You look like you've done that once or twice," Barry said as Ernie handed him the keys.

"Tell you somethin', my friend, this ain't my first rodeo."

"You sure?"

Ernie placed his right hand over his heart. "If I'm lyin', I'm dyin'."

Barry grinned and shook the old man's hand. "Thanks again, Ernie."

"Don't mention it, Detective," Ernie winked.

As Ernie climbed into his tow truck, Barry turned around and saw his mom standing behind him. She wrapped her arms around him and made a face when she smelled what was on his breath.

"Barry," Martha said softly. "You just got out of the hospital, and you've already started drinking."

"It was just one glass," Barry said, avoiding eye contact.

"You're riding with us."

"But I—"

"I said you're riding with us." Martha dug in her purse and pulled out a piece of chewing gum. She handed it to Barry, and said, "I won't tell your father, but you need to stop this. Promise me, Barry."

"What's the hold up?" Barry's dad asked from the driver seat.

"We're coming, Carl. Hold your horses, would you?" Martha said. Then to Barry, "Promise me."

"Okay, I promise," Barry said as he looked in her tired eyes. "But I only had one drink."

"One too many, Barry. Now let's go."

Barry followed his mother to the Lincoln and sat in the backseat.

Chapter 7

Denny Molasky woke up ten minutes till noon the next morning. The sun was shining brightly through the bedroom's window, and Elaine was no longer in the room with him. His tongue found the place in his mouth where his two front teeth had been. His gums were sore, but he forgot all about them when he saw that his hands and feet had been untied. Denny jumped out of bed and rushed to the window, opening it enough so that he could climb out and escape like he had the day before. Except, he didn't want to escape. He thought he had a minute ago. Hell, he could have sworn that was what he wanted to do, but as he found himself with the perfect chance to get away, he didn't. He pulled down on the window and closed it.

Why did I just do that? he thought.

He went to raise the window again, and this time he couldn't bring himself to even open it. *Why do I want to stay here? What did she do to me?*

Denny walked over to the mirror on the dresser. He looked at himself and thought he looked different somehow. It wasn't only the missing teeth, either. He was smiling, but he wasn't happy on the inside. Something was terribly wrong with him, and he could feel that whatever was happening to him was only getting stronger. He felt a severe shortness of breath, as if he was having an asthma attack. His heart rate sped up faster than he could ever remember it being before.

"Help," he said, trying to scream. But all that came out was a soft, "Help." He kept saying it as fresh tears rolled down his cheeks. Denny hunched over the dresser, the cold, sweaty palms of his hands bracing himself up. His eyes were closed now, and his head had drooped down as if it were too heavy to hold up.

"Help me. Someone. Anyone. Please," Denny said softly, feeling himself leave his body, feeling something or *someone* else take it from him.

Denny used the rest of the energy he had to look at himself one more time before he passed out. In the mirror's reflection, he saw that his skin had turned pale, but that wasn't what horrified him. He stared at his eyes in the mirror. His pupils weren't there. His eyes were blank, nothing but the whites of his eyes showing. He thought that they must have rolled back in his head involuntarily, but if that was true, how could he see himself?

Denny didn't get a chance to think that over, though. The next second, he hit the floor. The boy's eyes opened about an hour later, but the boy wasn't Denny anymore. Sure, a small part of him was in there, but a much larger part of someone else was running the show and pulling the strings.

The bedroom door abruptly opened. Elaine stood at the threshold, looking down at the boy that was once Denny. An eerie smile appeared on her face, then she said, "There's my boy. Come on, William. Let's get you up. We have plenty to do now, don't we?"

"We have plenty to do," William said.

Elaine bent over and helped the boy to his feet.

"Oh, William, it's been so long. I told you I'd bring you back one day, though, didn't I?"

Elaine said, holding him close to her. "I missed you," she said.

"I missed you too, Mama."

Elaine smelled his hair, looked around the room, and guided the boy into the living room.

"Come now," she said, "Do you remember what I told you we would have to do once I brought you back?"

The boy tilted his head up, looking as innocent as ever. "Hurt the people that hurt us?"

"That's correct, but first we need to be whole. We have to find your brothers."

She led him to the couch and sat down. William lay on his side, resting his head on Elaine's lap.

"We'll take us a little break today. We are going to need our rest to get your brothers here with us."

"But how are we going to get them?"

"Don't worry your little head about that," Elaine said, running her fingers through the boy's hair. "Mama has a plan."

The boy rolled to his back and looked up at the woman. She knew Denny was long-gone when she heard William say, "I love you, Mama."

* * *

On the other side of Abbott, the Kendalls' Lincoln pulled into a dirt parking lot. The parking lot of a locally owned seafood restaurant that had been in business since Reagan was in office. It's where Martha and Carl had celebrated many birthdays and even a few wedding anniversaries. Needless to say, it was their favorite restaurant.

Barry's parents hadn't told him where they wanted to eat lunch, but he didn't need to ask to know the answer. When people are on a first-name basis with the restaurant staff, it isn't hard to figure out, especially when you're a detective.

Barry got out of the car first so he could help his mother out. She held his arm as they walked into the restaurant. The three of them sat down in a booth near a large fish tank and were soon greeted by a server that had taken their order perhaps a hundred times over the years; she was a sandy-haired woman in her late forties that had been working there since she turned sixteen. Martha and Carl Kendall were the first couple she had ever served, and they knew this because she mentioned it to them on her first day.

"Martha, Carl, how are you two?" she asked, holding a Coke in one hand and a Sprite in the other.

"Just fine, Wendy," Martha said. "We brought our son with us this time."

"I see that," Wendy said. "It's been a little while since I've seen him. How are you, Officer Kendall?"

"I'm doing okay, ma'am. Thank you for asking."

"He's a detective now," Martha said, looking brightly at Barry. "We're so proud of him. Aren't we, Carl?"

Carl finished taking a sip of his Coke and put it down on the table. "Of course."

"Well, *Detective* Kendall," Wendy said. "I know what mom and dad drink. What would you like?"

"Water with lemon is fine. And just call me Barry, please. I'm off duty anyway."

"No problem, Barry," she said, then shifted her gaze to Barry's parents. "Martha, Carl, same as usual for your meal?"

"Yes, please," Martha said.

"And for your meal, Barry?" Wendy asked.

"I'll have the shrimp."

"Good choice," she said, then flashed a smile at Martha and Carl. "I'll be back with everything soon."

Wendy rushed off and went through a black door that led to the kitchen. When Barry saw the door close, he looked at his dad. "Do you remember the rental we cleaned out all those years ago?"

"You're going to have to be more specific. We cleaned out several from what I remember," Carl said, and took another sip of his soda.

"The worst one."

Carl's eyes shifted down and to his left as he thought it over. "Oh, right," he said, meeting Barry's gaze. "You know, I was upside-down on that one for a while."

"Do you remember the woman's name that rented it before she wrecked the place and left?"

"I remember what she looked like, but I don't remember her name. Why do you ask?"

Barry looked away as he said, "I think she may have something to do with this case I'm working on." He laid his eyes back on his father's. "Do you think you can find her name for me?

Maybe in an old rental agreement?"

Carl's brow furrowed as he leaned his elbows on the table. "How is she connected to this?"

"You know I'm not supposed to divulge that information. There are laws against that."

"I know. But you can't blame me for asking, right?"

"No," Barry paused. "So, can you check on that name for me?"

"I suppose I can. Hopefully I didn't throw it away. I normally throw paperwork ten years and older in the trash."

"Well, I hope you still have it. I think it'll help me out a lot with the case."

Carl nodded. "I'll check as soon as we get home."

"Thanks, Dad."

"Of course, Barry. So, she's really mixed up in this whole thing, huh?"

Barry was trying to think of something that would put an end to his father's curiosity. He didn't need to think for long, though. Wendy was coming out of the kitchen holding a tray full of steaming hot seafood.

Barry shrugged his shoulders and said, "Here comes our food."

* * *

After the meal, Barry conversed with his parents for a while, talking about him, his dad's new tenants, and his mother's health. Then, when they had run out of things to talk about, Barry was driven home. Once there, he hopped out of the backseat and waved at his parents as they backed out of his driveway. It was almost three in the afternoon, and he hadn't at all forgotten the dream. The image of the book sinking into the ground was as vivid in his mind as it was when he woke up this morning.

Before he left for Hole in the Woods, Barry went inside his house to grab a few things: his gun, a cup of coffee, and the Case knife Holly had given him as a gift over a decade ago.

He slid in behind the wheel of his Dodge Charger and started it up, taking one deep breath before putting the car in gear. As he drove on the road leading to Hole in the Woods, he thought about how long it had been since he was last out there. He went out to his and Holly's spot a handful of times after her death. Then, at some point, he just stopped going out there; it began to hurt too much. A few years after that, a wealthy woman from Tennessee purchased the property. It wasn't long after the purchase that she had a gate with a no trespassing sign installed down the little path on side of the road.

Barry thought back to the last time he was even near that gate. It was a couple of years ago, back before he had made detective. A trio of high-school kids had jumped the gate and ran in to explore the woods. Someone made an anonymous call, and Barry was the officer dispatch called to check it out. When he pulled up to the gate that day, he saw the kids as they were jumping back over it, just in time to bust them. Barry remembered the look on their faces when he pointed to the "No Trespassing" sign and asked them if they could read. The kids were wide- eyed of course. They were in stark fear of the trouble they might be in if Barry had taken them back to the station. Or worse, called their parents.

Barry didn't do either of those things, though, mostly because he didn't want to be a hypocrite. It wasn't all that long ago, he had thought back then, that he was just a teenager exploring the same woods. Although, there wasn't a gate or sign stating that they couldn't be back there when he was their age.

When Barry had asked what they were doing, one of the high school-ers spoke up immediately.

"We heard a girl died out here several years ago," the high-school kid said. "We just wanted to take a look around."

One of the other high schoolers said, "Yeah, but then we got creeped out by that tree with the initials on it. People say that she had carved her name there. After seeing that, we decided to leave."

"Don't believe that story. It's made up," Barry had told them. "You all need to leave now. If I ever see you guys out here again, you'll be leaving in the back of that police car."

The kids ran off, of course, and Barry never got called out there again. He figured the story had finally lost its allure for the high-school kids.

Around the end of his reminiscing, he realized he was on the road that led to Hole in the Woods. A road he hadn't been on in two years since he had run those high-school kids off. His heart began to beat a little faster as he applied pressure to the brake pedal, slowing the car down so that he could turn off the road.

The grass in front of the gate was almost four-feet high. Reluctantly, Barry put the car in park. He stared at the gate for ten seconds or so before finally stepping out of the car. The sun beat down on him as he walked up to the gate, touching the metal lightly. As he expected, the gate was as hot as a stove with the dial set to simmer.

Barry went back to his car, thumbed open the glovebox, and pulled out a pair of gloves. He kept them in there for two reasons: he never knew when he would need a pair of gloves. The other reason being that he thought the name was a fitting place to store them. He would normally grin at the irony of pulling his gloves out of the glovebox, but not now. Now he was trying to keep himself calm. His hands shook as he put the gloves on. He felt like he was doing something wrong. And in a way, he was. He thought he might find something out there by the tree that his and Holly's initials were carved in that could help with the case, but he was also told to take the day off.

"What Donaldson doesn't know won't hurt him, right?" Barry said under his breath as he began to climb over the gate.

As Barry's feet hit the ground on the other side, he felt like jumping back over the gate. The ground he stood on seemed wrong somehow. He looked back at his car and took a deep breath. A second later, he began walking the same path he had been on dozens of times when he was just a teenager.

After a few minutes, Barry stopped in his tracks. He stood there, frozen, as if he had just witnessed a murder. Except, that murder he saw playing out in his mind happened many years ago. His eyes were locked on the tree next to the place he and Holly had always called *their spot*. Everything looked just as it had the day Holly died, except the grass was a tad higher and the initials on the tree had darkened with age.

He began to walk again and, as he got closer, he saw his initials were still there right next to Holly's. Barry slowly made his way up to the tree. He didn't feel right. He usually had a grip on his anxiety. He could usually focus and push that feeling away like he had many times when he was an officer performing traffic stops. Barry knew he was alone and couldn't be hurt physically, but being physically hurt wasn't what worried him.

Barry took his gloves off and raised his right hand, running the tips of his fingers over the tree bark. He felt his eyes welling with tears as his fingers moved over the rough wood.

"Stop," he told himself, shaking his head.

The tears in his eyes dried up and disappeared as if on command. He looked over his shoulder at the small lake. It also looked the same, except for the vegetation growing up around its edges.

He closed his eyes and replayed that horrible day in his mind. He didn't want to; it was just something that happened.

Barry saw it all as his hand rested on the tree. He saw Holly reading that damn book aloud, and then he saw Elaine dragging Holly into the lake by her ankles as she screamed at the top of her lungs.

It was all too real.

Barry removed his hand from the tree and, as soon as he did, the memory began to fade away. He ran his hand down his face and sighed. His eyes found their initials again. In that second, he thought the letters needed touched up. He dug in his pocket, pulling out the same knife he had carved their initials with all those years ago. He opened the blade and did his initials first, working the blade in the bark carefully. After finishing his initials, he started working on Holly's. He was only a third of the way on the H when the knife fell out of his hand and landed on the ground, the entire blade stuck in the dirt. Barry saw how the handle protruded out of the ground and suddenly remembered why he had come out here in the first place.

Barry gripped the handle of the knife and yanked it out of the hard ground. He held it up, not believing what the knife's blade had pierced as it fell in the dirt. Barry carefully slid the little rectangular piece of paper off the knife's blade and read what was on it.

I'll see you soon.

Chapter 8

While Denny napped on the couch inside, Elaine sat out front on a wooden rocking chair. The same rocking chair she used to break the front door's oval window. Her eyes had been closed for perhaps ten minutes, but she wasn't sleeping; she was focusing on something deep in her mind. Through her supernatural abilities, she could see Barry walking around in Hole in the Woods. The images she saw were like those of an old movie reel. Elaine knew that Barry would go searching around the tree when she put that dream in his head the night he slept in the hospital. He was doing exactly what she wanted him to do. She was in his head, making him think of what happened all those years ago. The apprehension she saw in Barry's eyes as he read her message brought a smile to her face.

The image in her mind suddenly vanished. Her eyes flew open, sensing that someone was near her.

"Mama?"

She turned her attention to the little boy standing by the door.

"Yes? What is it?"

"I'm hungry," William said.

Elaine gave him a soft smile. "Of course you are."

She stared out at the wilderness surrounding the cabin. The smile gone. In its place was a far-away look. She gripped the arms of the rocking chair tight. Her nails dug into the wood as she quietly recited an incantation. After a short period of time, a turkey ran out of the woods and into the open area in front of the cabin.

Elaine's hands relaxed. The far-away look disappeared as she shifted her gaze back to the boy. "Eat up, William."

The boy's eyes shifted back and forth between Elaine and the turkey. "Are you sure, Mama?"

Elaine nodded. "I am."

William darted off the porch and pounced on the turkey. He wrestled it to the ground with the strength of a crazed full-grown man. Elaine swayed back and forth in her rocking chair, humming to herself as the boy broke the turkey's neck. William got on his knees, sinking his teeth into the turkey's leg. He ate away at the bird for a good fifteen minutes or so before his hunger was satiated. Then he looked back at Elaine, blood covering his mouth and chin. He left what remained of the turkey where it lay, walked up the front porch steps, and sat on her lap.

"When do we find my brothers?" he asked, staring up at her.

"Tonight," she said, gripping his shoulder. "But first, we need to find the right boys."

"I'm ready, Mama."

"You're still very new to this world we're in, William. This isn't like before. I've been here for thirteen years, waiting and learning. I believe we only have one chance at this. We cannot make mistakes this time. Go clean the blood off your face. If people were to see you like this, they'd call the sheriff and try to hurt us. Do you understand?"

"I think so, Mama."

"Good." She lifted him off her lap. "Now go clean your face. We need to leave soon."

William rushed inside. Elaine stood at the threshold, holding the door open and listened for water to hit the sink. When a minute went by and she didn't hear any water, she entered the bathroom. As she expected, William didn't know how to use the sink faucets. He was from the nineteenth century, and the house they lived in didn't have indoor plumbing.

"There's a lot you have to learn in very little time," she said as she turned the sink faucet on. "But you'll be fine as long as you listen to your mama."

"Listen to Mama," he repeated.

"Good," she said, placing a cloth under the running water. "Now hold still while I clean you up."

A few minutes later, Elaine and William were ambling out of the cabin and getting into the Suburban. As Elaine drove out to the hard road, William looked around, absorbing the future as he knew it. He watched as the other cars drove past theirs and asked what the signs on the side of the road were.

"Those signs inform you," she told him. "Some tell you to stop, and some tell how far until you get to the next town. They're nothing you should worry about, though. You just stay close to me."

They were nearing a shopping center and intuition told Elaine to pull in. They didn't get out of the Suburban. Elaine and William sat in the vehicle, waiting to see if the right boy—for her son or his brother to take possession of—would show up.

After an hour passed by, Elaine noticed two things: mostly girls were at the shopping center, and that the Suburban was starting to lean to one side. She opened the door and stepped out to find that her left rear tire was completely flat. She got back in the Suburban and opened her book of incantations. Nowhere in there was a spell for a flat tire.

She turned back to William, who was looking outside of the Suburban at all the people.

"William," she said.

His eyes left the people outside and focused on her.

"Would you like to help Mama with something?"

William's head bounced up and down with the enthusiasm of an obedient canine.

"Good. We need to get the spare out from under the car."

"What's spare?" William asked, furrowing his brow.

"Come on, get out. I'll show you," Elaine said as she opened her door.

They went around to the back of vehicle and looked underneath it. "Do you think you can get it down, William?" she asked.

A look rippled across his face as if he had just been asked a difficult question, then he got on his back and slid underneath the vehicle. She watched the boy grab hold of the tire and yank it down as hard as he could. The vehicle's rear suspension compressed a little, but the tire remained fastened. William tried again and let out a horrific growl.

"William, no," she said. "You can't be so loud. We mustn't bring attention to ourselves."

"Sorry, Mama," he said, his arms still wrapped around the spare tire. "It won't come down."

Elaine glanced over her shoulder and glimpsed a yellow sign far down the road. A sign that said "GENE'S TIRE SERVICE."

A smile crossed her face. "Come on out from there, William."

William released the tire and slid out from under the Suburban. He stood up, arms covered in filth, and looked at Elaine without saying anything.

Elaine stuck her hand out toward him. "Take my hand."

"What are we going to do now, Mama?"

"We're going to walk down the road to a place that will help us with our tire problem."

"What place?"

"Don't worry about that. When we get there, though, you let me do all the talking. Do you understand?"

"I don't talk."

"That's right," she said, and began walking.

When Elaine and William entered the parking lot at Gene's Tire, William jumped each time he heard an air tool echo from inside of the building.

"Easy, William," she said. "No one in there is going to hurt you. I wouldn't let them."

William shook his head, wary of the building, and followed her to the tire shop's front door. Elaine opened the door to see a pudgy man with thick glasses and a receding hairline. He was sitting behind an old desk with a computer on it, clipping his fingernails.

"Hey, there, how y'all doin'?" Gene asked, sliding his nail clippings off the table and into his hand.

Elaine ignored his question. "I need one of your employees to fix my tire. It's in the shopping center's parking lot just down the road," she said, smiling in an odd sort of way. A way that made Gene feel uncomfortable.

Gene threw the nail clippings in the trash can next to his desk and leaned back in his chair. "I'm afraid we're all booked up today," he said, narrowing his eyes at her. "But feel free to try another shop, ma'am."

Elaine walked up to the pudgy man's desk and raised her eyebrows, still smiling that profoundly odd smile. "I have a child, and we will not leave until you fix our tire."

Gene glanced down at the boy that used to be Denny Molasky. Even with his hair unkempt, his arms and shirt covered in filth, he noticed the boy. He knew it was Denny—it was a somewhat small town after all—and he saw on the news where he had went missing. Gene thought she had possibly drugged the boy.

Elaine saw it register on his face that he recognized William as Denny and reached into her pocket.

"Okay," Gene said, picking up the phone. "We'll get your tire fixed, lady. Just let me make a phone call real—"

Elaine's arm shot out and the phone fell from Gene's hand. "Hold him," she said to William. "Don't let him go anywhere."

William jumped over the desk and grabbed Gene by the arms, wrenching them behind his back. Gene tried to stand up, but the boy was too strong. To Gene, it felt like two full-grown men were holding him down.

"What the hell is this, huh? What're you doin'?" Gene said, raising his voice.

Elaine went around the desk. Her hand came out of her pocket. There was a little bottle filled with black liquid.

"Get that away from me," Gene said with wide eyes. "Don't come any clo—"

Elaine had him by the throat. She raised the bottle to his lips.

"Open your mouth," she said.

Gene pressed his lips together and shook his head no.

"Have it your way," she said, then lifted the fingernail clippers from his desk.

Elaine held the potion in one hand, the clippers in the other. She placed the bottle against his lips and worked the meat of his left nostril in between the blades of the clippers.

"Open your mouth," she said.

He shook his head hard, trying to free his nostril from the clippers. It didn't work, but it did upset her. She applied pressure to the clippers and before she could cut the meat all the way through, he opened his mouth to scream.

She poured a small amount of the potion in his mouth. He spit it out, but that was fine.

The potion only had to touch his tongue. He went to scream but Elaine clamped her hand over his mouth to stifle it. When his face began to settle, she let go and removed the fingernail clippers from the meat of his nostril. He looked up at Elaine, glassy-eyed, as the phone's dial tone continued to beep on and on.

"Let go of him, William," she said. Then to Gene, "Hang up the phone."

Gene did as she said. He didn't have a choice; the potion forced him to do anything she told him to. Until it wore off, he was hers.

"Now listen closely," she said, that eerie smile leaving her face. "You will now go in the garage and send out one of your employees to fix my tire. Do you understand?"

"Yes," Gene said in a somber baritone. "I understand."

"Good. Now go do as I said."

Gene stood up and briskly made his way through a door that led to the garage. Ten seconds or so later, he came back in with a lanky young man, perhaps in his mid-twenties, and said, "Trevor, you are to help this woman. Get the service truck. She'll tell you where her vehicle is."

Trevor noticed the red indentation on his boss's nostril and the dull look in his eyes. He was completely perplexed. "Um, okay," he said, and then glanced back at Elaine. "I'll meet you outside at garage-bay number three, ma'am."

"Wonderful," she said. And when Trevor left the room, Elaine ambled up to Gene as he stood there unable to move on two shaky legs. She put her mouth up to his ear, her lips almost touching his earlobe. She whispered, "Now you can sit back down in your chair and take a nap.

When you wake up, you won't remember any of this. Not me. Not the boy. Nothing. Do you understand?"

In the same somber baritone, Gene said, "Yes, I understand."

He waddled over to his chair, his legs trembling every step of the way, and sat down. As soon as he did, his head crashed down on the desk, and he was off to sleep.

Elaine held her hand out and William took it. She led him outside to garage-bay number three, where Trevor was loading a floor jack in the back of one of Gene's service trucks.

"May we ride with you?" she asked Trevor as she approached the service truck. Her strange smile was back, and Trevor began to feel uncomfortable.

"Yeah, sure," he said, looking at her, then down at William. "Uh, hop in. The door is unlocked."

All three of them got in the front seat of the truck; Trevor behind the wheel, William in the middle, and Elaine in the passenger seat. As they pulled out of the tire shop's parking lot, Trevor glanced at William and asked if he'd gotten dirty from playing outside. When William didn't respond, Elaine said in a kind voice, "He's a little dirty from trying to get the spare tire down. He's just too shy to say so." She patted William's shoulder. "He tried very hard."

"At least you tried, kid," Trevor said. "Most boys your age wouldn't be nice enough to even try to help their mom with something like this."

A minute later, Trevor was pulling into the parking lot. "Ah, there it is. I see it," he said, when he found the Suburban. He parked the service truck in an open spot on the side the flat tire was on. Trevor shut the truck off and slid the jack out of the bed while Elaine and William got out of the front seat. The lanky technician grabbed a square-shaped rod from the back of the service truck and slid it into a small opening on the Suburban's rear bumper. As soon as he began to crank it to the left, the spare tire came down on a cable.

William wore a frown on his face that looked as though he were at the beach and someone had just kicked over his sandcastle.

They each watched as Trevor placed the jack under the rear of the Suburban. In a few seconds, the vehicle's rear tires were inches above the asphalt. William's brow furrowed as he tried to understand how the vehicle had lifted into the air.

The trouble began right after Trevor started the air compressor.

"It's okay, William," Elaine said. "Be calm."

She felt him shaking under the palm of her hand. She had his shirt gripped tight. Suddenly, he began to jerk to the left and right. Every time Trevor used the impact wrench to take a lug nut off, William wanted to break free. Elaine held on tight, though. She didn't let him take off.

Trevor hadn't noticed William going mad to the right of him with the sound of the service truck's air compressor blaring behind him. He was also too focused with the task at hand. He checked the pressure in the spare tire and added air when he saw that it was a little low. Once he had the spare on the car, he took the impact wrench and ran the lug nuts back on.

As Trevor finished tightening up the final lug nut, Elaine lost her grip on William. Before she could get a hold on him, all hell broke loose.

William sank his teeth into Trevor's neck. Elaine saw Trevor's face fill with terror as he realized what was happening to him. Elaine was trying to pull William off Trevor, but the boy was latched on the tire tech like a bad dog. Finally, she shouted something—a spell perhaps—in William's ear. It took five seconds before he released Trevor. By then, the boy, Elaine, Trevor, and the pavement between the service truck and the Suburban were covered in Trevor's blood.

Tears streamed down Trevor's pale face as he screamed. Of course, with the roar of the air compressor, no one heard him. Before anyone saw what happened, Elaine opened the back door to the Suburban and slid William in. She knew this incident would bring lots of attention to her and William. Attention she had wanted to avoid. She couldn't put the blood back in Trevor's body. She was a witch, and a powerful one at that, but she wasn't a healer. Most of the incantations she knew were harmful to others. The one's that preserved and kept others alive were solely for her offspring. And those didn't bring them back from the dead; they merely kept their souls alive so that they could be placed in another person's body.

Elaine looked down at Trevor and saw that he was fading fast. The air compressor continued to blare as she opened the service truck's passenger door. Effortlessly, she bent down and picked up Trevor, tossing him in the front seat. He lay there staring at Elaine, trying to talk but unable to.

She spotted a pad on the dashboard. It was full of blank work invoices. She snagged a pen that was wedged in the window visor and wrote on the invoice. Elaine saw a few people coming out of the mall and walking toward her. In a hurry, she folded the paper and stuck it in Trevor's front pocket. "Sorry about my son. He can really be a pain in the neck sometimes," she said, and then slammed the door shut.

As she slid in behind the wheel of the Suburban, she put the vehicle in gear, ready to get the hell away from Trevor's soon-to-be dead body.

Then she stopped. A boy had snagged her gaze. The one she had been looking for before her tire went flat. His feathery blond hair was neatly parted to one side. He was holding the hand of a woman wearing an assortment of sumptuous jewelry that went well with her designer outfit. Next to her was a man in a gray pin-striped suit with slicked-back hair. They were walking to their car, a black four-door Bentley. As the little boy and his parents walked in front of the Suburban, they didn't see the blood on the pavement or Trevor's body in the front seat of the service truck. The boy's parents didn't see Elaine, either.

But the little boy did. The little boy only saw her for a second, but a second was enough.

"Thomas," she said, gripping the Suburban's steering wheel tight. "I've found you."

* * *

Barry stared at the note for nearly two minutes, and it would have gone on longer if his cell phone hadn't started ringing in his pocket. With his free hand, he reached into his front pocket and pulled out his cell. When he glanced down to see Eddie's name displayed across the screen, he tapped the green circle that would connect him with his long-time friend.

"Hello?"

"Hey, Barry, I just wanted to let you know that I'll be back in town tomorrow. Maybe noonish."

Silence on Barry's end of the line. He was staring at the note stuck on the blade of his knife again.

"Barry? You there, man?"

"Yeah," Barry said, taking his eyes off the note. He looked out at the lake instead. "I'm here."

"You sure? You sound a little funny."

"I just found a note."

"Okay. Are you going to make me guess what's on it?"

"No. Sorry. I think she's messing with my head."

"What do you mean? Where are you?"

"Hole in the Woods."

"For what reason? Do you think she would be hiding out there?"

"No, not really."

"Then why?"

"A dream I had last night in the hospital. I dreamed about this place. Do you remember the book I told you about? The one I found at my dad's rental."

"Yeah, of course. The one you said Holly read aloud before the witch came out of the lake. Kind of a hard thing to forget, honestly."

"Well, if you remember, the police never found the book back then."

"Yeah, I remember, Barry. Where are you going with this?"

"I dreamed that the book sank into the ground next to the tree I always parked my car next to."

"And did you find the book?"

"No," Barry paused. "But I did find a note."

"Right. The note. I almost forgot. What does it say?"

"I'll see you soon."

It was Eddie's turn to be silent.

"Eddie, did you—"

"Yeah, man, I heard you."

"I—I don't know how to stop her."

"We'll figure this out, all right?"

"Sure."

"Barry?"

"Yeah?"

"Get the hell out of there and go home."

"I will."

"See you when I see you," Eddie said before ending the call. Barry took the piece of paper off the knife's blade and stuck it in his pocket. He looked all around him, wondering if Elaine was watching him from afar. *Ridiculous*, he thought. *If she was watching, she would have already attacked me.*

Barry took one last look at the tree. His eyes locked on his initials there next to Holly's, thinking how much life had changed since the day he first carved those letters.

Barry began walking back to his car at a fast pace. Soon he was jumping back over the gate, and again he couldn't help but think of the teenagers he had reprimanded years ago. As he drove away from Hole in the Woods, he wondered if Elliot Deaver had made any progress on the Nancy McIntyre and Denny Molasky case. He doubted it, but he also hoped Elliot had found something to work with. He didn't want to go back to work starting exactly where he had left off. He looked down at his phone and remembered that he had Elliot's number stored in his contacts. Barry knew he wasn't supposed to do anything work related until the following day, but he just couldn't help himself. He found Elliot Deaver in his contacts and hit *Call*.

After the second ring, Officer Deaver answered. "Hello?"

"Hey, Elliot. It's Barry Kendall."

"And what can I do for you, *Detective?*"

Barry heard the emphasis Elliot put on the word but dismissed it. "I was wondering if you found any leads on Nancy McIntyre."

"Nothing yet."

"Where have you checked so far?"

"You know, Donaldson is letting me work this case my way until you get back tomorrow."

"So I've heard."

"If you've heard, then leave me alone, would you? Don't worry about where I've checked. The day isn't over. I could have the lady in custody by the time you come in tomorrow for all you know."

Barry knew Officer Deaver wouldn't find her. "Good luck with your search, Elliot. I just hope you have something for me to work with tomorrow, that's all."

"When I bring those two in tonight, you'll be demoted, and I'll have your job. You know that, right? You know I should have had that job in the first—"

Barry hit End and tossed his phone in the passenger seat. "That unfortunately went as expected," he muttered.

With nothing else left to do, Barry let out a deep breath and drove back home. By the time he pulled in his driveway, it was ten till five. He walked into his house, past the living room, and straight to the kitchen cabinet above the sink that he kept his liquor in. A few moments later, ice cubes clinked as he dropped them in the glass. Barry ambled to the living room, a glass in one hand and a whiskey bottle in the other. He placed each of them down on the coffee table and poured himself a drink. The whiskey wasn't the only thing on the table; his personal laptop rested on the other side. After a rather large sip, he flipped open his laptop. In the dim lighting, the screen illuminated his face. His laptop's background displayed a picture of him and Eddie at a car show a few years ago. That was something the two of them shared: a passion for cars. Although Eddie was undoubtedly more of an enthusiast than Barry. Around the time the two of them were working at Gene's Tire, Eddie had told Barry that he was going to open up a shop one day and hire Barry to work there. That dream of his didn't happen, of course. Eddie ended up getting his CDL, and Barry was too focused on getting in the police academy. Plus, Barry liked driving cars much more than turning wrenches on them. They remained best friends, though. Barry felt as if they always would be.

The day Barry's mother called him and told him she had cancer, Eddie was the first person he had called to tell and talk to about it. Other than his parents, Eddie was all he had.

Barry pulled up his go-to search engine to work on finding more information about Elaine. He was thinking of the right keywords to type when his phone began to ring in his pocket.

This time, it was his dad. Before answering, he took another sip of his whiskey.

"Hey, Dad."

"Hey, guess what I found?"

Barry sat the glass down on the table, and said, "Your mind?"

"Very funny. Don't you remember asking me to find that woman's name that rented from me all those years ago?"

Barry's eyes became large and round in an instant. "You found her name?"

"Yep."

"Well, what is it?"

"Melinda Henley."

Barry typed the name into the search engine. "Any information on her?"

"Just your basic lease agreement information: her date of birth, where she was working at the time, how much she made each month, how many children would be living with her."

"Can you give me all of that info?"

Barry's dad told him Melinda's date of birth, along with where she worked, which happened to be at the local post office. Lastly, Barry asked how many kids she had.

"Just one," Carl Kendall said. "She was about your age at the time from what I remember."

"Her name on there?"

Barry heard papers being sifted through on his dad's end of the line. "No, I'm afraid it's not."

"That's okay. The information you gave me should be good enough. Thanks a lot, Dad."

"Yeah, of course. No problem at all."

"How's Mom?"

"Tired. She's sleeping in the recliner next to me."

"I'll try to come see you guys a little more often."

"That sounds great, Barry. I know your mother would love to see you more."

"It'll probably have to be after this case, though."

"Oh. Yeah, I—uh," Carl cleared his throat. "I understand."

"Thanks again," Barry said, trying to sound grateful. "I've got to get back to work on this case."

"Okay, Barry. I'll let you go."

"Bye, Dad."

By the time Barry ended the call, his laptop had already brought up a dozen different people with the name Melinda Henley. He knew it would take him hours on end to find the correct Melinda this way. Fortunately for Barry, he had a laptop with a much more thorough database that only law enforcement had access to. Barry looked at the glass of whiskey, deciding he better not drink any more just yet. It sat on the table while he hurried out to his car.

Barry slid in behind the wheel of his Charger and flipped open his laptop, immediately typing in Melinda Henley's name and date of birth. His eyes were glued to the screen as it loaded the next page. Finally, as the screen loaded, he saw the woman his dad had rented to all those years ago. The woman that left without telling his dad she was moving. The woman who left a book on witchcraft in her shed that would flip Barry's world on its head.

He stared at her picture for a minute or so, memorizing her features. According to her date of birth, the woman was forty-nine. For that age, Barry thought she looked quite young in the photographs. He couldn't find a time stamp, but because of the quality, he figured they were from eight-or-nine years ago. He continued looking through the database and discovered something that he didn't expect to see. It was written in all-caps: DECEASED.

Barry sat back in his seat with his hands on the top of head, fingers interlocked, and let out a sigh. After a few seconds, he began scrolling to see what else he could find now that he wouldn't be able to contact Melinda Henley. Barry was counting on her to give him the answers to all his questions about Elaine. The question he wanted to ask her first, though, was, "Why'd you leave the book?"

Barry would never be able to ask her that question now, and he was just seconds away from slamming the laptop shut when his eyes found a section that showed all the places Melinda Henley had lived.

She was born in Adams, Tennessee, and according to the information on the screen, she lived there until she was thirty years old. The first Florida town she lived in was Clearwater. White sand and clear blue water must not have been what she was looking for, though, because only a year later she moved to Abbott, where she lived in his dad's rental property for a couple of years. After that, it said she moved back to Tennessee; however, this time Melinda settled in Blountville. The database showed her address, but Barry didn't need it; he saw something near the very bottom of the page that would do just fine: her daughter's name.

Her name was Aidy Henley.

As the sky began to darken around him, he typed the daughter's name into the database. Barry thought, for just a moment, he was looking at the same picture of the woman he had just typed in only a couple of minutes ago, but it wasn't. This woman looked even younger, her hair was dyed a dark red, and her skin appeared to be a paler complexion than her mother's. The first sentence he read showed that she had lived in all the same locations as her mother, except for one.

It seemed that Aidy had moved back to Florida soon after the death of her mother. Now Aidy lived in Tampa, Florida, a city only a half-hour drive from Abbott.

Barry looked at the darkening sky again, and then at the digital clock on his car's dashboard.

It read 6:08 p.m.

Barry put the address into his GPS and left his driveway without a second thought. In another thirty minutes or less, he would be knocking on Aidy's door.

* * *

When the couple with the little blond boy got into their Bentley, Elaine followed them from a distance. She was careful not to get too close. William, who had possession over Denny's body, sat in the backseat with dried blood around his lips still. His gaze was focused on the vehicle in front of them; the vehicle that his soon-to-be little brother was in.

After a few miles, the Bentley turned down a side road. Elaine slowed the Suburban down and watched as the Bentley stopped in front of a fenced-in yard with a large metal gate. Within a second or two, the gate swung open, and the Bentley drove down the asphalt driveway to a three-story colonial house that sat at the end of the road.

Elaine memorized the house and its address.

"We'll come back in a few hours, William," Elaine said. "When we see the lights go out, we'll remove your brother from that house. He'll be back with us again."

"Thomas," William said. "Back with us."

"He will be."

"I miss him."

"As do I, William. As do I."

They drove back to the cabin out in the woods. Elaine set the bed up with restraints as she did with Denny. She'd give him the same potion she gave the first boy and recite the same incantation that would bring back her youngest son, Thomas. Once she had Thomas back, she'd be not only stronger but twice as dangerous.

After Elaine got the bed ready for the little blond boy, she saw William sitting upright on the couch, staring at the floor. He looked as if nothing at all was going on upstairs.

"William, are you okay?"

His eyes snapped up and met hers. "Yes, Mama."

"What are you thinking about?"

"I don't know."

Elaine walked over to the couch and sat down next to him. "You can tell mama what you're thinking about."

William nodded as if he understood, but he stayed silent.

"Are you thinking about your brother?" she asked.

William nodded.

"Soon," she said, giving his thigh a few pats. "We just have to wait a while longer."

Elaine opened her book of incantations, the one Holly read to summon her thirteen years ago. Elaine read for hours until it was dark out. William sat beside her on the couch and stared at the floor again. Around nine o'clock, Elaine closed the book and placed it on the night-stand. She glanced over at William, who was beginning to drift off to sleep, and said, "It's time to go get Thomas."

* * *

Barry made it to Tampa in twenty-eight minutes. He was parked outside of an apartment complex a couple miles north of Ybor City. He had her address and apartment number, but he didn't know exactly what to say to her. He had questioned many people over the years, but this was different.

Barry stepped outside of his car and heard an engine revving in the distance, followed by unintelligible shouting. He walked up to the apartment complex, his hand resting on the butt of his Glock.

According to the information on the laptop, Aidy's apartment was on the second floor. Barry found the stairs and proceeded up them in a hurry. When he made it to the second floor, he passed a drunk couple stumbling down the hallway, but managed to slip past them without an incident. He thought the fact that he looked like a cop might have helped with that.

He checked the apartment numbers as he walked down the hallway. When he finally made it to Aidy's door, he felt a ping of unease. Barry took a deep breath, then he rapped his knuckles against the door three times and waited. After a short period of time, the door swung open.

Aidy stood there in a tank top and pair of black leggings that accentuated her hourglass figure. She looked exactly like the photo he saw of her earlier: dark red hair, pale skin, and resembled her mother.

Barry said, "I'm—"

"I know who you are," Aidy said with a snap.

Barry opened his mouth to speak, but the words escaped him.

"Well, don't just stand there," she said. "Come in so we can talk. I'm sure you have a multitude of questions."

Barry followed her to the couch in the small living room. He sat down and looked around at all the cardboard boxes, noticing the walls and most of the apartment was bare and lacking décor.

"Can I get you something, Barry? A water or—"

"No, thanks," he said. "And how do you know my name? How do you know who I am?"

"Already with the questions, huh? You know, I could ask you the same thing now, couldn't I? And better yet, how'd you even find me?"

"I asked first."

"And you'll answer first, if you want to know more."

Barry met her eyes again and felt something. He couldn't exactly say what that feeling was, although he was pretty sure it was akin to dismay.

"Fine," he said, and took a deep breath. "I'm a detective for the Abbott Police Department. I found your name and looked you up on my laptop. It gave me the address to your apartment. I'm working a case where a woman went missing and—"

"And you think it has something to do with Elaine?"

Barry raised his eyebrows. "So you know her?"

"Know *of* her, yes. I'm related to her, on my dad's side."

"Who's your dad?"

"I don't know," she said, looking down at her coffee table. "He left shortly after marrying my mom. I was only two years old. I don't remember what he looked or even sounded like."

"I'm sorry to hear that."

"I know Elaine killed her too," Aidy said. She was looking down, but Barry could see tears developing in her eyes. "That's why I came to Florida. To find you. I was going to get an Uber to Abbott tomorrow."

"Your mom, you mean?"

Aidy nodded.

"I'm sorry."

Aidy bit her bottom lip and shifted her gaze up to Barry. Elaine had murdered someone each of them loved. He felt her pain.

"Why'd you come to Florida to find me, Aidy?" Barry asked.

"To warn you," she said. "And help you."

"What do you mean by that?"

"By now, you surely know that she wants to kill you too."

"Yes, that much I know. But how can you help me?"

"Well, first of all, I know why she wants you dead. Do you know why?"

"Because I found her book on witchcraft, I'm guessing."

Aidy blinked away the tears and smirked. "Being a detective, I really thought you'd be closer than that."

"I can't find any information on her. Believe me, I've looked."

Aidy stood up. "Come on. Follow me."

"Where to?"

"I want to show you something."

Barry stood up and followed her to a small bedroom. He saw an unmade bed, a dresser, and more cardboard boxes.

"You just move in, I take it?" Barry asked, standing by the door's threshold.

Aidy opened the dresser's top drawer, moved a few items of clothing, and pulled out a black leather book.

"Yeah, a few days ago. I left Tennessee after my mom's funeral."

Barry stared at the book, frozen in place.

"Hey," she said, knitting her brows together. "Are you okay?"

"Is that the book?"

"What are you talking about?"

"The book," he said, pointing. "Is it Elaine's?"

"No. This one was my mom's."

"Your mom was a witch too?"

"Yes, but she was good. That's why Elaine killed her."

"Your mom was a good witch? Those exist?"

"Not all witches are bad. Some of us are good and some aren't, just like normal humans," she said. "Although, I must admit that my mom did have a dark past."

"Wait. Some of us? Are you telling me you're a witch?"

Aidy smiled softly and sat on the edge of the bed, patting the spot next to her. "Come sit."

Barry stood still by the door's threshold.

"Oh, come on. I promise not to put a spell on you," she said, dropping Barry a wink.

"This isn't funny," Barry said.

"Never said it was." Aidy patted the edge of the bed again. "Now come sit if you want to know why she wants to kill you."

Barry acquiesced and sat down next to her.

Aidy eyed him as he sat down. Her arms rested on the book in her lap. "Comfy?" she asked.

"Sure."

"I felt it would be best for you to hear all of this while sitting."

Barry gave her a look that said, *I'm waiting.*

"Okay, so in the mid eighteen-hundreds, Elaine was killed by your great-great-grandfather for practicing witchcraft. His name was also Barry."

"You're serious?"

"Yes, look it up on one of those ancestry websites if you'd like. And him killing her isn't the worst part. Before he drowned her in a lake, he and his deputies drowned her three children in front of her."

"His deputies? He was a sheriff?"

"A sheriff that loathed anyone who practiced witchcraft. After the Bell Witch incident, the local police didn't take any chances with witches. They were killed as soon as they could prove they were witches, and sometimes before they could prove it."

"I read about the Bell Witch while trying to find information on Elaine. That took place in Adams, Tennessee."

"Yes. That's where my mom and I are from."

"Don't tell me you're related to the Bell Witch."

"Not that I'm aware of. My grandma was a witch that practiced black magic. She wanted my mother to follow in her footsteps, of course. And she did for a little while. My grandma introduced my mom to my dad. My dad told her about your great-great grandfather killing Elaine. He told my mom the whole story, and he gave my mom a book. A book that was handed down generation to generation. A book that was ultimately meant for you to open."

"I don't understand, Aidy. How'd your dad get the book in the first place?"

"He's how I'm related to Elaine. He's kin to her. That's what my mom told me anyway."

"How, though? Did Elaine have a sister or brother that also practiced witchcraft and just somehow flew under the radar?"

"That's the part I'm not sure of," Aidy said. "My mom never told me *how* he was kin to her. I always assumed a cousin or something."

"Yeah, maybe," he said. "Okay, so your dad told your mom the story about my great-great grandfather killing Elaine and her three sons?"

"Correct."

"And your mom somehow found me and saw my dad's rental ad online?"

"Also correct."

"Then, when the time was right, she moved away, leaving Elaine's book for me to find?"

"Not quite."

"What do you mean?"

"Like I said, my mom was a good witch. She didn't leave the book for you. My dad did."

Barry's brow furrowed as he thought it over. "Why would he leave it for me?"

"My mom said he's a talented wizard. That he has good in him, but that someone has also ingrained loyalty to Elaine and her plan in him."

"Her plan to kill me?"

"Yes."

"Because of something my great-great grandfather did a long, long time ago?"

"Hit the nail on the head."

"Hardly seems fair, does it?"

Aidy nodded in assent. "What your great-great grandfather did shouldn't be your problem."

"But?" Barry asked.

"But it is."

"How, though? How did your dad know I'd take that book home?"

"I don't know. I'm nowhere near as powerful as he is."

"We need to find him."

Aidy laughed. "Good luck with that."

"What makes you say that?"

"He's a powerful wizard. If he doesn't want to be found, he won't be."

"I suppose you're right," Barry said, then was silent for a few moments. "Did he make you and your mom move out of my dad's rental?"

"Yes."

"He was the one that trashed the place, too, wasn't he?"

Aidy nodded. "It was his way to get us to leave sooner."

"And you never saw him?"

"No. My mom said he found her outside of the grocery store one day. He told her what had to happen. He told her it was time for Elaine and her three boys to return."

"Three boys. That must be why she took the Molasky boy."

"What do you mean?"

"Elaine kidnapped a twelve-year-old boy the other day."

Judging by the shocked look on Aidy's face, this was news she didn't know yet. "She's bringing them back one at a time."

"Which means she's going to kidnap two more innocent children."

Aidy didn't say anything. She just shook her head.

"Do you know what she's going to do to the kid?"

"Not exactly, no. If I had to guess, though, she's apt to use some sort of mind-controlling incantation, enchantment, or maybe even something worse."

"What do you mean, worse?"

"Worse as in, casting one of the forbidden spells. One that actually puts the soul of someone, whether they're dead or not, in another person."

A rational person would have laughed and called her insane, but Barry had seen things he couldn't explain with rationality. As soon as the words were out of her mouth, Barry just knew that was what Elaine was planning to do.

"I have to call Donaldson," Barry said.

"Who's that?"

"My sergeant."

"And tell him what exactly? You think he's going to believe some crazy story about a witch coming back to seek revenge against you and your family?"

"I'll start with the idea that she may try to kidnap more kids. And as far as the witch talk goes, I'll have to have hard evidence if I want to prove it to my sergeant."

"And what hard evidence do you have?"

"Just you so far."

"Which isn't good enough evidence for your sergeant, is it?"

"No, but I have this," Barry said, taking a folded piece of paper out of his pocket and handing it to Aidy.

She unfolded the note and read what was written across it.

I'll see you soon.

"She knows you're looking for her," she said, handing the note back to Barry.

"Yeah, I gathered that."

"What's your plan if you do find her?"

"Kill her before she kills me."

"Not a bad plan. Easier said than done, though. I think you'll need my help."

"What makes you say that?"

"Well, if she hurts you, I can help heal you. Most of the spells my mom taught me were healing spells."

"You don't know any spells that do harm?"

"Just one. It can incapacitate or stun someone transiently."

"That could come in handy."

"Yeah, only Elaine would counter that spell easily."

"I guess I have my work cut out for me."

"An understatement."

Barry checked his watch. "I have an early morning ahead of me. I better get going. Thank you for shedding some light on this whole situation."

"You're welcome."

Barry nodded and lifted himself off the bed. When he reached the door, he said, "Are you worried she's going to try to find you?"

"Yeah," she said. "But you're the only one that knows I'm here."

"Let's hope you're right about that," Barry said, and handed her a card with his number on it. "Call me if you need me."

"Okay," Aidy said, glancing down at the card. "I just put my number in your phone."

Barry pulled his cell out and saw her phone number stored. "How the hell?"

Aidy met Barry's eyes again. "I'm a witch, remember?"

"Not sure how I forgot."

"Onset dementia probably."

Barry smiled at that one. "Good night, Aidy."

"Good night, Detective."

Barry left her apartment and walked back down to where his car was parked. When he sat behind the wheel of his Charger, it dawned on him that he had just had a conversation with an actual witch. Not your arche-typal witch, though. Aidy wasn't an old crone with a prominent wart on her nose or forehead; she was his age, kind, and easy on the eyes.

From down the road, Barry either heard a car backfire or someone fire off a shotgun round. He looked around and didn't see anyone with a gun, so he put the car in gear and headed home. Barry tried to go to bed early that night, but his thoughts kept him awake. After an hour or so, he went into the kitchen and made himself a drink. The alcohol allowed him to stop thinking as much. He got back in bed and fell asleep in a few minutes. Barry's alarm was set for 7 a.m., but his phone began to blare its ringtone an hour and a half before the alarm was set to go off.

Barry answered on the third ring. "Hello?"

"Barry, it's Donaldson."

Barry sat up in his bed. "What's going on?"

"I have something here you need to see."

"Can you give me a hint?"

"Rhymes with Nancy McIntyre."

"I'll be right there."

* * *

Elaine piloted the Suburban down the side road she had driven down earlier that day. It was 9:12 p.m., and in just a minute or two, she'd be in front of the gate that led to the three-story colonial house she had fol-lowed the Bentley down just hours ago.

The Suburban's brakes squeaked as Elaine brought the vehicle to a stop. William sat in the passenger seat, staring out of the window at the house. It was well lit with lots of outdoor lights. And even though she was behind the fence, a hundred yards or so away, Elaine could see that two lights were still on in the house. The light shining through the windows were on the second story, but that didn't worry her in the slightest. She didn't know which room was the boy's and she didn't know which room was his parents', but as soon as one of the lights went out, she'd have a pretty good idea. She knew it was customary for the child's light to be turned off first, just as soon as his mom or dad tucked him in and flipped the switch off before heading back to their own room.

Elaine gripped the key in the ignition and turned the Suburban off. There wasn't much traffic on the road at that time of night, especially since the house was the only thing on that stretch of road. The vehicle's headlights were off. She had pulled onto the sidewalk, close to the fence, in a dimly lit spot between two streetlights.

"Want to help Mama?" Elaine asked William.

William nodded with enthusiasm.

"Good. You stay here," she said, opening the car door. "Now, when you see me coming back with Thomas, I want you to start the car. Okay?"

"How do I do that?"

"It's easy. Now watch." Elaine twisted the key until it turned over and fired up. "See. Now you try one time."

Elaine turned the vehicle off again. William shuffled in his seat, reaching over to grip the key. He twisted it and jumped a little when the Suburban started up.

He met her eyes and said, "That was fun, Mama."

"Yes, now remember what I told you." She turned the vehicle off again. "Have the car running when you see me coming back, just in case Thomas and I are seen by the people that live in the house."

"Who are those people, Mama?"

"Not important, William. What is important is that we leave the car off. We don't want to draw too much attention to ourselves. Now do you remember what you're supposed to do when you see me and Thomas?"

"Turn the car on?"

"Precisely," she said, pinching his cheek. "I'll be back soon. Be ready."

Elaine opened the sunroof and stood on top of the Suburban. The old witch was incredibly agile for her age; she leaped over the fence, oddly cat-like, landing on her feet and hands. When she stood back up, she looked at William sitting in the Suburban, then she spun around and made her way up to the house. She was careful to keep near the darker sections of the property, staying out of well-lit areas. As she neared the house, she noticed the security cameras fastened to every corner. In the last thirteen years, she had learned a lot about this new world, but it was only a couple of years ago that she learned about security cameras. She knew very little about them, other than that some were motion-activated and had night vision. She stayed on the edge of the property, far enough away that the security cameras, if they were motion-activated, wouldn't detect her movement.

She sat next to a thick bush on the fence line, watching the house's windows until one of them went dark. After ten minutes or so, Elaine let out a deep, slow breath as the light behind the window closest to her went out; she knew which room was the boy's now, and she knew she needed to move fast.

Elaine walked the fence line to the back of the house, where she saw a large oak tree. She didn't spot a camera pointed at the tree and knew she had found her way up into the boy's window. With ease, Elaine made her way up the tree, climbing a branch that jutted out over the back of the house. She landed on the roof with an unnatural quietness. It was as if she weighed nothing at all.

Elaine walked along the edge of the roof, and when she got to boy's bedroom, she gripped the cameras from above and ripped them off the house. With the wires no longer intact, she let them fall to the ground.

The boy's window was right beneath her. There was another section of the roof that served as an eave for the first story. She jumped down to that section, which she did just as quietly as before, and put her hands on the window. With her palms pressed against the glass, she tried to move the window, but it was locked. Elaine let out a grunt of annoyance and tapped softly on the glass with her nails.

The boy didn't answer, and she knew she couldn't risk being any louder. She closed her eyes, searching for the boy's mind. Being so close in proximity, it didn't take long to find him.

He was already asleep, dreaming sweet dreams of playing video games.

In the boy's dream, he sat in his leather recliner playing a newly released game on a large flat screen TV. When Elaine's face popped on the screen, he thought it was all part of the game.

"Thomas," she said. "I need you to wake up."

"Who is this character on the game?" he asked himself.

"I'm your mother."

Thomas's eyes widened. "You can hear me?"

"Of course I can, Thomas."

"Why are you calling me that? My name is Phillip."

Elaine cringed on the screen when he told her his name. Now her eyes narrowed and looked deep into his eyes through the TV's screen. "Wake up and go to your bedroom window. Open it for Mama. I have a present for you."

"A present," Phillip said, his eyes lighting up.

"Open the window. Wake up and open the window," she said.

Phillip snapped awake. Darkness surrounded him, except for the nightlight plugged into the outlet next to the window, the window Elaine was on the other side of. Phillip heard her tapping lightly on the glass now. The boy slid out of bed, not bothering to turn on the ceiling-fan light, and took tentative steps toward the window.

"Open the window if you want to see your present," Phillip heard from outside his room. He was standing in front of the window curtains now, spreading them apart. He took a deep breath before lifting the blinds. When the blinds went up, he saw no one. Phillip rubbed his eyes with the backs of his hands and looked out of the window again.

Still no one.

Phillip reached toward the window. His fingers found the locks and flipped them open. When he lifted the window all the way up, he stuck his head through to look around outside. He looked to the left and right and saw no one, but he did see a vehicle parked by the gate in front of his house. He couldn't tell if it was a car or a truck being so far away; however, in that moment, the thought of the vehicle vanished from his mind. From below his window, he felt a hand wrap around his throat and pull him out of the house. The boy went to scream, but Elaine mumbled another incantation as she held the boy's mouth. The boy yelled at the top of his lungs, but no sound came out; not even a whisper.

"Don't worry, Thomas," she said, stroking his feathery blond hair as she held him on the eave of the house. "Mama is here."

The boy tried to shout again. No sound came out.

Phillip was still in his pajamas. He began to cry as he struggled to get away.

"Don't be scared, my child," Elaine said, tightening her hold. She spun him around so that his eyes would meet hers. "I'm not going to hurt you. Understand?"

The boy shook his head as if he did, but he still continued to cry. Elaine's eyes widened and began to softly recite an incantation. As soon as she started the spell, the boy stopped his mewling and stared intensely at Elaine as if he were looking through her.

"Time to go, my boy," she said, that strangle smile once again displaying itself.

She took Phillip by the hand, leading him to the edge of the roof. With the cameras removed, she didn't bother going to the back of the house; she put the boy in her arms and jumped down to the grass as she did with Denny from the burning house. If she were an ordinary human being, the impact alone would be enough to break one's ankles, but Elaine had a supernatural advantage that others simply did not.

Elaine didn't waste a second as she landed in the soft timothy grass; she put one foot in front of the other and walked back to the fence line. When she reached the dark section of the property near the fence line, she spun around to see if anyone heard her or noticed the boy missing. The light that was on in the boy's parents' room went out just seconds after she reached the fence line. She grinned, knowing she hadn't been heard or seen, or so she had thought.

Elaine noticed the boy's eyes still had that faraway look. She lifted him up on her shoulder and carried the boy back to the Suburban. As she got close, she heard the engine start up; William had remembered what she told him.

William went through the sunroof as Elaine had earlier. He stood on top of the Suburban and grabbed the boy when Elaine lifted him over the fence. Once William had him, Elaine pulled herself up and over the fence and stood on top of the Suburban again.

"Get back in the car. I'll hand Thomas down to you," Elaine told William.

William did as she said and put the boy in his lap as he sat down in the passenger seat. Elaine slipped in behind the wheel, smiling eerily as she looked at the two boys next to her.

"Where we going, Mama?" William asked.

"Home, my child. We're going home."

Chapter 9

Barry pulled his Charger into the station at ten till six. He stepped out of the car and made his way up the sidewalk. His shirt was untucked and he hadn't shaved, but he was there. Donaldson stood out front next to the door, smoking a cigarette. His shirt was tucked in, but his face looked haggard, as if he hadn't slept much himself.

"Thought you quit?" Barry said.

"I did, as far as my wife knows," Donaldson replied.

"How bad is it?"

"Bad, Barry."

"Worse than Denny Molasky?"

Donaldson closed his tired eyes and shook his head. "Let's go inside," he said, putting the cigarette out on the bottom of his shoe. "We're going to need some coffee."

The two went to Donaldson's office and sipped on their coffees. Donaldson sat his down and placed his elbows on his desk, rubbing his temples with his thumbs. He let out a deep breath and said, "We have a shit show on our hands."

"Nancy got another one?"

"Try two. Well, one isn't exactly a kid. He was in his early twenties. Still a kid to me."

"Deaver didn't get any leads on her either, did he?"

"No, he didn't."

"That's why you called me in early."

Donaldson stopped rubbing his temples and crossed his arms as he straightened up in his seat. "How are you going to find this woman, Barry?"

"How do you know it was her?"

"The parents emailed me the video from a hidden camera. It was in a tree next to the fence by the road."

"Show me the video."

Donaldson spun his laptop around so that Barry could see it. It showed Nancy McIntyre jumping over the fence. Then he fast forwarded to the part where she was leaving with a small child."

"Whose kid is that?"

"Gerald and Clair Carter's eight-year-old son, Phillip."

"Oh shit."

"Oh shit is right."

"She took the son of the wealthiest family in town. What'd they say to you?"

"Clair told me that she had woken up in the middle of the night. Her bladder was full. Something about some medical problem she has. Anyway, she peeked in her son's room and saw that the window was open. She immediately woke up Gerald, who opened the app on his phone to check his cameras. He found that two of them weren't working and that someone had ripped them off the house. Then he saw her on the hidden tree camera, which he immediately sent to us. He gave me an earful this morning. They both did. Being lawyers, and hysterical, they threatened to sue the department if we didn't get their child back safely in under twenty-four hours."

"As if the judge will go for that."

"Who knows, Barry? Gerald Carter didn't become rich by being bad at his job. We have to find this kid today, dammit."

"Okay," Barry said, steepling his fingers. "What about the other one?"

"Other what?" Donaldson asked, taking another sip of coffee.

"You said, 'Try two.' Who's the other one?"

"There was a murder in the parking lot of the mall down the road from Gene's Tire. The murder victim worked at Gene's. He was on a service call to fix a tire for the damn woman, and she killed him for no apparent reason. It just doesn't make any sense."

Donaldson drank the rest of his coffee and placed several photographs along with a piece of paper on his desk so that Barry could see them. Barry lifted the first photograph up to get a better look. He didn't recognize the guy in the picture, but he could tell that his neck had been bitten.

"What the hell," Barry said. "You're sure she did this?"

"In broad damn daylight."

"Is that a bite mark on his neck?"

Donaldson nodded.

Barry looked at the other pictures. He held two of them up now. "How didn't anyone see her do this?"

"Beats the hell out of me, Barry. I can't say I've ever worked a case this strange before.

We don't know what her motive is, and, most importantly, we can't find her *or* the two missing kids." Donaldson lifted the piece of paper off the desk before Barry had a chance to pick it up. "I haven't even told you the strangest part, Barry."

Barry stared at him, listening intently.

"I really don't understand this at all." Donaldson read what was on the paper to himself one time before handing it over. Barry looked at it. He saw that the paper was an invoice slip from Gene's Tire. He saw Nancy's bloody fingerprints on the corner where she had been holding it. His heartrate doubled when he read what was written across the paper in black ink.

You're next, Barry.

* * *

When Elaine parked the Suburban in front of the cabin, she told William to bring his brother inside. The spell Elaine used on Phillip Carter was starting to wane, but for the most part, he wasn't fighting back much. Elaine looked up at the night sky and said, "Get him to the back bedroom. I'll be there in a minute to prepare his transformation."

It was nearly ten o'clock when Elaine and William got Phillip tied to the bed, the same one Denny Molasky had been tied to not that long ago. Denny had become William, and if everything went the way Elaine wanted it to, Phillip would become Thomas.

"Now what do we do, Mama?" William asked, looking innocently up at Elaine.

"We wait, my child. We wait until midnight. Then, when everything is just right, I'll recite the spell that will put Thomas's soul in this boy," she said, patting the top of his head.

Phillip blinked his eyes several times from the bed. A look of understanding crossed his face, and his voice had returned. "Where am I? Who are you? Who is he?"

"I'm your mother," Elaine said, showing her teeth.

"And I'm William."

Phillip's eyes darted back and forth between the two. "Why'd you tie me up?"

"Oh," Elaine said, walking up to the boy's bedside. She ran her hand over the boy's face, moving his feathery blond hair from in front of his eyes. "It's for your protection. I wouldn't want anything bad to happen to you, Thomas. No, I couldn't handle that again."

Phillip's brow furrowed. He looked at Elaine as if she were insane. "You're not here to protect me. I want to go home! Let me go!"

Phillip shouted and shouted. "Let me go! Let me go! Let me go!"

William gave Elaine a quizzical look. "Why's he saying that, Mama?"

"He just doesn't remember who he is, William. It's up to us to remind him."

William moved next to Elaine by the edge of the bed. "It's okay, Thomas. Mama is going to help you like she did me. You don't have to be scared."

Phillip spat on William. It hit him just above his right eye. The spittle started to run over his eyelid and then down his cheek. Elaine grimaced. William brushed off the spittle with his hand and wiped it on his jeans.

"Why'd he do—"

Phillip's head twisted to the right as Elaine slapped him hard on the left side of his face.

Phillip's eyes met hers. She could see that he was dazed, and that a red mark under his eye had started to swell.

"That's no way to treat your brother, Thomas."

Phillip was too disoriented to hear or respond to her.

"We were going to keep you company, but now I think we'll leave you to think about how rude you were to William." She grabbed William by the shoulder and motioned him out of the room. "I'll be back in a couple of hours. I hope you'll be in a better mood, or else the transformation could be quite painful."

Elaine closed the door behind her. Phillip was still dazed and didn't hear anything she had said. William let Elaine guide him to the couch.

"You should get some rest, William," Elaine said.

"No, I want to help you with Thomas," he said as he sat down on the couch.

Elaine smiled as if her murderous son were a perfect angel. "You're such a good boy, William, but Mama knows best. And Mama says you need your rest."

William nodded and rested his head on the edge of the couch. Within a few minutes, his eyes closed and he began to snore an eerie, creepy snore.

Elaine sat in the recliner next to him, flipping through pages in her book of spells. She was not only a vengeful, evil witch, but also a studious one; a witch that kept her eyes on the prize. Elaine wanted to strangle

Barry. She wanted him to suffer through the same pain his great-great grandfather caused her and her children.

To get revenge, though, she would need her boys. *Mama's boys.*

After rereading the spell she needed to perform that night for the twentieth time, two beams of light shined in through the cabin's front window and landed on her face. She closed the book, squinted, and put a hand in front of her eyes to block the blinding lights. She rose up from the couch, hardly disconcerted, and walked over to the window. Parked outside was a dark-colored truck pulling a mid-sized camper behind it. She heard the vehicle's engine shut off, but the headlights stayed on. Elaine thought for a second that the blond boy's parents had somehow followed her to the cabin. That thought went away as soon as she heard two car doors shut, one after the other. In the yellow glow of the truck's headlights was an old couple that looked to be in their seventies. The man held a wood-colored cane, and the woman held him by the arm as they walked up to the front door. Elaine still stood at the window, watching them as they neared the door. Keys jangled in the old man's hands as he tried to find the right one.

"Are you sure you left it on the nightstand, Hank?"

"I know where I left it, Dolores. I'll grab it, and then we can get back on the–"

"Whose vehicle is that, Hank?" Dolores said, looking behind her. "Is it the cleaning lady's?"

"I don't know. I didn't even see it when we pulled in."

"I don't think it's the cleaning lady's car. It wouldn't make sense for her to be here at this time of–"

"Dolores, the window," Hank said. "Someone broke in."

"We better leave and file a police report."

"But what about–"

"Shhh," she said, listening. "I heard something. It sounded like a little boy."

From inside the cabin, Phillip began to yell for help.

"Hear that, Hank?"

Hank's brow furrowed for a few seconds as he listened to the boy's cries for help.

Then suddenly, the cries stopped.

"We need to go in," Hank said. "That little boy could be hurt."

Dolores nodded and squeezed Hank's arm. "Then we'll file the police report."

Hank twisted the doorknob to see if it was unlocked. He realized it was as the door swung inward. It was dark inside. He used his cane to make his way in the house. Dolores still held his arm but now she was holding on tightly, as if afraid he'd float away.

Hank leaned his cane against the wall, reaching for the light switch. When he flipped it on, he saw a young boy lying down on the couch.

"Are you okay, son?" Hank asked. "You alone in here?"

William's eyes flicked between the old man and his wife. He looked at them the way a bird looks at a worm. His mouth began to salivate.

"Hank, stay back. There's something wrong with—"

William leaped at Hank, mouth open, arms outstretched. Hank brought his cane up just fast enough so that the William's teeth sank into his cane instead of his throat. Dolores screamed as Hank tried to keep the deranged boy from killing him.

"Run to the truck, Dolores!" Hank shouted. "Leave!"

Dolores turned around and glanced outside. The truck's headlights had been turned off.

Elaine was walking up to the cabin.

"There's a woman outside, Hank!"

William's teeth were still locked on the cane when he pushed Hank into his wife, whom he toppled over and brought down with him. The old couple were both on the floor now by the door's threshold. Hank tried to keep pushing the cane up and away from him, but William's relentlessness began to wear the old man out. He was struggling to keep William away.

The boy removed his teeth from the cane, grabbed it with both hands and wrenched it away from Hank.

"Please," Hank said. "Don't do this."

William was on Hank in a second. The boy's teeth were just inches from Hank's neck when he felt a powerful hand grab him by the hair. William looked up to see Elaine. She seemed proud.

"That's my boy," she said. "Get up. I have plans for these two."

William obediently stood up.

"Get some leftover rope from the bedroom. We're going to save these two for tomorrow. One for you, one for Thomas."

"Yes, Mama," William said, and ran off into the bedroom.

Hank was taking deep breaths, as was Dolores.

"Why are you doing this?" Hank asked.

"What do you want?" Dolores added. "If it's money, we'll give it to you. Please, just let us go."

Elaine shifted her gaze down at the old couple. "I just want my boys."

Hank and Dolores exchanged a look, confused and terrified.

"I want Barry Kendall to feel the pain I felt when my boys were drowned in front of me."

"Who's Barry Kendall?" Hank asked.

"A man whose days are numbered." A savage smile appeared on her face.

"I got it, Mama," William said as he ran in with the rope.

"Good. Tie them up. Put them in the bathroom."

"Now wait just a damn min—" Hank began to say before Elaine made a gesture with her hand. Hank's mouth still moved. His lips and tongue still worked, but no sound came from his mouth.

Dolores let out a small cry as she watched her husband try to talk. "What did you do to Ha—"

Elaine made the same gesture with her hand and Dolores's voice was gone. Her mouth was moving but words were not coming out. Elaine had taken their voices, and William tied them up quicker than a boy scout with a vest full of merit badges could have.

William dragged Hank into the bathroom first. Then he came back and got Dolores. Elaine sat on the couch again, her book of spells flipped open on her lap. William walked around the coffee table and sat on the couch next to her.

"Did you shut the bathroom door?" Elaine asked William.

"Yes, Mama."

"Good," she said, and glanced at the clock on the wall. It was 10:30 p.m.

William rested his head on her lap, and she read over her spells again. They did this until 11:58 p.m.

Elaine glanced at the clock.

"Are you asleep, William?"

"No, Mama."

"Get up, then. It's time."

Each of them stood up, making their way to the back bedroom. Phillip was no longer struggling to get out of the restraints. The little blond boy's eyes looked tired, his face completely drained, as if he had been trying to undo the restraints for the past two hours. His head was lowered but he raised it up slowly when he noticed Elaine had entered.

"One minute to go, Thomas," she said. "Are you ready?"

Phillip didn't respond.

From behind Elaine, William said, "Don't worry, it doesn't hurt too bad."

Phillip started to cry. He couldn't move. "I just want to go home," he said, his lips trembling as each word came out of his mouth.

"But, Thomas," Elaine said, spreading her hands out before her. "You are home. You're with your true family."

Before Phillip could say another word, Elaine began her incantation in a clear, loud voice. Neither Phillip nor William knew what the words meant, but it was clear that something was happening. Each of them could feel it.

As Elaine continued on with the spell, she dug into her pocket and pulled out another vial full of red liquid, just like the vial she had made Denny drink the night before. She walked up to the side of the bed.

Phillip was frozen in fear, hardly moving a muscle. She leaned over him and said, "Open up. You drink this and it's all over."

Phillip pressed his lips together and closed his eyes. Elaine squeezed his nose, cutting off his air. When he went to open his mouth to breathe, she poured the red liquid down his throat. She didn't let go of his nose; in fact, she squeezed even harder. Phillip had no choice but to drink the red liquid. After he did, he was able to breathe again. Elaine held his nose for a few moments, only releasing it when she was sure he had swallowed her potion.

The witch watched as Phillip's eyes became heavy. In seconds, the boy was out.

"Come, William," she said. "Let your brother rest. Tomorrow morning, he will know his true self. Thomas will be alive again, just like I promised all those years ago."

William stared at the blond-haired boy in the bed and heard a buzzing sound coming from another room. "You hear that, Mama?"

"Hear what?"

The buzzing was gone now. "I thought I heard something." He licked his gums where his two front teeth were missing, then said, "When do we find my other brother?"

Elaine grabbed him by the hand, tilted her head, and said, "Soon, William. Soon."

Chapter 10

When Phillip woke up the next morning, Elaine and William heard him screaming from the bedroom. It sounded as if the boy were having a root canal procedure without the aid of a local anesthesia injection.

Elaine had slept in the recliner next to the couch where William had fallen asleep. She looked over at him and said, "I think Thomas has him now. Would you like to go see your brother?"

William lifted his head up. "Yes, Mama."

"I know it has been a long time, but I kept my promise, didn't I?"

William nodded.

"I knew I'd be able to bring you all back one day. When your older brother comes back to us, the wait will be over. We'll find and kill Barry Kendall when the time is absolutely right. Then we can live the lives that were taken from us because of his family."

"That sounds nice, Mama," William said, getting up from the couch.

When they entered the room, the blond boy's hair was matted to his head from sweating all night. His teeth were clenched tight, but he relaxed when his eyes found Elaine's.

"Mama," the blond boy said.

"That's right, Thomas. Welcome back."

"That William?" Thomas asked.

"Of course it is," she said, moving William in front of her. She rested her hands on William's shoulders. "I know you boys look a little different now, but you're still my boys."

Thomas grinned from the bed. Elaine let go of William's shoulders and ambled up to Thomas's bedside. She began to undo the restraints. She started with his arms and untied his legs last. Thomas sat up, shifted his legs to the side of the bed, and stood up. He almost fell over, but Elaine caught him before he hit the floor. He wasn't all there just yet.

"Sit back down. You're not ready yet, my child." She checked the clock on the wall.

"Give it another hour. By then, I think you'll be okay."

"I'm hungry, Mama," Thomas said, holding his stomach.

"Don't fret, child. There's a meal for you and your brother locked away in the bathroom. The meat is aged, but I'm afraid it'll have to do."

Thomas laid back down, his stomach growled. The growls coming from inside of him sounded horrifying. It was like a bad dog was trapped inside of his stomach and wanted out.

"Rest, Thomas. We'll come back soon."

Thomas closed his eyes and took deep breaths.

A buzzing sound came from within the cabin. William said, "I hear that buzzing noise again, Mama."

"I don't hear a buzzing noise," she said.

William pointed. "I think it's coming from the bathroom."

Just then, Elaine had an epiphany. "Their cell phones! Come with me, William."

They ran down the short hallway to the bathroom door. Elaine swung it open to see the elderly couple still lying on the linoleum, their eyes becoming large and round as soon as they noticed Elaine and William staring down at them.

"Get their phones out of their pockets, William."

"I don't know what phones is, Mama."

"Move," she said, shoving him aside. "I'll do it."

Elaine removed the phones from Hank's and Dolores's pockets. The incoming call on both cell phones displayed the same name: Eric.

There were several missed calls on each of their phones. Elaine tried to scroll through the messages on Dolores's phone, but it was password protected. She tried Hank's phone next. No password. She scrolled through and it didn't take long for her to realize that this Eric person was worried about the two people she had William tie up and stow away in the bathroom. She saw that the first couple of text messages and phone calls had been from last night. She recalled William mentioning something about a buzzing noise, but she hadn't been able to hear it. Elaine stared at the screen, reading the last text message Eric had sent to Hank. It was from thirty minutes ago:

Something isn't right, Dad. I thought maybe you and Mom might have gotten tired and stayed at the cabin and fallen asleep. This isn't like you guys to not respond in the morning, especially Mom. I've contacted Abbott PD. They'll be there to do a welfare check. I really hope you guys are okay.

Elaine was still staring at the screen when William said, "When can we eat them, Mama?"

"Why couldn't I hear their phones, but you could?" she asked aloud.

William shrugged his shoulders.

Elaine turned the cell phones off and threw them on the bathroom floor, shattering the screens. She slammed the door and said, "This is bad, William."

"What's bad, Mama?"

Just then, they heard a car pulling in the driveway outside. They ran to the window to see a tall man with dark sunglasses and a chiseled jaw get out of the police car. It was Officer Deaver.

Deaver saw the black truck towing the camper. Then he saw the Suburban and grinned.

He pressed a button on the radio mike clipped to his lapel and said, "Send backup. I think I found Nancy McIntyre."

* * *

Barry put the piece of paper down on the desk in front of Donaldson. He didn't realize his hand was covering his mouth until Donaldson said, "Move your hand away from your mouth, Barry, and tell me how Nancy knows your name. Why does she seem to have it out for you?"

Barry moved his hand and met Donaldson's eyes. "You wouldn't believe me if I told you, Sarge. In fact, you'd think I was crazy."

"Dammit, Barry, I don't have time for this. Tell me what's going on. Don't beat around the bush, either."

Barry thought over how to say what he needed to without making himself sound like an absolute lunatic.

"I'm waiting, Barry. I know you know something about this lady that you're not telling me."

"Fine," Barry said. "But you're going to think I'm bat shit."

"Already do. But let's hear what you have to say anyway."

"Do you remember when Holly died all those years ago out in Hole in the Woods?"

"Yeah, I do. I recall that's what you kids called those woods at the time too."

"I'm sure you know what I told the police back then, also, right?"

Donaldson's brow furrowed. His mouth turned into a frown. "What does that have to do with an insane woman kidnapping random kids and killing people?"

"She's back. The woman that killed Holly. She's back."

Donaldson leaned back in his chair and crossed his arms. "Are you telling me that Nancy McIntyre is the one that drowned Holly in the lake?"

"No. I'm not saying that."

"I thought I told you not to beat around the bush."

Barry took a deep breath. "It's not Nancy who's behind all this. It's a witch. Her name is Elaine. When Holly read what was written in her book all those years ago, Elaine appeared from the lake and dragged her in." Barry bit his lip.

"And?" Donaldson said.

"And I think she's taken over Nancy's body to carry out some crazy plan. She's kidnapped two kids now, Sarge. There's a reason for it. The police never found the book Holly had read, but I remember what was written on it."

"And what was written on it, Barry?"

"Elaine, the mother of three. Don't you see? She's doing something with those kids. I don't know what, but I think it has something to do with me."

"Why the hell would those kids have something to do with you?"

Barry broke eye contact with Donaldson. Looking down at his hands, Barry said, "I spoke with someone last night. She told me why Elaine wanted me dead."

Donaldson sat up in his chair, arms still crossed.

"A couple hundred years ago, in Adams, Tennessee, my great-great grandfather apparently drowned Elaine in a lake for practicing witchcraft."

"Uh-huh. So where do the three kids come from in all of this?"

"She told me that he drowned the three kids in front of Elaine before drowning her."

"And who is *she*?"

"Her name is Aidy Henley. She is the daughter of the woman that rented my dad's trailer. I found Elaine's book in the shed behind the trailer when she took off and left out of nowhere. It was meant for me to find. Aidy is Elaine's great-great granddaughter."

"You remember when you said I thought you'd sound bat shit?"

"I do."

"Well, you're right," Donaldson said, resting his elbows on the desk as he leaned forward. "I mean seriously, Barry, do you really expect me to believe this stuff?"

"I was hoping so, but if I'm being honest, I knew you would be skeptical. Hell, I would be too."

Donaldson put his head down and sighed. "Barry, you know I love you like the son I never had, but I really think you need time off. You're obviously not well."

"I'm fine. And I don't need time off. What I need is to find Elaine before she does more harm to others, or before she kidnaps another kid."

"Listen to yourself. Do you really think you sound fine? And how do you know she'll kidnap another kid? For all we know, she could be in another state by now."

"She's taken two kids. The book says she's the mother of three. I know she'll kidnap another one, and I have a strong feeling she isn't in another state."

"Uh-huh. Why is that, Barry? And please, don't tell me it's because of what your great- great grandfather did two hundred years ago. I'm not buying it."

"Just like the local PD didn't believe me all those years ago when Holly was killed. I know what I saw, dammit. And you saw the paper she left behind. It has my name on it."

"You know what I think?"

Barry motioned for Donaldson to continue.

"I think Nancy is psychotic. I think she is even more bat-shit crazy than the story you're telling me about this witch nonsense. But what I also think is that she knows your history somehow. She knows that you thought you saw a witch, and now she's using that knowledge to her advantage. It's clear to me that she's messing with my best detective's head."

"That's not the case, Sarge."

"Unfortunately, Barry, is it. And I'm taking you off the case."

Barry slammed his fists down on the desk. "This isn't a good idea!"

Donaldson startled and glared at Barry. "You slam your fists on my desk again and we're going to have a problem."

111

Barry remained silent, staring down at the desk, his hands in his lap now. "Take the week off."

"I don't need a week off, Sarge," Barry said softly.

"You don't have a choice. Take a week off or I'll have to terminate you."

Barry looked up and met Donaldson's eyes. He could see that Donaldson was dead serious. Barry rose from the chair he was sitting in without another word. He began to walk out of Donaldson's office. Before he went out the door, Donaldson spoke up.

"Barry," he said.

Barry turned around.

"Don't go looking for her."

Barry nodded and walked out.

He made it to his police-issued Charger and glanced down at his watch. It was 7 a.m. A Bentley pulled into the station and parked next to him. Barry sat in the driver's seat with the car door open. He was just about to close it, but he stopped when he saw Gerald Carter walking briskly toward him. Gerald's wife, Clair, followed closely behind.

"You're the detective here, right?" Gerald asked, pointing at Barry.

"Yeah."

"What the hell are you doing sitting on your ass, then?" Gerald reached in the car and poked Barry in the chest. "Find my son."

"Gerald," Clair said from behind him.

Gerald ignored her.

"So help me God, I'll sue this department dry if anything happens to him."

"Gerald," Clair said again.

Gerald ignored her. "Why the hell are you still there sitting on your ass doing nothing, Detective?"

Barry tried to speak but Gerald cut him off again. "I'll have you terminated. I know people. I know your boss, and I'm about to go have a word with him, so just keep sitting there looking like an idiot."

"Gerald," Clair said.

"What!" he finally responded.

"I'm upset too. This isn't the person who took Phillip, though."

"You don't think I know that? My problem is that he isn't doing his damn job. He should be out looking for our son, not sitting here wasting our tax dollars."

"I understand that you're furious, Mr. Carter," Barry said.

Gerald glowered down at Barry. "Of course I am. You think you understand how I feel?

Your child ever been kidnapped? Huh? That ever happen to you?"

"I didn't say I understood how you felt. I understand that you're mad at everyone and everything. I get that. I've been there. And I'm sorry, but I'm not the detective on that case."

"Then who the hell is?" Gerald asked, clenching his fists.

"My guess would be Elliot Deaver. I've been told to take a week off, so if you'll excuse me, I'll be going on my way."

"Deaver isn't a detective. I know every cop in this place. I know that you're the lead detective. Why would Sergeant Donaldson take you off this case and give you a week-long sabbatical? That's absolutely ludicrous."

"I have to agree."

"So, you're just going to let this woman get away with kidnapping two children? You can live with yourself knowing she has them and may even ki–," Gerald paused. "Hurt them."

"I didn't say I was going to stop looking for her and those kids."

"So, you are on the case."

"I'm not supposed to be."

"Why not?"

"Donaldson's orders."

"And you're going to disobey his orders."

"Yeah," Barry said. "And if he fires me, I'm going to need a good lawyer."

"You find my son, Detective, and I'll represent you pro bono."

"I'll do my best."

"Sorry about earlier," Gerald said as he straightened up his suit.

"Don't mention it."

"If you need anything, please let us know," Clair said.

Barry nodded and closed the car door. Gerald knocked lightly on the window. Barry rolled it down.

"Here," Gerald said, handing Barry a rectangular piece of paper. "It's my business card. I've written my personal number on the back. Call me if I can help in any way."

Barry nodded and backed out of the parking spot. He rolled up his window and pulled out on the main road. As he left, he saw Gerald and Clair Carter making their way into the station. He had a feeling Gerald would give Donaldson a big helping of litigation threats. The image of Gerald abruptly rushing in Donaldson's office almost made him smirk. He was upset at Donaldson, but he also understood his skepticism. Barry was a little mad at himself for not being able to convince Donaldson, but it was pointless to brood over something that couldn't be changed at that moment. He needed to think. He wanted a drink. There was a pub on the other side of Abbott that he and Eddie had been to a hundred times. It opened at 11 a.m.

Barry drove around Abbott for four hours, looking for Nancy's Suburban. He had no leads, nothing to go on at all. He checked a dozen of cult-de-sacs, back roads, private drives, and camp sites. He asked several people walking on sidewalks if they'd seen a woman and two kids driving around in an early 2000s Chevy Suburban; just about every single one sported a confused expression as they shook their head, indicating that they hadn't.

At ten-till-eleven, Barry had had enough. In the past, driving around and asking townspeople had worked for him countless times. People would see things happen and break out their cell phones, recording all the excitement; however, no one had caught a single video of Elaine. Barry thought he'd check the mall's parking lot that Trevor had been killed in. He knew Donaldson and the local PD already examined the scene, but he wanted to check it out himself. Gene's Tire truck had been towed away already when Barry entered the parking lot. They still had the spot the truck had been in cordoned off. He'd parked his car a few spots down from the cordoned-off one. He went inside to speak with the security staff; they told him the cameras didn't reach as far as the spot Gene's Tire truck had been parked in. When he went back outside, where Trevor had been murdered, he walked to the spot to look around, hoping to find something. Anything. There was nothing except a dark stain where Trevor had bled on the pavement.

Barry returned to his car and backed out of the parking lot. He drove straight to the pub. He walked in a little before noon and sat at a high-top table that looked outside at the cars in the parking lot as well as the front door. Barry always took the seat that had a clear view of the front door; it was a cop thing.

A minute later, a blonde in tight jeans and a black V-neck came up to him and said, "What'll ya have?"

Barry ordered a beer and looked at the menu for a few seconds. Then he felt his pocket vibrate. He pulled his phone out to see that he had a text message from Eddie.

I'm back in town. You working?

Barry answered immediately.

Yeah. Not on the clock, though. I'll explain later. Long story.

Barry saw three dots dancing on his screen that indicated Eddie was typing.

Little early for a beer, don't you think?

Barry stared at the message for a few seconds before spinning around. A man wearing denim jeans and a Tampa Bay Lightning T-shirt sat at the bar. His brown hair was combed over neatly, not a hair out of place.

"Good to see you, Barry," Eddie said from the bar.

Barry's eyes narrowed in on him. "Eddie? Where the hell did you come from? I didn't see you when I walked in."

"I was in the restroom. I couldn't believe you were here when I walked out," Eddie grinned. "Had to mess with you a little bit."

Eddie grabbed the glass of water in front of him, stood up, and met Barry at the high-top.

"You okay?" Eddie asked, taking a seat across from Barry. "You look like shit."

"I feel like it too."

"What's going on?"

"My sergeant is making me take a week off."

"What for?

"I told him the truth about Elaine. He thinks I'm overworking and that she's messing with my head."

"And is she?"

Barry's brow furrowed as he thought it over. "I'm sure she's trying to."

"You're still going to look for her, aren't you?"

Barry nodded as the blonde in the tight jeans sauntered up and placed the beer he ordered in front of him. She glanced at Eddie and said, "You want a drink?"

Eddie held up his glass of water. "I'm good for now. Thanks."

"I'll check back in a few," the blonde said before walking away.

Barry drank a quarter of the beer, looked at Eddie, and said, "I met someone yesterday that might be able to help us with Elaine."

"Is it someone I know?"

"A girl named Aidy Henley. I met her last night. She has an apartment a couple miles north of Ybor City."

"And?"

"And she's a witch. She's related to Elaine, like her great-great granddaughter or something. She basically told me that Elaine wants me dead. She even knew why Elaine is out to kill me. That part I couldn't figure out."

Eddie looked across the bar, appearing to think over the information for a few seconds before returning his gaze to Barry. "You believe her?"

"Yeah, I do. I kind of already knew Elaine wanted to kill me before she—"

"No, Barry, I mean do you believe she's a witch?"

"Oh. Yeah, I do. She sort of proved it."

"Proved it?" Eddie smiled, interlocked his fingers, and placed his elbows on the table.

"Do tell."

"She put her number in my phone somehow."

"So that makes her a witch?"

"You think I'm crazy now too? She knew a lot about me and Elaine, okay?"

"Okay, so let's say Aidy is a witch. How is she going to help us with Elaine?"

"I don't know, Eddie, but there aren't exactly people lining up to help me. Donaldson thinks I'm losing my mind, and now I'm not even sure you believe me."

"I believe you, Barry. I don't know about this Aidy person yet, though."

"Elaine killed her mom."

Eddie's eyes grew wide as he sat back in his chair. "Are you sure?"

"Yeah, I've verified it."

"How?"

"Law enforcement software. When I searched for her, it showed that she was deceased."

Eddie looked horrified.

"Eddie," Barry said. "You good?"

Eddie found Barry's eyes. "What are you going to do?"

"I don't know. But I have to find her soon, Eddie."

Eddie nodded. "How do we find her?"

Barry drank another quarter of his beer and set it down on the table. "Not sure. You got any ideas?"

"Aren't you the detective?"

"Nah, I'm off for the week," Barry said, smirking.

"Better call that girl and see if she has any ideas, then," Eddie said, standing up.

Barry finished the rest of his beer and placed a twenty-dollar bill under his glass. Eddie and Barry walked out of the pub and stood next to his Charger.

"Never took you for a Dodge guy," Eddie said, glancing at the car.

"It's what the department issued me," Barry said as he dug his cell out of his front pocket.

"Could be worse, I guess."

"How?" Barry said. "A witch has come back from the dead to murder me. How the hell could it be worse?"

"Oh," Eddie said, thumbing back at the Charger. "I was talking about your car."

Barry let out a sigh. "Eddie, let's focus, please."

"Sorry. What's the plan?"

Barry scrolled through his phone and found Aidy's number.

"Can you meet me at my place in a couple of hours, Eddie?"

"Yeah, sure. Should I bring anything?"

"Just your thinking cap."

Eddie smiled and placed a hand on Barry's shoulder. "We'll get through this, Barry."

Barry nodded. "See you in a couple of hours."

"See you when I see you," Eddie replied, dropping Barry a wink before heading to his car around the side of the building.

Barry still had his phone out. He texted Aidy a question:

Can you meet me at my house in two hours?

Barry saw the dancing dots appear on the screen and received a reply five seconds later.

Yes. Send me the address. I'll take an Uber.

Barry sat down in the driver's seat of his car and sent her the address. He caught a glimpse of himself in the rearview and didn't like what he saw. He saw fear in his eyes. Not just fear that Elaine would succeed in her plan to kill him, but fear that he wouldn't be able to find her in time before she took another child from their home. Fear that she'd kill another innocent person. Fear that he'd fail; fail the way he did when he wasn't able to protect Holly. Barry tossed his cell phone into the passenger seat, took a deep breath, and headed home.

* * *

"Go get your brother, William. Hurry," Elaine said, shooing the boy away. Deaver had his gun out as he walked up to the cabin. By the time he made it to the front steps, William was back with Thomas.

"There's a man outside. Tell him you're scared and want to go home. Run to him." She paused for just a second and hugged them. "Then you can eat him."

William and Thomas nodded and ran out the front door. Deaver raised his handgun and then lowered it when he saw the boys running out of the house.

"We're scared," William told him.

"And we want to go home," Thomas added.

"It's okay, boys," Deaver said. "Are any of you hurt?"

"No," William said. "Just scared."

"Stay behind me. I'll get you both home safe. Is the lady that took you still in the house?"

"I don't know," William said.

"Stay here while I go inside," Deaver said, then made his way up to the front door. When he gripped the doorknob, his eyes lit up from an immense pressure on his neck and forearm.

William's teeth sank into the flesh on Deaver's neck. The boy had jumped on his back and wrapped his legs around the officer's mid-section. Thomas's teeth were burrowed deep in the flesh of Officer Deaver's forearm, the one that held the handgun. Deaver writhed and tried to shake the boys off, but they wouldn't release him. As blood began to run freely from his neck and arm, an overwhelming feeling of being light-headed and weak soon told hold of him. He dropped the gun and collapsed to the ground, where he felt the boys still biting down hard. His body went into shock, and the pain subsided a little. He felt numb to everything, except for the fact that his life was coming to an end. Before darkness took him completely, he looked up at Elaine. Through his half-lidded eyes, he saw her kneel next to him. She held the truck keys in one hand and her book in the other. She looked down at him with that eerie smile. He held her gaze for a few seconds, then his head lolled to the side. Deaver was gone.

Elaine walked over to the truck and started it up. "Let's go, boys!" she yelled over the noise of the truck's idling engine.

William and Thomas raised their heads, their mouths full of Officer Deaver's flesh.

"We have to go now!"

The boys let the meat fall from their mouths and ran over to the truck.

"We can't stay here any longer. It isn't safe."

"Are we in trouble, Mama?" William asked as he climbed in the vehicle.

"We won't be as long as we leave right now."

"Where are we going?" Thomas asked, climbing in behind William.

"Where it all started, boys. Barry won't find us there because he's afraid to go back. Now get in the back seat and keep your heads down. We have a little drive ahead of us."

Chapter 11

Barry sat on the leather couch in his living room, thinking about Elaine nonstop. His mind wouldn't quit. He thought about the shed where he had found Elaine's book. He thought about the rental and everything he and his dad had thrown away. Then he wondered if going back to the rental would give him some solution or maybe even an idea on how to stop Elaine. He didn't know what he could possibly find there to help, but he didn't know where else to start. He dialed his dad's number.

Carl Kendall answered on the second ring. "Barry?"

"Hey, Dad, is the single-wide trailer on Spring Street still vacant?"

"Yeah, has been for the last month and a half."

"Can I borrow the keys?"

"What's this about?"

"Nothing too concerning."

"It concerns me, Barry. It's my property."

"I just want to make sure we didn't forget anything."

"Since 2006? Barry, we got it all out. What is it you're thinking we missed?"

"I don't know. I really don't. Can I just borrow the keys to put my mind at ease?"

Carl sighed. "Keys are here. Let me know if you end up finding anything, I guess."

"Thanks. I'll be by later," Barry said, and hung up.

A few minutes later, Barry heard a knock on the door. He got up from the couch, grabbed his Glock, and stuffed it in the holster clipped to his waistband. Then he walked quickly to the front door. When he opened it, he saw a pale-skinned woman with shoulder-length red hair. A leather messenger-style bag hung from her shoulder. Her eyeshadow matched the black outfit she was wearing perfectly, and her lips were even a brighter red than her hair.

"Detective," Aidy said.

"You're a little early."

"Only an hour. I think the earlier we start on this the better."

"I suppose you're right."

Aidy stood in front of Barry, looking him up and down. "So can I come in?"

"Oh, sorry. Yeah, right this way."

Barry held the door open and closed it behind them. Aidy found the living room and sat down on the couch, propping her feet up on the coffee table as if she had been a guest at Barry's dozens of times.

When Barry sat down on the couch across from her, she said, "So what's the plan?

"Well," Barry said. "I just got off the phone with my dad. The single-wide you and your mom rented thirteen years ago is vacant. I'm thinking when Eddie gets here, we'll head over to the rental to see if we can find anything."

"Who's Eddie?"

"My friend. The only one who believes me about Elaine."

"Does he know about me?"

"Yeah. I told him about you."

"And you told him that I'm a witch?"

"Yeah, why wouldn't I?"

"Did he believe you when you told him I was one?"

"Not completely, no. What's with the questions?"

Aidy took her feet off the coffee table and crossed her legs, her fingers interlocking just under her knee cap. "So, your plan is to just go to the single-wide trailer I used to live in? And do what?"

"What do you suggest we do? I've already driven all over Abbott looking for her vehicle. No one has seen her, the kids, or the Suburban."

"I don't know. Doesn't the police department have some sort of plan for you to go on?"

"That's not how it works. And my sergeant doesn't even want me on this case now because of what I told him."

"You told him the truth, didn't you?"

"Yeah."

"I bet he thinks you've lost your mind."

"Yeah."

"What'd he say to you?"

"He told me to take a week off or else he would terminate me."

"And you're obviously going against his command."

"Obviously."

Aidy smirked for a second before staring off at the wall behind Barry. The smirk had left, replaced by a look of sudden insight.

"Aidy, are you okay?"

She continued to stare off. "I just remembered something. I can't believe I forgot about it."

"About what?"

Aidy met his eyes. "That single-wide out there on Spring Street. I left something in the trailer. In my old bedroom."

"Something that could help us find Elaine?"

"I doubt it, but who knows. It should still be where I left it."

"What should still be—" Just then he heard a car pull in his driveway. Barry rose from the couch without another word.

"Hey, what's going on?" Aidy asked when Barry started to leave the living room.

"I think Eddie is here," he said, still walking toward the front door. "Sounds like his car."

Barry opened the front door and looked out. Eddie was getting out of a silver two-door Nissan; a car Eddie had modified years ago to sound like a racecar. After all the work he had done to it, it pretty much was one.

"Haven't seen Gretchen in a while, have you?" Eddie asked, thumbing back at the Nissan.

"Nope," Barry said. "You're seriously still calling your car that?"

Eddie shrugged. "Baby has to have a name, right?"

"You're a strange one, Eddie. Anyway, come on in. I have someone you need to meet."

Eddie followed Barry inside, closing the door behind him. When they made it to the living room, Aidy was gone.

"And I'm the strange one, huh?" Eddie said.

"Yes," Barry said, looking around the room.

"Being that you have an imaginary friend now, maybe Donaldson was right to take you off the case, Barry."

"That's not funny. She was sitting on the couch when I left to meet you outside."

"Just went to the little girls' room, boys," they heard from the hallway. Aidy walked around the corner, locking eyes with Eddie. "Do I know you from somewhere?" Aidy asked.

Eddie stared at her for a second. "Possibly. I'm a long-haul truck driver. I've been to every state at least four times."

"Ah," she said. "I know where."

"You do?"

"School. I remember seeing you in line behind us at the front office. My mom was helping me change my schedule."

Eddie's eyes became large and round. "Holy cow. I do remember that. I was trying to get an extra period of Power Mechanics but they wouldn't let me." Eddie glanced at Barry for a second. "Small world, huh?"

"I'm Aidy, by the way."

"Eddie. Nice to see you again."

"Okay, good, we're all aware of who's who now. Are you guys ready to go?"

"Go where?" Eddie asked.

"The trailer I used to live in," Aidy said.

Eddie's eyes became large and round again. "The place you found Elaine's book?" he said, looking at Barry.

"Only plan I could come up with. Not like we know where she's hiding."

"Okay, I'll meet you guys there," Eddie said, digging his keys out of his pocket.

"You're not riding with us?" Barry asked.

"If Elaine is there waiting for us, do you think it'd be wise for all of us to be in one vehicle?"

"I highly doubt she'd there waiting for us."

"Have you checked there yet?"

"Not yet."

"Then how can you highly d—"

"Okay, I see your point," Barry said. "We'd be sitting ducks if she happened to be there. You know, I can't believe I didn't think to check that trailer when I was driving around earlier searching for her."

"Do we have something to protect ourselves with if she is there?" Aidy asked. "I may be a witch, but I'm nowhere near as powerful as Elaine."

Barry raised his shirt, revealing the Glock in his waistband. "There's a shotgun in the car too."

"Who needs spells when you have bullets, right?" Eddie said.

"Which reminds me," Barry said, going into another room. He came back holding a pistol in a brown leather holster. He handed it to Eddie. "Remember how to use one of these?"

"It's been almost a year since you took me to the gun range."

"Just don't point it at yourself."

"Hah-hah," Eddie said, not really laughing. "I remember how to shoot, Barry."

"Good," he said. "We have to stop by my parents' house to get the keys first."

Eddie glanced back at Aidy with a smirk. "Things are getting serious. Already meeting his parents, huh?"

Aidy's cheeks turned scarlet.

"Shut up, Eddie," Barry said, turning a little red himself. "Let's get going. We're burning daylight."

* * *

Elaine piloted the truck across town. It was her first time ever pulling something behind a vehicle. The camper's tires took a beating, hitting curb after curb on every ninety-degree turn she took. Luckily for her, none of the tires blew from the impacts; although, a few wheels were surely bent.

Despite her inability to avoid curbs, she made it to the other side of Abbott around 2 p.m. Up ahead, in her field of vision, was the turn she needed to take. The road was a dirt path without a street sign. She slowed the truck down and turned off the hard road. As she continued down the narrow path, thin branches screeched until they snapped from the size of the truck and camper. This went on until she reached a clearing. She looked ahead and saw the galvanized gate. When Elaine looked past it, where the trees circled around the lake, that eerie smile appeared across her face.

"We're here, boys," she said, reaching down to put the truck in park.

She stepped out of the truck and walked up to the gate. William and Thomas followed closely behind. Elaine looked out at the lake again. She ran her hand down the metal gate until she found the lock and chain. She gripped the lock and shifted her gaze to William and Thomas. "Do you boys think you can open this for Mama?"

William took the lock from her, examining it while Thomas pulled on the chain. The boys tugged as hard as they could. William even tried to chew through it.

After thirty seconds or so, she said, "That's enough, boys. I have another way to get through. Get back in the truck."

Elaine slid in behind the wheel, put the truck in gear, and floored it. There was a loud metal on metal sound as the gate broke off its hinges and fell to ground. Elaine ran it over and then stopped as soon as the truck and camper had passed over it. She got out, the boys following right behind her again.

"William, you and Thomas help me set this gate back in place."

The boys were quick to help. The hinges were broken, though. All they could do was lean it against the wooden corner post it used to be connected to.

Elaine began to walk back to the idling truck. "Come, boys. I have good news to tell you as soon as we get settled."

Elaine pulled in next to a tree, not far from the small lake. The grass all around them was at least four feet tall. Elaine shut the truck off and stepped out, taking a deep breath as she looked around. This place was always the backup plan. Elaine knew that Barry hardly ever went to Hole in the Woods. And she knew he wouldn't think to look in a place that he had been just a day ago when he found her note. She had seen him here. She remembered watching him as he found the note. The horrified look on his face as he read it. It made her want to close her eyes and see what Barry was up to now.

Elaine walked around to the passenger side and opened the door to the camper. She heard the boys walking around the truck now. They were standing next to a tree; a tree with a heart carved in it. Elaine looked at the tree and then closely at the lake. The same lake she had drowned Holly in. Her plan was finally in motion. Thirteen years in the making. She was stronger than ever. She couldn't help but laugh. The boys laughed, too, but they had no clue as to what was so funny.

Elaine opened the door to the camper. There was a bed and small couch near the front, a booth in the middle, and a kitchenette in the very back. She waved the boys over and held the door for them as they stepped inside.

She found two boxes of cereal in one of the overhead cabinets. She gave one to William and one to Thomas. "You boys eat. I'll be right outside. Don't disturb me. What Mama is doing is important. Understand?"

They both nodded.

Elaine exited the camper and sat in the truck's driver seat. She leaned back, closed her eyes, and exhaled slowly. She focused on Barry. All she could see was darkness, at first. Thirty seconds passed by. Then she saw him at his house, answering the door. She saw him talking to Eddie before inviting him in. Elaine couldn't believe what she was seeing. The girl she had killed in Tennessee. Elaine focused harder.

"No, it's her daughter," she said aloud, her eyes still closed.

She watched as Eddie and Aidy met each other. She saw the three of them walk out the door. Then something happened. Elaine's vision began to blur. She saw nebulous figures get in two separate vehicles. When Aidy closed the door after getting in Barry's car, her vision went from blurry to absolutely nothing. They were gone.

"She kicked me out," Elaine said, becoming enraged. "I knew I should have ended her too!" She couldn't hold back. She slammed her fist on the dashboard repeatedly until it cracked.

Elaine closed her eyes again, focusing hard. She saw Aidy sitting next to Barry for just a second, and then they were gone again. Elaine screamed and, through her rage, tried to focus on Barry again. No matter how hard she focused, all she saw were the back of her eyelids. Total darkness.

When she opened her eyes, she stared through the front windshield as if Barry and Aidy were standing in front of the truck. She gritted her teeth as her bloodshot eyes continued to glare at the windshield. "Stupid girl," she said, seething with anger. "You'll pay for this."

* * *

Aidy and Eddie stood on either side of Barry as he knocked on his parents' front door. After a short while, the door swung inward, and Carl Kendall said, "Whoa, didn't know you were bringing company." Carl's eyes found Eddie's. "Hey, haven't seen you in months. How's life treating you?"

"Pretty good, sir," Eddie said. "Just driving semi and keeping Barry here out of trouble."

"Well, you haven't been doing a great job at the latter." He smiled. "No offense."

"None taken. How's Mrs. Kendall?"

"I'm fine," Martha said, appearing behind Carl. "Edward, come give me a hug."

Eddie obliged and embraced Barry's mom. "Good to see you, Mrs. Kendall."

Martha held Eddie at arm's length and said, "I told you years ago to call me Martha, you know."

"I know," Eddie said, grinning. "I told you the same thing about calling me Eddie instead of Edward."

"Fair enough," she said, then shifted her gaze over to Barry. "Come give your mother a hug."

She closed her eyes as she wrapped her arms around Barry. When she opened her eyes, her arms were still wrapped around her son. She noticed Aidy standing a few feet behind Eddie.

"Who's your friend, Barry?" she asked.

Aidy stepped forward and stuck her hand out. "I'm Aidy."

Martha took her hand in each of hers. "So nice to meet you." She glanced at Barry. "Why don't you three come inside for a little while? I'll make us some coffee."

"Mom, we really need to be go—"

"We'd love to," Aidy said.

"Great," Martha said. Then to her husband, "Can you help me in the kitchen, Carl?"

"Of course, dear. I'll be right behind you." Carl glanced at Barry. "You guys can take a seat in the dining room. Just take your shoes off at the door."

As soon as his parents started toward the kitchen, Barry shot a look at Aidy. "What the hell?" he said. "This wasn't the plan."

"It's not like we'll be here all day. We'll still have time to check the trailer before it gets dark out," Aidy said.

"Yeah, Barry," Eddie said. "Your parents should meet the new woman in your life anyway." Eddie's grin was ear to ear.

Aidy blushed again.

"Eddie, remind me why we're friends again?"

"Who else is going to help you on your witch hunts?"

Barry tilted his head toward Aidy.

"Already replacing me." Eddie crossed his arms and feigned sadness.

Barry rolled his eyes. "You guys know we don't have time for this? The faster we—"

"We don't have time to spend ten or twenty minutes with your mom?" Aidy asked, her face grave. "You know what I'd give to spend just another minute with my mother? Take it from me, Barry, the case can wait. For a little while, anyway."

Eddie stopped kidding around and looked at Barry. "She's got a good point."

"I know she does." Barry sighed. "Come on, let's go inside."

A few minutes later, Barry, Aidy, and Eddie took their seats in the dining room. Aidy's eyes wandered around the room and spotted a picture of Barry and Holly hanging on the wall. It was from a homecoming dance. Barry was wearing a turquoise long-sleeve button up that matched the color of Holly's silk dress. He held her hand and had one arm wrapped around her waist in the typical school dance pose.

"That girl in the photograph," Aidy said. "She looks familiar."

Without even glancing at the picture, Barry nodded and said, "That's Holly. Elaine murdered her when she was sixteen."

Aidy looked at Eddie, who was shaking his head in a you-shouldn't-bring-her-up kind of way.

Barry's mom and dad entered the dining room, each of them holding two cups of coffee.

"I put an ice cube in each one, so it'd cool down faster," Martha said.

"Thanks, Mom," Barry said as she gave him his cup.

Carl handed a cup to Aidy and one to Eddie. Everyone took a sip and then Martha said, "So, what are the three of you up to today?"

Eddie and Aidy shifted their gaze to Barry, who was still sipping on his coffee. Barry was about to say something when Carl cut in. "Barry wanted to borrow the key to the rental out on Spring Street."

Martha shot Barry a look. "Why do you need the key to that old trailer?"

Barry nodded his head in Aidy's direction. "She used to live there when she was a teenager."

"Wait a minute. I thought you said you wanted to make sure we didn't forget anything in there?" Carl said.

"Yeah, that's right. Aidy hid something in her old bedroom. We just want to see if it's still there."

"I'm afraid it probably isn't. A few years ago, that place got a total remodel on the inside: new carpet, new paint, and even new ceiling fans throughout the whole place. The outside hasn't changed much, though."

"It'll be there," Aidy said. "I'm almost sure of it."

Carl arched a skeptical eyebrow for a few seconds. Then he dug in his pocket and pulled out the key to the rental. He slid it across the table to Barry, and said, "Hope you find what you're looking for."

When Barry grabbed the key, his phone started to ring. He looked at the screen and was surprised to see Donaldson calling him. He answered it immediately.

"Hello?"

"Barry, you busy?" Donaldson asked. He was almost sure he heard Donaldson take a drag on a cigarette after the question.

"Visiting my parents. What's up?"

"It's Deaver."

"He not doing as good a job you thought he'd do?"

"He's dead, Barry."

Barry's eyes went wide. "Dead? How?"

"Nancy did it. We have witnesses." Donaldson coughed a few times. "We found an elderly couple tied up in the bathroom of a cabin on the outskirts of Abbott. Neither one will say a word. As much as I hate it, especially after telling you to take a week off this morning, I need you to work this case. You up for it?"

There was a hesitation on Barry's end. Donaldson noticed.

"You there, Barry?"

"Yeah, I'm here."

"Well?"

"Send me the address. I'll be there as soon as I can."

Barry ended the call and looked up. Everyone was looking at him.

"Everything okay?" Martha asked.

"Not really," Barry said, looking at Aidy and Eddie. "She killed one of our officers."

"We have to get to her before more people get hurt," Aidy said.

"And do what?" Eddie asked.

"Who's *her*?" Carl asked.

"No one," Barry said. "Everyone, calm down." Barry felt his phone vibrate. Donaldson had sent him the address. "I have to go."

"What about the rental?" Aidy asked.

Barry handed the keys to Eddie. "You two check it out. Call me if you find anything."

Barry rose from his chair and went around the table. He hugged his mom and said, "I'm sorry."

Martha forced a smile, "Go ahead, Barry. They need you."

Before Barry could turn to leave, she grabbed his arm. "Just do us all a favor."

"Yeah, of course," Barry said, discerning the seriousness in her eyes. "What is it?"

"Be careful."

* * *

An ambulance was leaving as Barry pulled in the cabin's driveway. He saw Nancy McIntyre's Suburban first and felt a chill run down his spine. Beyond the Suburban was a forensics van, another ambulance, and half a dozen police cars.

Barry parked his Charger behind Nancy's Suburban. When he shut the car off, he looked over his shoulder and saw Donaldson walking toward him.

"Well," Barry said as he opened the car door. "Any idea what happened?"

Donaldson shook his head. "You have to see it for yourself."

Barry followed Donaldson over to Deaver's car. In front of it, on the ground, was a white sheet covering Deaver's body.

As Barry got closer, he noticed spots of the cloth were stained red. Donaldson kneeled next to Deaver's body and lifted the sheet up. Barry couldn't look away. The bite mark on Deaver's neck was far worse than Trevor's. It looked as if a coyote had mauled him. Deaver's arm was just as bad. A large chunk of muscle had been removed on his forearm. The radius bone was visible, and as if that wasn't horrible enough, it also appeared to have been chewed on.

"You think Nancy did this?" Barry asked.

"I don't know what to think anymore, Barry." Donaldson placed the sheet over Deaver.

"Forensics find any prints? DNA?"

"Yeah, two sets of prints."

"Whose?"

"Denny Molasky and Phillip Carter. Their prints are all over the cabin."

"What about Nancy's?"

Donaldson threw his hands up. "Not one single print," he said, then pulled a cigarette out of a pack in his breast pocket. He cupped his hands, lit it up, and took a drag. "Doesn't make any sense, does it?"

"No," he said, "It doesn't. How'd Deaver find her out here in a cabin?"

"Welfare check," Donaldson said, jetting smoke from his nostrils. "We found an elderly couple tied up in the bathroom. They can't talk. We can't figure out why. We spoke to their son; he's the one who called in the welfare check. And get this, Barry, he said neither one is mute. Paramedics haven't got a clue why they can't utter a single word."

"Have they already been taken to the hospital?"

"The older gentleman just left. He was a little banged up. Apparently, he had wrestled the Molasky boy off him with his cane. His wife told us the boy was trying to bite him."

"How'd she tell you if she can't speak?"

Donaldson gestured as if he were writing with an invisible pen.

"Ah. Is she still here?"

Donaldson thumbed behind him. "She's in the back of that ambulance. I think we got all the information we could from her already."

"I'd like to ask her a couple questions of my own, if that's all right."

"Knock yourself out," Donaldson said, pulling out his cell phone to make a call. When he placed it by his ear, Barry walked over to the ambulance.

The back doors to the ambulance were wide open. The elderly lady was lying down on a stretcher, writing on a notepad. After she finished writing, she handed it to the paramedic sitting next to her.

"Excuse me," Barry said, showing his badge. "Can I have a word with her for just a minute?"

The paramedic lifted his head up from the notepad and shot a look at Barry. "Your sergeant has already asked her every question in the book. She needs to get to the hospital and rest. She's been through an extremely traumatic experience, don't you understand?"

"I understand more than you could ever imagine. I know the woman behind this atrocity better than anyone here. That's why I need to have a conversation with her."

The paramedic sighed and stepped out of the ambulance. "Her name is Dolores. You have five minutes. Don't cause her any more distress."

134

Barry didn't respond as the paramedic walked past him. He was focused on what he needed to ask the woman.

As he sat down next to Dolores, her eyes found him. He showed her his badge and said, "Hello, ma'am. I'm Detective Barry Kendall with the Abbott Police Department. From what I've been told, you are unable to speak."

Dolores nodded.

"This woman and the two kids you saw, they didn't seem normal at all, did they?"

Dolores shook her head.

"Is she the reason you are unable to speak?"

Dolores gestured for something to write on. Barry handed her a small notepad with a pen.

She scribbled on it with a shaky hand. *She took my voice from me. Hank's too. I don't know how she did it. They don't believe me.*

Barry read what she had written and glanced up at Dolores. "I believe you. She took something from me too."

Her hand shook as she wrote something else. *Do you know how to stop her?*

Barry read what she had written and looked down at his hands in his lap. "I'm still working on figuring that out. Did you ever see her holding a black leather book, by chance?"

On the pad, Dolores wrote: *No. But she did mention your name.*

Barry stared at the written words. "What'd she say about me?"

Dolores bit her lip and shook her head.

"It's okay. You can tell me."

Dolores looked at Barry and took a deep breath before writing on the pad. *That your days are numbered.*

"I had a feeling she was going to make her move soon," Barry said. "She didn't mention where she would be going when she left the cabin, did she? Could you hear them talking?"

I don't know where they went. But I heard her tell the boys something about their older brother. Something about when he came to them. I can't remember exactly. I'm sorry.

As Barry read the last of it, the paramedic appeared at the back of the ambulance. "Five minutes are up, Detective. I need to get Dolores to the hospital now."

Barry looked at Dolores and nodded. As he got up to leave, she grabbed his wrist. She scribbled on the pad in a hurry. *Will I get my voice back?*

"If I can find her, I think so," Barry said, and turned around to exit the ambulance.

He walked back over to the driveway. He saw his sergeant sitting in the passenger seat of Nancy's Suburban, going through her glove box.

"Well, the old lady tell you anything she didn't tell me?" Donaldson asked, still going through the glove box.

"Just that my days are numbered."

"What the hell are you talking about, Barry?"

"The lady said she overheard Nancy talking. Nancy said my days are numbered. She even used my name, according to Dolores."

"I don't know what you did to piss her off, Barry, but watch your back. Nancy is obviously off her rocker."

"I'll be sure to keep my eyes peeled."

"Dammit, Barry, I'm serious. Deaver's dead. Now she's saying you're next."

Barry nodded then shifted his gaze to the Suburban's glovebox. "You find anything in the Suburban that could give us any idea as to where she went?"

Donaldson slammed the glovebox closed. "Not a damn clue. We know she took the elderly couple's truck and camper, but where they took it," Donald threw his hands up. "Who the hell knows."

In Donaldson's right hand was several pieces of paper and a picture. "What's that in your hand?"

Donaldson shuffled the papers. "Just her registration and proof of insurance papers. Looks like a few bank statements too. Lady bought a lot of stuff online, let me tell you."

"That a picture?" Barry asked, pointing behind the bank statements.

"Yeah, there's one here." Donaldson said. "It's not of her, though."

"Can I see it?"

"Sure," Donaldson said, handing it to Barry.

Barry knew who the man in the picture was immediately. It took him a few seconds to recognize the woman. He flipped it over and saw that the date of the photograph was from December of 1992. Barry flipped it back over and stared at the photograph. The woman in the picture was a young Melissa Henley; she was holding an infant in her arms. Barry knew the infant in the picture was Aidy, but what froze him in place was the man in the aged photograph. His arm was wrapped around Melissa, and he was looking down at Aidy just as a new father would.

"Barry? You all right?"

He stuffed the picture in his pocket. "I—uh. I need to make a phone call," Barry said and walked briskly over to his car.

Barry sat in the front seat of his car, dialed Aidy's number, and peeled out of the driveway.

Chapter 12

Eddie parked his Nissan in front of the trailer Aidy used to live in. When Aidy got out of the car, she looked around the property, seeing what had changed about the place and what had not. The front steps leading up to the door were different; she noticed that right off the bat. The trees had been trimmed up, but the trailer was mostly the same; the vinyl siding was still white, the window screens had a few more rips and tears than she remembered, and the shingles on the roof were just a little more faded than they had been thirteen years ago.

She made her way up the steps and slid the key in the lock. For a second, it felt like she had gone back in time to when she was sixteen, getting home from school. That feeling went away as soon as they entered. Aidy looked slowly around at the bare walls and new flooring. To her left, the kitchen still looked the same except for the painted cabinets and newer appliances. She turned to the right, walking down the narrow hallway until she reached her old bedroom. It was so much smaller than she remembered. She thought of all times she would just lay in her bed and read books or listen to music. She thought of her mom coming into her room to ask her if she wanted to share a bag of popcorn and watch a movie. Other thoughts popped into her head, but they faded away when she heard Eddie say something behind her.

"What?" Aidy asked, turning around to face Eddie.

"I asked if you were all right."

"Oh," Aidy said, "Yeah, it's just . . . I haven't been here in so long."

"Evokes old memories, doesn't it?"

"Yeah, but not all of them are pleasant."

"What do you mean?"

"I see my old room, but I also see what it looked like when my mom and I got back from the store to find the place turned upside down."

"What happened?"

"My dad happened. He wrecked the place when my mom told him she didn't want to move again."

"I imagine it was hard to see your things thrown all over the place."

"Yeah," she said. "It was. I had already hated my dad for not being around, and then he comes back to ruin the trailer. All so Elaine's plan could take place." Aidy took a deep breath and ran her hand through her hair. "I wish my mom would have been brave enough to stand up to him."

"Maybe he was in a bad place," Eddie said. "You know, mentally."

"You know what really gets to me?"

Eddie shook his head.

"He left when I was a toddler. Then he comes back, but not to say hi or anything. He comes back to run us off. I never even saw or heard from him after that."

"That's a really crappy thing for him to do."

"Yeah," Aidy says, looking at the closet. "I hope your parents treated you better."

"Well, our situations are quite similar. I don't know who my dad is either."

"Your mom raised you too?"

Eddie nodded and leaned up against the bedroom wall, crossing his arms. "She did. The best she could, anyway."

"Guess we both got dealt a shitty hand, huh?" Aidy said as she ambled over to the closet, kneeling next to the floor register.

"What are you doing?" Eddie asked, ignoring her question.

She lifted the floor register and set it aside. "I woke up one day and found a locket sitting on my nightstand. When I opened it, one side of the locket was blank; just white paper where a picture would be. On the other side was some writing. It said that when I was ready, I'd be able to see what the locket held within it. I've been learning new spells since then, some from my mom and some from the spell book she left me. When I asked her about the locket, she acted as if she had never seen it before. She attempted to reveal what was in the locket. After the third or fourth incantation, she gave up. She told me to get rid of it. That it could be bad news." Aidy's arm was elbow-deep in the floor's air duct now. "I couldn't get rid of it, though. I was too curious. I hid it in here and taped it down so I wouldn't lose it."

Eddie watched, no longer leaning on the wall, his arms loosely crossed.

Aidy felt the tape and began to peel it. "It's still here. I can feel it under the tape." Aidy brought her arm out of the air duct and held the locket up. "You know, I actually forgot about this until earlier today. I can't believe I'm actually holding it."

"Can I see it?"

Aidy stood up and handed it to him. Eddie held it in the palm of his hand and smiled.

"Rose gold. This is pretty nice."

Eddie gave it back to Aidy. She met his eyes and said, "Yeah, I suppose that's part of the reason I could never get rid of it."

"What's the other part?"

"I have a feeling my dad left it for me. Like he wanted me to work on my spells until I could figure out how to reveal what's inside."

"Like maybe whatever is inside will help with the Elaine situation?"

"I don't know. It could be that. That would be nice, wouldn't it?"

"Yeah, it would. Do you think you can figure out the spell that's keeping the picture inside hidden?"

Aidy looked down at the locket in her hands and smiled. "Yeah, I have two in mind. One of them is sure to reveal the image." She kneeled on the carpeted floor and set the locket down in front of her, hovering her hands over it while reciting the first incantation.

Eddie narrowed his eyes on her, his arms no longer crossed.

The locket began to vibrate, but the picture inside remained blank.

After a few moments, Aidy sighed and looked at Eddie. "I really thought that one would do it."

"Try the next one," Eddie said. "You can do this."

She took a deep breath, cracked her knuckles, and started the next incantation.

This time the locket vibrated until it began to flip over repeatedly. It bounced on the carpet as if it were made of rubber. Then, as she finished, the locket came to rest. She went to pick it up but stopped when her cell phone started to ring. She saw that Barry was calling her.

"Barry?" she answered.

"Aidy, are you around Eddie?"

"Yeah, why?" Aidy asked, picking up the locket to see if the spell had worked.

"I don't know how, but I think he's your dad. You need to get away from—"

All she heard was dial tone. She heard what Barry had said, but all she could do was look at the picture in the locket. It was the same one Donaldson had shown Barry. The photo of Melinda, Eddie, and Aidy.

After a few seconds, Aidy's eyes shot up at Eddie. His hand was outstretched.

"We need to talk, Aidy."

She lifted herself off the floor and ran toward the door, but Eddie blocked it before she could escape. Like an animal in fear for its life, Aidy shrank away from him and backed herself in the corner of the room.

"You bastard...You're here to finish what you started, aren't you?" she said, her hand rising. In a quick burst, she shouted the incantation she planned on using to incapacitate Elaine.

Eddie countered it easily enough and performed one of his own. As Aidy had told Barry, her father was a powerful wizard. Aidy went to her knees, trying to fight what was happening to her. A couple of seconds later, her eyes closed. She fell to the ground, the locket falling from her hand.

* * *

Aidy woke sitting upright against a corner in her old bedroom. Her hands had been tied behind her back. She felt tired but alert at the same time. Eddie wasn't in the room, but she heard his footsteps as he walked down the hallway. When the door swung open, the man that she had recently discovered to be her father ambled in.

"Why?" Aidy asked.

"Why what?"

"Why are you still loyal to her? I don't understand."

"To Elaine?"

Aidy nodded.

"She's a powerful witch, Aidy. I don't expect you to understand."

Aidy looked around the room before meeting her father's eyes again. "Why did you leave when I was a baby? You left my mom to raise me alone."

"I suppose I owe you an explanation," Eddie said, sitting down with his back against the wall. "At a very young age, it was instilled in me to do exactly what my mother told me to do. I was what people would nowadays call a mama's boy. She would tell me to jump, and I would ask 'How high?' That sort of thing." Eddie placed his right hand on the back of his neck, staring at the empty closet. "Before Barry's great-great grandfather drowned her and my brothers in that lake, she gave me her book. She told me how she cursed it, that I would have to make friends with a Kendall—the right one, as she put it—and I knew that right one was Barry. I knew it because we became best friends in an instant. I tried befriending his grandfather and even his dad. Neither one was interested. But Barry was different from his old man and his grandfather. Barry didn't have an ego. He was cordial and lacking just the right amount of self-esteem. It was easy to deceive him. Hell, I was the one that introduced him to Holly."

"And then she read the spell that ultimately brought Elaine back."

"That wasn't the plan, but that was how it happened."

"Wait a minute," Aidy said, looking at the carpeted floor. It all started to make sense to her. "If Barry's great-great grandfather drowned your mother and brothers then you're—"

"Elaine's oldest son. I'm the one she entrusted to bring her back from death with a spell she put in her book of incantations."

Aidy stared at Eddie, looking incredulous. "But his dad saw you earlier. Doesn't he remember you trying to become his friend all those years ago?"

Eddie interlocked his fingers and rested them in his lap. "Wizards have ways of making people forget. You may even know the spell I'm thinking of."

"I don't," Aidy said, and then, "Are you going to kill me?"

Eddie's brow furrowed. "Of course not."

"What about Barry? That's what all this is about, right? Revenge. That's what she wants."

"Yeah, that is what she wants. That's why she wanted me to bring her back. It's why she waited all these years after I helped bring her back. She wanted to make sure she wouldn't make any mistakes. She wanted to get stronger, and let me tell you, Aidy, she's stronger than ever."

Eddie and Aidy both heard a car pull into the driveway. A second later, they heard a car door slam followed by heavy footfalls slapping against the front steps.

"Aidy!" Barry shouted. "Where are you?"

She looked at Eddie. He nodded as if to say it's okay.

"Don't come in here, Barry. Eddie—"

Before she could say another word, Barry burst into the room, his nine-millimeter pointed at the man he thought was his best friend.

Chapter 13

Eddie remained seated against the wall. His hands were up. And his eyes were locked with Barry's for what seemed like a minute.

Eddie was the first to break eye contact. He glanced at the gun and saw that Barry's forefinger was resting on the trigger. "Going to shoot me?" he asked him.

Barry breathed in deeply through his nose and said, "You've always been there. We've spent countless years together. Why now?"

"Why what?"

"You know."

"Why are we seeking revenge now? Why are we coming after you for something your great-great grandfather did a long time ago? That it, Barry?"

Barry's heart pounded inside of his chest. He chanced a quick glance at Aidy before saying, "Yeah. That's—"

Eddie was on his feet, pouncing on Barry before he could shift his gaze. He slammed him against the wall, wrestling for the gun. Eddie gripped the handle and managed to press the magazine release, which caused the magazine full of hollow-point bullets to bounce off the carpeted floor. Barry still had one round in the chamber; Eddie knew this and went to wrench the gun from him, but as he did, Barry lifted it and slammed the butt of the weapon against Eddie's skull. It split him open, and blood began to trickle down his face. Still holding Barry against the wall, Eddie squeezed the wrist that held the nine-millimeter and kept it pinned against the wall.

He tried to pin Barry's other arm on the wall, but Barry swung and landed a left hook just above Eddie's right eye. Eddie fell to a knee, still holding Barry's wrist that held the gun. Barry quickly went to knee Eddie in the face, but Eddie caught it, lifted Barry and slammed him on the ground.

As Barry's back connected with the trailer's floor, the wind was knocked out of him. He could hardly breathe, and he felt woozy; it took him a few moments to realize that his head had also connected against the trailer's floor. Barry looked up at Eddie, who was holding him down, and saw blood slowly dripping from his face. What Barry found eerie in that moment was that Eddie didn't look mad or even in pain; he looked as calm as ever.

When Barry was able to breathe regularly, and when the wooziness subsided, he noticed something that he hadn't before about Eddie. He was holding his gun, and Eddie had it aimed directly at him.

Barry turned to look at Aidy. She was struggling to get up to help. Tears were running down her face. He saw her yelling, but he couldn't hear her. When he looked back at Eddie, the gun went off.

The round that was still in the chamber put a hole in the floor about six inches from his head. Eddie tossed the gun aside, looked Barry in the eyes, and sat with his back against the wall again.

"Maybe now we can talk, now that you know I'm not here to kill you."

"You could have, though," Barry said, beginning to sit up. "Why–"

"Why didn't I tell you in the first place? You wouldn't believe me. The only way to prove it to you was to show you that I could kill you and then let you live. I didn't see any other way."

Barry stared at Eddie for a few moments, trying to determine whether or not that made sense. "If you're not here to kill me, then you're here to facilitate Elaine killing me."

"That used to be true."

"What do you mean?"

"It's a long story."

"I got time."

"You don't though, Barry. Not a lot of time, anyway."

Barry looked over at Aidy again. She was no longer struggling to get up. She had given up on that around the time the gun went off. She was looking wide-eyed at Barry, speaking but her vocal cords weren't working.

"Why can't she talk? What'd you do to her?"

"Just put her on mute while we had our little tussle," Eddie said, and then motioned his hand toward Aidy.

The rope tied around her wrists came undone. When the rope hit the carpeted floor, her voice was back. "Why'd you do that?" she asked.

"So that I could explain myself to Barry without interruption."

"Well, you haven't done much of that yet."

"I was in the middle of telling you when Barry arrived, wasn't I?"

Aidy's eyes narrowed. "Continue on."

Eddie placed his hand over the split on his forehead. In a matter of seconds, the wound stopped bleeding and completely disappeared. After that was taken care of, he shifted his eyes over to Barry.

"What do you know about your great-great grandfather, Barry?" Eddie asked.

"Did you just—"

"Focus, Barry," Eddie said. "Now, what do you know about your great-great grandfather?"

"Only what Aidy told me about him," Barry said, still staring incredulously at Eddie. "He killed Elaine and her sons for practicing witchcraft."

"Not all of her sons."

"How did you survive?" Aidy asked. "I was never told."

"My mother knew that the sheriff had been planning to make an example of her. She handwrote a spell in her book of incantations and entrusted me with it if she was killed. But she didn't think he'd have the audacity to kill her children too. The way the sheriff and the towns-people saw it, we were tainted. And to some degree, he was right. My mother was practicing witchcraft as her mother had done before her, and she was teaching it to me and my younger brothers."

"Did you ever meet your grandmother?" Aidy asked.

"No. My mother told us she was murdered by the same kind of men that wanted to kill her," Eddie said, and then noticed Barry staring at the floor with his arms crossed in front of his chest. "You okay, Barry? I hope you didn't hit your head too hard."

Barry looked up, his arms remaining crossed. "I'm just having a hard time accepting this."

"I've been trying to figure out a way to tell you, and I had planned on doing it today when we all went out here. Then the plan changed when you got called in. I figured, what better place to tell you that I'm Elaine's son and Aidy's father than this trailer, where it all started for you? But then you found out anyway. I'm sorry I didn't come clean sooner," he said, looking back and forth between Barry and Aidy. "To both of you."

"Hold on," Barry said. "Did you just say that you're Elaine's son?"

Eddie nodded. "Her oldest son."

Barry had never in his life seen Eddie look so serious. "I don't under-stand," he said.

"I'll tell you everything, Barry," Eddie said. "Just tell me where you'd like to start."

"Why didn't you come clean sooner? Why wait until now? I don't get it."

"She watches me. All these years, she's been watching me. But now," Eddie said, "Elaine thinks it's Aidy blocking her from seeing me, even though I've been the one doing it."

"I wouldn't even know how to do that," Aidy said.

"Elaine doesn't know that, though," Barry said. "Right?"

"Exactly," Eddie said. "But she knows Aidy is a witch."

"So, if she watches you, then she knows where I live, right?" Barry asked.

"She does. But I've warned her not to do anything stupid. She's known for years and hasn't tried anything. I've been watching her just as much as she's been watching me and not once have I had to step in to stop her. But now she's summoned my brothers. Now she's the strongest she'll ever be. And, honestly, I don't think she'll listen to me the way she did when she was weaker."

"Why'd you let her recover? Why'd you let her get so strong?"

"Because, if I kill her . . . I die too."

"What do you mean by that?" Barry asked.

"It's part of the spell," Aidy said, "Isn't it?"

Eddie nodded. "If I die, so does she. And vice versa. It's how I've managed to live for so long."

Barry ran his hand through his hair as he thought it over. "So there's no way to stop her without you dying?"

"Possibly."

Barry squinted as if trying to read Eddie's thoughts. "What are you thinking?"

"When I realized she had to be stopped, I spent almost every night working on a spell that would put her back in the book without killing her. I don't know if it'll work or not, but it's the only plan I have. If I perform it incorrectly, it could send me in the book with her, being that I'm attached to the original spell."

"Let's say this plan of yours works," Barry said. "Let's say she goes back in the book and stays trapped there. What happens to the kids she took? What happens to Nancy's body?"

Eddie drew in a long, deep breath before saying, "I don't know."

"Those kids can't get hurt, Eddie," Barry said. "You have to figure out a way to get rid of her without hurting those kids."

"Look, I'm going to meet her tonight, after I leave here. I'll tell her the plan is to wait until you're sleeping two days from now. Then we'll make our move to finally seek revenge on what your great-great grandpa did to our family."

"And she really thinks killing me will somehow make things better?"

"No, but she thinks it'll set things right. Even the score."

"That's absurd. My great-great grandfather and I aren't the same."

"You're that man's blood, Barry. You work in law enforcement just like he did. You both even go on witch hunts."

"I'm only looking for her because she killed Holly, took possession over a middle-aged woman, and kidnapped two kids. It's not like I do it for sport."

"I know that, but to Elaine it doesn't matter. *You* are what she wants. Her mind was made up years ago."

"Okay, so she's going to come to my house in two days?"

"Yes."

"And you're sure she'll stick to that plan?"

"She wouldn't risk ruining everything she's worked for over the years to execute the plan a day sooner. She knows she needs me for the plan to work. She needs her boys."

"I don't get it, though. Why does she need the three of you?"

"We make her complete."

"God help me, I almost feel bad for her," Barry said, pinching the bridge of his nose with his thumb and forefinger.

"Don't. You're not the one at fault. Although, she doesn't see it that way. In her eyes, someone has to pay. But . . . "

"But what, Eddie?"

"But I'm not going to let that person be you. We've been through so much together through the years. I've been alive a long, long time, Barry, and I've never had a friend quite like you." Tears began to develop in Eddie's eyes as he said, "All the weekends we spent working on our cars together, laughing at ridiculous inside jokes or our favorite movie references. Our friendship was real. I won't let her kill you, Barry. I'll die before that happens."

Barry sat there looking at Eddie wipe the tears in his eyes before they had a chance to fall. Barry knew exactly what Eddie was talking about. Even though Barry was primarily concerned with his job, he never stopped hanging out with Eddie. He was just always there. And suddenly it dawned on him how Eddie had such a natural ability to fix cars. He had been alive longer than Henry Ford had been making them. A multitude of possibilities rushed through his mind, but he shoved them away. He needed to stay focused. His life depended on it. If he lived, he could think of those things later.

"Now I know why you got the job driving a semi-truck," Barry said.

"It was a good excuse to be gone for days at a time," Eddie said. "I visited my mother regularly. She wanted me to stop spending so much time with you, anyway. When she searched her mind and saw us together, she could tell my laughter was genuine, and she became worried I'd turn on her."

"What about my mom?" Aidy asked, her eyes fixed on her father. "Why did Elaine kill her now after all this time?"

Eddie closed his eyes and took another long, deep breath. "Elaine saw her as a threat. She had a suspicion that your mom might help Barry learn the truth about me. That Barry might kill me just to end her life. I told her that wouldn't happen, but she drove to Tennessee and . . . well, you know the rest."

Aidy covered her eyes with her hands as tears ran down her cheeks. "How could you have let that happen? How could you let her die?"

Eddie glanced at Barry and sighed before pushing himself off the carpeted floor to his feet. He kneeled next to Aidy, placing a hand on her shoulder, but she instantly gasped and shrank away from his touch as if his fingers were as hot as fire.

"Look, I didn't know she was going to do that. If I had, I would have killed her then, even if it meant I'd die. I've stayed away from you and your mother to protect each of you. I knew if Elaine thought that I loved you and your mother more than I loved her, even for a second, that she'd kill you both; that's why I had to stay away. I had to prove it to her. But what she doesn't know is that I watched you both from a far. When Barry was in high school and so were you, I kept an eye out. I remember those girls cornering you in the hallway during your lunch break; they made fun of the clothes you wore. They made fun of the way you walked and the shoes on your feet. Do you recall what happened after they swatted those books out of your hands?"

Aidy looked up, her eyes staring at the wall, going back to that day, trying to remember the event that took place. She had finished eating lunch with her best friend in high school, Deb. She normally went to the library with Aidy after eating their lunches, but on this day, Deb had a book club meeting to attend. Aidy left the library with a couple of books Deb had recommended. On her way to store them in her locker, a trio of girls surrounded her in the hall. They were the archetypal pretty-but-mean girls that would marry young, land rich husbands, but still be unhappy long after their inevitable divorces. The image of the three girls was as vivid as ever in Aidy's mind. After they accosted her, called her ugly, weird, and every other hurtful name in the book, they swatted the books out of Aidy's hands and took a step closer to her. There was nowhere for her to run. Every exit was sealed tight until, almost simultaneously, the three girls hunched over, holding their abdomens. An audible growl came from their stomachs, then, without another word, the girls shuffled away to the nearest restroom.

"That was you," she said, now facing Eddie. "You made them—"

"Have to desperately find a toilet," Eddie grinned. "Yeah, that was me."

Aidy shifted her gaze to the wall again with a wistful smile. "They never messed with me again after that. They were too embarrassed."

"That's because the spell I used gave them that feeling any time they got close to you."

A snort of laughter escaped Aidy. "I can't believe you did that," she said.

Eddie took Aidy's hand and looked her in the eyes. "When you were born, something inside of me changed. The only love I knew was my mother's, but when I saw you for the first time, that all changed. You and your mom were all I could think about. But you have to understand, even after so many years, my love for my mother still existed. Even though she's incredibly evil, she's still my mother, and I was in ways beyond comprehension still loyal to the woman. When I made your mom leave this trailer, I wasn't thinking straight. I thought my mother would allow me to have you and your mother in my life. That she'd let me have a family, but that wasn't the case. I was foolish to think otherwise. Elaine was inordinately jealous of you and your mom. I knew she'd snap and seek out to harm each of you if I didn't do something; so, I left you. As hard as that was for me, it was the only way I could keep you both alive."

Aidy wiped her cheeks with the backs of her hands and closed her eyes. "Give me a minute to process all of this."

"Does Elaine know that you found out about Melinda?" Barry asked.

"I didn't know until you told me at the pub."

Barry's eyes widened with insight. "That's why you looked the way you did when I told you about Melinda's death."

"It wasn't easy trying to hide the fact that I was in utter shock. But I managed. It took everything I had to play it cool."

"If she can drive to Tennessee to murder someone without you knowing, how do you know she won't try to kill me or Aidy without telling you? How can you be so sure?"

Eddie stood up and crossed his arms. "That was a mistake on my part. A mistake I'll never forgive myself for," he said, shifting his eyes over to Aidy. "I won't let that mistake happen again. Not with you guys."

"Okay," Barry said, standing up to be eye-level with Eddie. "So, what's the plan?"

"If you shoot and kill her, I die as well. That's plan B."

"And Plan A is?" Barry asked.

"We ambush her tomorrow night. I know a spell that will incapacitate even her. When she's out, I'll perform the spell that should put her back in the book."

"What do you need us for if it's that simple?"

Eddie gave him a tight-lipped smile. "My brothers."

"I thought you said—"

"I'll be very weak after performing such a spell. Look at Elaine after the spell she put in the book for you to read. She had just a short amount of time to kill Holly before disappearing. I doubt you know this, but it almost killed her doing what she did to Holly. She was so weak when I found her. It took Elaine a year to walk again, and it's taken years for her to regain her strength. The one I'll be performing won't take me years to regain my strength; however, it may take a few weeks. I'll need you two to not only handle my ravenous brothers, but to help me recover."

"So we ambush them tomorrow night," Aidy said, standing up. "How?"

"That's where Barry comes in to play."

Barry nodded. "I have a couple of flashbangs at my house. We could sneak up and alert you. Then, you can exit the camper, break a window, and throw in the flashbang. After the first one goes off, I'll throw in the second one. Then you can perform the spell before her vision comes back."

"What's a flashbang?" Aidy asked. "And what about the kids?"

"It's a less-lethal device that stuns the enemy when it explodes. Basically, a loud bang followed by a blinding flash of light."

"And if I'm right," Eddie said, "once Elaine is in the book, the spell she put on the boys will wear off. I don't know how long that'll take, though. Could be minutes, hours, days—hell, maybe even a week."

"Okay," Aidy said, running her hand through her hair. "Let's say we're able to put her back in the book. Then what?"

Barry looked at Eddie, waiting for his response.

"Then I'll keep the book in a safe place, where no one will find it."

"Why not just destroy the damn thing?" Barry asked.

"Because," Eddie said, "she'll live in the book. She dies, I die. Remember?"

"Oh, right."

"If I happen to die, though. There's only one way to destroy the book."

"How?"

"The same way Elaine was killed. Drown it."

Barry nodded. "Makes sense."

"Yeah," Eddie said, looking out of the window. "I need to go meet up with her. She's expecting me."

"So you know where she is, then?" Barry said.

Eddie turned around and met Barry's gaze. "Where it all started, my friend."

"Hole in the Woods."

"She's parked that truck and camper she stole out there. You'll have to come from the woods to execute the flashbang plan."

"I know a good place to hide the car on the shoulder of the road."

"Good. We better get going," Eddie said, and walked out of the room. Barry followed Eddie down the front steps. "One more thing, Barry."

"What is it?"

Eddie peered over at Aidy standing at the front door's threshold. She was taking in one last look before locking the door behind her. Eddie was still watching her when he said, "If anything happens to me, Barry, I need you to take care of her."

"Nothing is going to happen to you."

Eddie shifted his gaze back to Barry and smiled. "Tell me you'll take care of her anyway."

"You've got my word."

"Thanks," Eddie said, then his smile widened even more.

"What?"

"I can tell you like her, you know."

Barry shot him a look. "How—"

"What are guys talking about?" Aidy said as she walked up behind Barry.

Eddie's wide smile was still there. "Barry and I were discussing that when this is all over, we have a lot of catching up to do."

Aidy gave him a soft smile. "Yeah, I look forward to it."

"Oh," Eddie said, patting his pockets. "I almost forgot." He dug his hand in the front pocket of his jeans and pulled out the locket from earlier. "This is yours."

Eddie stepped behind Aidy. She lifted her hair up with one hand as if about to put it in a bun. Eddie wrapped the necklace around her, clasping it, the locket resting just above her breasts.

When she let her hair down, she gripped the locket tight.

"You know, I wish we had more time to talk about—"

"It's okay," Aidy said. "We'll have time later to talk."

Eddie could see the pain he'd caused from his absence in her life. Behind those big hazel eyes of hers were years of pain and resentment that couldn't be fixed in a single conversation.

"Yeah, you're right," Eddie said, watching her walk to the passenger side of Barry's car. When Barry started to walk toward his car, Eddie reached out with his right hand and took him by the shoulder. Barry saw the weariness in his friend's eyes. "If it comes down to shooting Elaine," Eddie whispered. "Don't hesitate."

"I won't have to," Barry said, placing a hand on Eddie's shoulder. "Because you're going to put her ass back in that book."

Eddie nodded. "Keep Aidy with you tonight. Keep her safe. I'll be in touch."

Barry gave Eddie's shoulder a squeeze, and then the two friends walked back to their cars. When Barry sat behind the wheel, Aidy fixed her eyes on him. "What was that all about?" she asked.

"Just old friend stuff," he said as he put the key in the ignition. After starting the car, he felt his cell phone vibrate in his pocket. He pulled it out and saw that the text message was from Eddie. It read: *See you when I see you.*

Barry looked where Eddie had just been parked and found that he was gone already. He spun around in his seat and spotted the Nissan's taillights going down the road. Barry was still trying to process everything he learned in just a modicum of time. He glanced over at Aidy; she was looking down at the picture in her locket as if she were still trying to process it all too. He took a deep breath, put the car in gear, and backed out of the driveway.

Chapter 14

Elaine opened the truck's door and stepped out, slamming it behind her. When she stepped foot in the camper, she saw William and Thomas sitting at the booth across from each other. They looked toward Elaine, then down at the mess scattered across the floor. She glanced at the torn-open boxes on the camper's floor, realizing the boys had scarfed the cereal down as soon as she left.

"I hope your appetites have been satiated," she said. "Because you two will need to be focused for this plan of ours to work."

"What plan, Mama?" William asked.

"Your brother will be here before long to go over it. He has been undercover for a long, long time, you see. He has gained Barry's trust. A lot has happened since you two were taken from me. Your brother, Edward, not only brought me back, but he's also helped me devise a plan to end Barry's life once and for all."

Thomas sat up and met Elaine's gaze. "I remember Edward."

"You remember what he used to look like, Thomas. As I've said, it's been a long time. He will look different to you, but he's still your older brother. He's the one I trusted all those years ago. And now I know I made the right decision."

Elaine went over to the window, raised the blind, and took a look outside of the camper. "We all need to rest. Very soon we'll go to Barry's house while he's sleeping. I'll incapacitate him and bring him back here.

When he wakes up, he won't be able to move. Edward and I will have tied him to a chair. You boys will take turns feeding on him. Then, after he's begged me to end his life, I won't. I'll wait. I'll wait until he has suffered far too long, just like I did. When I feel he's close to death, we will take him to the lake, where he'll die the same way the girl he loved did."

"When will Edward be here?" William asked.

"Soon," she said, then sat on the small couch in the front of the camper. "Come here, boys. Rest your heads. We have a busy night ahead of us."

Elaine sat upright, William's head resting on her thigh. Thomas's head rested on the other. In a few minutes, they fell asleep. Elaine's eyes became heavy. She knew Eddie would be meeting her in just a few hours. She looked down at the boys sleeping on her. They didn't look exactly like William and Thomas from so many years ago, but the resemblance was close enough to meet her standards. What mattered most was that her actual boys were there with her, anyway. Elaine tilted her head back and closed her eyes. A minute later, she was dreaming of what she would do to Barry.

Hours later her dream came to an end as a noise coming from right outside the camper woke her. She rose from the couch. The boys stirred but continued to sleep. She walked as quietly as she could to the window. When she lifted the blind to look outside, she noticed the sky had darkened and that a man was gripping the door handle of the camper. As the door began to open, Elaine raised her arms, her fingers splayed out. She was ready to incapacitate her assailant, but realized it wouldn't be necessary when she saw the man enter the camper.

"Hello, Mother," Eddie said casually.

"Shhh," she said, lowering her arms. She walked past Eddie and exited the camper "Come out here. Let your brothers rest."

Eddie glanced at the two boys sleeping on the couch. They didn't look exactly like the brothers he remembered, but he knew they were living inside of the two boys. Without taking a second look, he closed the door softly.

"Come with me," Elaine said, reaching for Eddie's hand. "We need to talk."

Eddie took her hand and let her lead him to the edge of the lake. When they reached it, she let his hand go and stared out at the full moon reflecting on the water. A smile appeared across her face.

"After all these years, Edward, it's finally time."

Eddie continued to stand next to her, resting his eyes on the lake as well. "It's been a long, hard road," he said. "Difficult to believe we've come this far."

Elaine shifted her gaze over to her oldest son, her smile fading. "Do you still believe our plan will work with this interloper that has attached herself to Barry?"

Eddie's brow furrowed, but he kept his eyes on the lake. "I don't see her as much of a threat."

"You know the girl that's helping Barry, don't you? I mean, you must know—"

"I know who she is, Mother."

"And?"

"I left her and her mom a long time ago to focus on bringing you back, didn't I?"

"You did. But she has your blood, Edward."

"My loyalty lies with you," he said, turning toward her, looking Elaine in her eyes. "Just as it always has."

Elaine watched his face, trying to detect any signs of deceit or dishonesty, but Eddie's facial expression didn't show any of that.

"You know she's been blocking me from seeing her and Barry. Whatever it is they are planning on doing, I can't see it."

"She's not even a quarter as strong as we are, Mother. I wouldn't worry about her too much. Aidy's mother was a much stronger witch."

"Was?" Elaine said. "So, you know she's dead, then?"

"Barry told me."

"She had to be stopped. She was going to—"

159

"I don't care that you killed her," he said impassively. "But not telling me what you were doing did bother me. I should have been informed."

"You're right. I thought you would object to it, though."

"It was a risky move, Mother. A risk we didn't need to take. She obviously isn't the one you should have killed anyway. Aidy is the one helping Barry learn all there is to know about you. She's the one blocking you out and trying to ruin our plan."

Elaine looked at Eddie with an odd grin. "I think we should execute the plan tonight while they're sleeping. I'm tired of being blocked out, and I'm tired of waiting."

"That isn't a good idea. They know you're coming for them. They'll be ready for you tonight, and maybe even tomorrow night too. The best thing to do is wait until they let their guard down in a few days."

"He could find us in a few days, Edward. You know as well as I do that Barry and the local police department are scouring the town."

"Listen to me. Barry isn't going to find you in the next few days. You're safe here as long as you do as I say and don't go on any more solo missions that could get us all caught." Eddie put his hands in his pockets and shifted his gaze back to the lake. "You know, you're not the only one that has been waiting a long time for this plan to finally take place. We're so close to ending this thing. Our family will be whole again. That's all I want."

Elaine watched Eddie for a few seconds as he stared off at the water. "I suppose you're right. You've helped me get this far. I'll try to be patient."

From behind the two of them, a light emitted from the camper. They spun around to see William and Thomas stepping outside. Elaine waved the boys over. They ran toward them with what Eddie perceived as an odd obedience. The same odd obedience he used to have.

"Boys," Elaine said, wrapping her arm around Eddie, "we're whole now. Your brother is here."

The boys stared at Eddie, dumbstruck.

"You look different, Edward," William said.

"Yeah, different," Thomas agreed.

"Well, guys, it's been long time since we last saw each other. I'm sure you both know that," Eddie said.

"We do," William said, nodding. "Don't we, Thomas?"

"Sure do," he said.

Eddie smiled, but behind the smile wasn't happiness. When he looked down at the two young boys, he feared for their lives. Not his brothers, but the boys those bodies belonged to. He knew bringing Elaine back was a mistake, but it was too late by the time he realized it. Now the lives of his daughter and best friend were at stake. And, in Eddie's mind, it was all his fault. He brought her back, which allowed her to not only kill Holly and take over a middle-aged woman's body, but also kidnap two innocent children. Shame and guilt overwhelmed Eddie. Those emotions crossed his face for just a second, and she noticed.

"Edward," Elaine said, her eyes wide. "Are you okay?"

Oh no, Eddie thought. His guard was down momentarily. He could feel her digging around in his mind. It felt as if her claw-like fingers were sifting through the thoughts in his head, his secret to help his best friend and daughter doing its best to stay hidden.

"Yes, Mother," he said, "I just—"

Eddie heard her shout something he discerned as an incapacitating spell. A second later, he tried to counter it, but with the boys on his mind he wasn't ready. The spell took him by surprise, and he fell flat on the ground.

* * *

Eddie woke up two hours later inside of the camper. He was sitting upright in a chair, head lolled down, chin in his chest. He felt like he had just been hit in the jaw by a heavyweight boxer. As focused on the pain as he was, he didn't notice the tightness around his arms and legs. He didn't realize what exactly had happened, but he would soon.

When Eddie opened his eyes and raised his head, he saw Elaine sitting across from him. William and Thomas sat on either side of her, their heads resting in her lap. He looked down again, and understood that he was tied to the chair. He couldn't move his legs or his arms.

"What is this all about, Mother?" Eddie asked.

"It's about you being dishonest with me. It's about you lying."

"What are you talking about?" Eddie asked. "Lying about what?"

"For starters," she said. "I know it isn't your daughter that's blocking me from seeing them."

Eddie remained silent.

"I've been watching her and her mom for longer than you know. I gave you the benefit of the doubt, Edward. I thought that maybe the girl had learned how to do it without me knowing. That there's no way my first born was blocking me out—why would he, right?"

"I'm not the one—"

"You thought you could do these things without me knowing. You thought I wouldn't find out. Well, that was somewhat true. You had me fooled for a while. But then I learned, just like you have over the years. I learned how cell phones worked, Edward. I learned how they can hear us if the person on the other end knows how to turn one's microphone on."

Elaine pulled her cell phone out. It was an Android in a black case. She tapped the screen a few times and then held it in front of her. His conversation from earlier in the trailer with Barry and Aidy played before him. It started from the fight that broke out, then she skipped ahead to Eddie telling them the plan to trap her in the book, then she skipped all the way to them leaving the rental property.

Eddie's eyes were wide with fear. His heart was pounding against his ribcage. He knew he had messed up. He should have left his damn phone in the car, but he didn't.

"How'd you listen in on my phone? Who taught you how to do that?"

Elaine gave him a cold stare. "I didn't listen in on your cell phone." She moved the boys' heads aside and stood up. In just a few quick steps, she was right in front of Eddie, digging in his front pocket.

"What are you doing?" Eddie asked.

"I should have done this sooner," she said as she held his iPhone up in front of him. "Oh, and I already found this." She went over to the counter and picked up the nine-millimeter Barry had given Eddie at his house earlier. She pointed it at Eddie and said, "I don't know why you would even carry one of these, Edward. It doesn't make any sense."

"Don't point it at me."

"Why not?"

"I know we haven't discussed guns much, which is exactly why you shouldn't be handling one. If you accidentally shoot and kill me, you die, too, remember?"

"Of course I remember," she said, scowling at him. "I'm the one who created this spell you and I are stuck in."

"Good," Eddie said. "Now tell me how you heard my conversation from earlier."

Elaine cackled in amusement. "Look at you. Commanding me from the chair you're tied to. You've let Barry and that girl twist your mind. We could have lived forever, Edward. Now I don't know what to do with you."

"How'd you listen in on my cell phone?"

She fixed him with that strange smile and set the gun and his iPhone on the booth's table.

"Again, I didn't listen in on *your* cell phone."

"Then—"

A man opened the door and stepped into the camper holding a lit cigarette in his right hand. "We heard you on Barry's cell phone. I learned how to activate the phone's mike a while back when we were investigating a homicide last year. Came in handy today, didn't it?"

Eddie saw the man standing in front of him. He knew he looked familiar. He wore a blue oxford, but what really caught Eddie's eye was the badge on his belt.

"You're," Eddie said, trying to think of the man's name.

"That's right," Sergeant Donaldson replied.

Chapter 15

"Why are you helping her?" Eddie asked, his eyes locked on Donaldson's. "I don't understand."

Elaine whispered something in Donaldson's ear and instantly his eyes became glassy. The cigarette fell from his mouth and hit the floor. Elaine quickly stomped it out. Donaldson's mind seemed to be far, far away.

"Ah," Eddie said. "I see what you've done."

"I had to," she said, lifting the same vial of red liquid she used on Gene up to Donaldson's mouth. She put a single drop of the potion on his tongue. "When I became suspicious of you, I had to come up with a back-up plan, didn't I? Just in case I was right about you—which I was. Luckily for me, this man found my potion at the cabin we were staying at. He took the top off and smelled what was inside. That's all it took. I found him in my mind and told him what to do from there. He showed Barry the picture of you with Melinda and Aidy. I told him where I was, and that if he brought my potion back to me, I'd give him a taste of it. I told him the girl was blocking me out so that I couldn't see you, and he kindly revealed to me that we would be able to hear you on Barry's phone if you were near him. Imagine my surprise when I heard you tell Barry the truth. Sure, I was disappointed, but I still had two boys that were loyal to their mama. And even with you out of the picture, Edward, I still have someone here that is close to Barry." She tilted her head toward Donaldson.

"I know you don't agree with me on this—which is why I had to go behind your back in the first place—but killing Barry isn't right. Think about it, he isn't the man that murdered you and my brothers. He isn't the man you should be going after."

"Well, Edward, you didn't exactly kill the man I should be going after, did you?"

"I tried. We've been over this already. The man nearly killed me when he realized I was your son. I got away by the skin of my teeth, and then I went into hiding to recover."

"And what about Barry's great grandfather, his grandfather, or even his father? You had plenty of—"

"I wasn't ready. It took a long time to get my strength back. After I had it back, I didn't have the courage."

"And when you finally did, you met that girl . . . Melinda."

Eddie nodded. "I wanted to live a normal life for a while. And I did. But at some point, I had to bring you back. The spell you put on your book wouldn't leave me alone. I'd try to sleep, and the damned thing would nag me until I thought I'd go crazy. I knew the only way to shut it up was to get Barry to open it and read it. I wanted it to be someone else's problem. Then you were back. You had some sort of power of me. It took years for it to weaken."

"You betrayed me, Edward."

"You're wrong."

"Excuse you?"

"You betrayed your children. Thomas and William are living through two kids' bodies that you stole. Think about those boys' parents. You're no better than Barry's great-great grandfather. And you made me carry this burden for so many years. Your spell's success was based on whether or not I'd be able to pull off getting a Kendall to read your spell aloud. Barry may not have read it, but he was present. You hurt him enough then when you killed Holly.

There's no need to continue this any further. Eddie shifted in the chair he was tied to. "Look at where we are now. You have me tied to a chair, you've kidnapped two innocent kids, and you've killed innocent people to get what you want. Who do you think is wrong now? Who has betrayed whom?"

Elaine ran her hands through her hair as she thought about what Eddie said. She looked over at William and Thomas and then at Sergeant Donaldson. Finally, she shifted her gaze back to Eddie. In what seemed like a practiced monotone, she said, "Barry has to die."

"And then what?" Eddie asked.

Elaine's brow furrowed. "Then I have to figure out how to get rid of you without killing myself, I suppose. I'm sure I'll figure something out. Perhaps I'll work on a potion. It'll take time, but that's something we have plenty of, isn't it? In the meantime, I'll keep you weak. Weak just like I used to be."

Eddie glanced at William and Thomas and then rested his eyes on Elaine. "You're too far gone. The whole police department is looking for you, you know? You won't get away with this. And if Barry see's you, he'll kill you."

"No, he won't," she cackled. "He knows that if he does, you'll die along with me. I heard you tell him that."

Eddie gritted his teeth.

"The real question is this: whom do I kill first?"

Every muscle on Eddie's body tightened as he tried to lift himself from the chair.

"Barry?" she asked before narrowing her eyes. "Or your daughter?"

Eddie shouted a spell that should have incapacitated her, but nothing happened.

"Edward, do you really think I wouldn't use a spell of my own? One I never taught you. And now I'm glad I didn't."

"What'd you do to me?" Eddie's eyes were welled with tears of rage.

"It's a rather difficult spell. Luckily for me, you were out and kept very still."

"What'd you do to me!?"

"Your ability to cast a spell is gone."

"What the hell are you talking about? That's impossible."

"I thought you said it would only last for a little while, Mama?" William asked.

Elaine's head snapped toward him. "And I thought I told you not to speak unless spoken to."

"Sorry, Ma—"

"Quiet! I've had enough of this. Tonight is the night it all ends. When I'm finished," she said, looking back at Eddie, "I'll come back to deal with you."

"I hope he kills you," Eddie said. "Even if it kills—"

Eddie's shoulder's slumped as his head lolled forward. Elaine effortlessly incapacitated Eddie with a spell she had taught him when he was just a boy; an oldie but a goodie. With Eddie out, she went to the camper's door and opened it. The boys rose from where they were seated and walked out. At the snap of her fingers, Donaldson became alert, but he was still under her control.

"Come now," she said to Donaldson, motioning him along. "We have a busy night ahead of us."

Donaldson exited the camper and waited outside. Elaine glanced at Eddie one more time.

Then she slammed the door closed behind her.

***

Elaine sat behind the wheel of the truck, watching Donaldson in the rear-view mirror as he unhooked the camper. William and Thomas sat in the backseat, peering through the back window, also watching Donaldson. While he was winding the crank to raise the camper off the truck's hitch, Elaine turned the key in the ignition and looked at the time. It was 10:15 p.m.

A few seconds later, Donaldson slid into the passenger seat.

"We're ready," he said, not bothering with the seatbelt.

"Good," Elaine said, then put the truck in gear.

Elaine drove past Donaldson's car and down the road that led to the gate, which Donaldson had left open. As she pulled out onto the hard road, she was careful not to exceed the speed limit.

"So, what are we doing?" Donaldson asked. "Barry has a security system at his house. How exactly do you plan to get inside?"

Elaine smiled. "That's easy. He trusts you. You'll knock on the door. He'll answer. I'll step out from behind you and cast a spell to make him go to sleep."

"What about the girl?"

Elaine scoffed as if he had to be joking. "That girl is no match for me. She'll be easier to take down than Barry."

"Then you want to bring them back and kill them in front of Edward?"

"That is correct. But I want to make sure they suffer first—especially Barry. He'll endure the pain his great-great grandfather should have received by my coward son."

Elaine made a right when she needed to make a left to get to Barry's house.

"Where are you going?" Donaldson asked. "Barry's house is a few miles back that way."

"I know that," she said, scowling in his direction. "I have something I need to do first."

Five minutes later, Elaine piloted the truck into a driveway that was cordoned off with caution tape.

"This is Nancy McIntyre's house," Donaldson said. "What are we doing here?"

"Just sit here while I go inside," she said, shutting the truck off. "I won't be long."

Donaldson, William, and Thomas watched Elaine walk up to the house. The porch light near the front door was the only light on outside. They saw her grip the doorknob. When she twisted it and realized the door was locked, she waved her hand over the knob a few times. After a moment's hesitation, she gripped the doorknob and twisted it. This time, the door swung inward and Elaine went inside, closing the door behind her.

"What's Mama doing in there?" Thomas asked.

William raised his hands up as if to say, *How should I know?*

Donaldson kept his eyes on the door. After a minute or two, the front door opened and a pale-skinned woman with long white hair and a dark red dress shuffled out. In the scant light, the boys in the backseat could just barely see the mother they'd remembered from long ago.

The truck's interior lights came on as she slid back in the driver's seat. She flipped her hair to one side and looked back at her smiling boys. They were as giddy as a couple of kids on Christmas morning.

"I found this dress in her closet," Elaine said.

"Smart move," Donaldson said. "The guys won't be looking for you."

"I've had a lot of time to think this through."

Donaldson nodded, then asked, "What'll happen to Nancy McIntyre?"

Elaine pursed her lips as she thought it over. "She should wake up not remembering much. At least, that's what has happened in the past."

"Where to now?" he asked.

Elaine gave him that strange, eerie smile of hers and started the truck. "To do what I've been wanting to do for a long, long time."

Elaine backed out of the driveway and began driving to Barry's house.

* * *

From inside the camper at Hole in the Woods, still tied to the chair, Eddie's eyes flew open. He woke remembering exactly what had happened: Elaine was leaving with Donaldson, William, and Thomas to kill Barry and Aidy. With absolutely no idea how long he had been out, he began to panic. His heart pounded, he struggled to control his breathing, and his eyes darted from left to right, looking for a way to get out of the chair he was tied to. On top of the counter next to him, he saw a set of knives beside a mini fridge. Only he didn't have a way to reach the knives with his hands still tied tightly behind him.

He tried to thrust himself closer to the counter. To his surprise, he and the chair slid about an inch or so. He thrusted himself and the chair forward again. He was headed for the cabinet below the counter. His hope was that he'd find something sharp enough to cut the rope restraining him. He was two feet away from the cabinet now, but he'd have to do a complete one-eighty to attempt to open the cabinet with his tied-up hands. He thrusted himself and the chair up again and tried to spin. It worked. He only spun an inch or two, but he was making progress. He needed another six or seven inches when he toppled over on an attempt to spin around. As he came down, the side of his head slammed against the floor.

He closed his eyes and gritted his teeth, trying not to curse and failing. He couldn't move now. He laid there and listened to the camper's generator steadily hum along, wondering just how much gas was left in the tank before it ran out and left him in total darkness. He thought the situation was hopeless. Barry and Aidy were going to be killed. He just knew it. They weren't expecting an attack from Elaine and her boys tonight. And Eddie knew she'd use Donaldson to throw Barry off guard. For all Eddie knew at that moment, his best friend and daughter could already be dead. And the thought of it made him grit his teeth even harder.

He was on the verge of giving up. For a few weak seconds, he figured his only option was to stay tied up on the floor until Elaine came back with horrific news. Then he remembered something he wished he would have before he fell trying to get to the cabinet: his iPhone was on the booth's table.

Eddie had taught his mother the basics about cell phones. He showed her how to dial a phone number, send a text message, take a picture, and send it to another cell phone; however, she didn't know how Siri worked or that it even existed.

The way Eddie had fallen, he could see the booth's table but not what was on top of it.

He took a deep breath, hoping like hell she had left the phone, and then said, "Siri, call Barry Kendall."

After a slight hesitation, Eddie heard the *beep-beep* sound an iPhone makes right before Siri says something. His eyes became large and round, then, "Calling Barry Kendall," came out of the phone's speaker.

Eddie listened to the phone ring and waited.

"Dammit, Barry, pick up!"

It continued to ring.

His heart sank when he got Barry's voicemail.

"Barry, you have to get out of there. Elaine and the boys are coming to your house tonight. She found out I was helping you, and she—"

Eddie stopped when he heard a woman's voice come out of the iPhone's speaker. "The voicemail box is full and cannot accept any messages at this time. Goodbye."

Chapter 16

Barry was still thinking about Eddie and everything he had recently learned as he pulled into his driveway. A normal person would have a severely difficult time wrapping their head around the fact that their long-time best friend is the son of a witch that wants to kill him. And while Barry *did* struggle with that realization, his police training kicked in and kept him focused. He worried about the here and now and not on the things out of his control. He thought how he could combat a witch that had the ability to easily cast a spell to disarm or even incapacitate him. He knew he couldn't shoot her without killing Eddie. Then he thought back to the flash bang idea, knowing it would only disorient her for so long—and that was if their idea went according to plan, which Barry knows doesn't always happen from his years on the job. He needed some sort of back-up plan. Something to fall back on if the flash bang idea didn't work. He frowned as he thought it over. Then a smile appeared when the words left his mouth.

"Military-grade OC spray."

Aidy stared at him from the passenger seat. "What are you talking about?"

"That's how we can disorient her."

"You think that'll work?"

"Have you ever been OC sprayed?"

"Of course not. I take it you have?"

"It was hands down the worst part of the police academy."

"Okay, so you use the OC spray on her," she said, crossing her arms. "Then what?"

"Then I'll have to get her hands behind her back so I can cuff her."

"Only one problem with that."

"Going to make me guess?"

"The problem is she can recite an incantation even with her hands cuffed behind her."

"Doesn't she have to be focused or see me or something for the spell to work? You know, like wave her wand around in some elaborate way?"

Aidy gave him a look that screamed, *You've got to be kidding me.* "You've been watching too many witch movies."

"Well, I don't know. That's why I'm asking you."

"Witches and wizards can cast spells without a wand. Hollywood made wands *a thing*."

"Okay, so if she can't see me from the OC spray, can she still hit me with one of her spells?"

"I suppose if you stayed out of her line of sight well enough that would keep the spell from attaching itself to you."

"But?"

"But suppose the OC spray doesn't work on her?"

"Why wouldn't it?"

"I don't know. She's barely human at this point. What if she is impervious to it?"

"We can't worry too much about the what-ifs," Barry said, stepping out of the car. "Look, let's go inside and we'll try to get something figured out."

Aidy followed him up to the front door, which he unlocked and held open for her.

"Such a gentleman," she said as she stepped inside.

Barry went in and locked the door behind him. "Depends on the person you ask." He checked his watch and saw that it was 7:15 p.m. "Are you hungry?"

"After everything that went down in that trailer, not really. Are you?"

Barry shook his head. "How about a coffee, then?" Barry asked as he ambled toward the kitchen.

"Cream, no sugar."

When they entered the room, Aidy walked over to the kitchen island and leaned against it while Barry brewed the coffee.

Barry glanced over to find Aidy fiddling with the locket around her neck.

"Hell of a day we've had."

Aidy looked up, still holding the locket in her hand. "I can't remember the last time I've experienced so much excitement. I surmise you must be used to excitement in your line of work."

"Excitement is one word for it, but I'm not exactly used to *this* kind of excitement." Barry said, handing her a mug.

She looked down at the steam coming from the coffee and smiled. "You missed your calling as a barista, you know?"

"Yeah, that's what they keep telling me."

"Who tells you that?"

"Random witches I invite over for coffee."

"Ahh, and I thought I was the witty one," Aidy said, then took a sip. "Do you really think this plan will work out the way we want it to?"

Barry met her eyes for a second and then looked away. "Honestly?"

"Out with it."

"I don't know."

"That's reassuring."

"You wanted honesty."

"It's the best medicine, but sometimes it leaves a bad taste in your mouth. This is one of those times."

"I thought it was the best policy?"

"Huh?"

"You said it was the best—never mind. Look, I do think we have a chance. I feel even more confident after learning the truth from your dad—I mean Eddie." Barry felt his face go hot. His complexion reddened. "Sorry, I—"

"It's okay," she said, then cast her gaze at the floor. "You know, I spent so many nights wondering where my dad was, why he wasn't home with me and mom. I wondered what he was doing, if he'd ever come back. Today I learned the truth . . . and it hurts. It hurts because he actually cares about me, but because of Elaine he couldn't risk being with us. He couldn't risk her becoming consumed with jealously and killing me and mom."

"He stayed away to protect you both."

Aidy nodded as she blinked back tears. "Life just isn't fair, you know?"

Barry thought back to the day Holly was murdered in Hole in the Woods. Then he thought about the day his dad called him on the phone and told him that his mother has cancer.

"Yeah," he said. "Unfortunately, I do."

Barry took a sip from his mug and leaned against the counter opposite of Aidy. She was a few feet in front of him, still looking down. "I'm scared."

"I'd be worried if you weren't."

"Aren't you scared?" she asked.

"Of course," he said. "But I'm pissed off too."

She looked up now. "So am I."

"That's understandable." Barry took another sip of coffee. "You know what that makes us, though?"

Aidy shrugged her shoulders.

"Dangerous."

Aidy chuckled. "I think she might have us beat."

"What makes you think that?"

"I know you have years of experience in law enforcement, but she has many more years in practicing witchcraft. She's been obsessed with you for how long now?"

"I see where you're going," Barry said. "But I still think we're a danger to her. And I think she knows it. If not, why didn't she just cast a spell on me when I found her in the house with Denny Molasky? Why not kill me then? She had the opportunity, and she chose to flee."

"Maybe she wasn't strong enough because she hadn't turned Denny yet; maybe she needed the rest of her boys. Or maybe Eddie told her she had to wait until the time was right. Regardless, she is stronger than ever now. Eddie even said so."

"Yeah, but she'll be missing one of her boys when we ambush her tomorrow night. She'll be strong, but we'll be stronger. Plus, we have Eddie."

Aidy shook her head. "I just don't know, Barry."

Barry sat his coffee down on the counter. "Maybe we should talk about something else. We'll have plenty of time to worry about Elaine tomorrow before we execute our plan."

"What else is there to talk about?"

A faint smile appeared across Barry's face. "I have some stories about Eddie if you want to hear them."

"Sure." Aidy sat her unfinished cup of coffee on the counter next to Barry's and walked out of the kitchen.

"Where are you going?"

"To sit in the living room. Are you coming or not?"

"I'll be there in a minute," he said, walking toward the hall. "I have something I think you'll enjoy."

A couple of minutes later, Barry ambled into the living room holding several photographs in his hand. He sat next to Aidy and handed her the pictures. The first one she held up was of Barry and Eddie, years ago, before Barry went to the police academy. Barry stood there with his shoulders slumped, looking exhausted. Eddie had an arm slung over Barry's shoulder, grinning ear to ear.

"That was my first day working at Gene's Tire," he said, pointing at the photograph. "Eddie made the job look easy, but I can assure you, it's not."

"You look like you're about to pass out in the picture."

"Look at the next one."

It was of Eddie standing in front of an expensive car at a car show giving the camera a smile and two thumbs up.

"What a dork," Aidy said as her lips formed into a soft smile.

"Just wait until you see the next one."

Aidy and Barry continued to look at pictures and talk about Eddie. Then, after they had gone through all of the photographs, Aidy rested her head on Barry's shoulder. She started talking about her mom. She told Barry about all the places they had moved, all of the spells her mother had taught her, and all of the fun times they'd had together.

Without Barry even realizing it, a couple of hours had passed by. Then he noticed that Aidy was starting to doze off. When she stopped talking, he glanced over and saw that she had fallen asleep. He felt sleep coming to him as well, but before he closed his eyes, he looked at Aidy again. Since Holly, he hadn't had any feelings for anyone but her. Something was changing, though, and Barry knew it. The longer he watched her sleep, the more he realized what he was feeling.

The weight of Aidy's head on his shoulder was the only thing on his mind at that moment; not Elaine, not Eddie, not even the craving for alcohol. Just simply the warmth of a girl he met a day ago.

He leaned over to the end table and flipped the switch on the lamp, surrounding them in darkness. Barry closed his eyes and sleep came quickly.

Twenty minutes later, his cell phone began to ring.

* * *

Barry was in a deep sleep, as one often is when they first slip away into a dream. He didn't fully open his eyes until the fourth ring. His eyes hadn't adjusted to the darkness yet, but they didn't need to; in front of him, resting on the coffee table, was the rectangular glow of his cell phone.

From where he was seated, he couldn't make out the name or number displayed across the phone's screen.

On his shoulder, Aidy was beginning to stir. He gently moved her so that her head rested on one of the couch's pillows. While he was doing this, he realized he had missed the call.

Barry leaned forward, lifted his cell from the table, and sat back down. After letting out a deep breath, he saw the missed call notification from Eddie. His thumb was hovering over the icon to call him back when his phone began to ring again.

"Eddie?" he answered.

"Barry. You're alive. Thank God," Eddie said.

"Yeah. Why wouldn't I be?"

"Listen, I don't have much time to explain, okay?" Eddie said, not giving Barry time to respond. "Elaine is on her way over there right now. Get Aidy and get the hell out of there!"

It felt as if the blood running through his veins had been replaced with some sort of liquid anxiety. For a few seconds, he couldn't even move. He didn't know if it was his police training or fight or flight, but he flipped the lamp on, stood up, and ran to look out of the front window.

"Barry? Say something," Eddie said.

"I'm here. Where are you?"

"I'm in Hole in the Woods, tied to a chair inside of a camper. She found out about me helping you guys," Eddie said. "She'll be there any minute. And, Barry, she put a spell on your sergeant. He's with her. I think she's going to pin the murder of you and Aidy on him. Just get out of there and come untie me!"

"Donaldson?"

"Yes!"

Barry saw headlights coming down the road in front of his house.

"Shit," he said.

"What?"

"I think they're here."

"Go, Barry, now!"

"I am. Hold tight."

Barry ended the call and slid the phone in his pocket.

"Aidy, wake up!"

She was in a much deeper sleep than Barry had been in. He ran over and shook her awake.

"What the hell, Barry?" she said, rubbing her eyes.

"Elaine is pulling in the driveway. We have to go now."

Her eyes went wide. "That's not funny."

"I'm serious," he said, running to his bedroom. "Put your shoes on and meet me at the back door."

Aidy was near tears when she got up, scrambling to find her shoes.

Barry grabbed his nine-millimeter, shoved it in its holster, and fastened it to his belt. Then he opened his gun safe, remembering to get a large canister of OC spray, but forgetting all about the flash bang. Before he left the room, he slid his shoes on and put two sets of keys in his front pocket.

Barry went to the front window again. He looked out and saw Donaldson walking ahead of Elaine. Barry knew it was Elaine, even though she didn't look like Nancy anymore. The boys were nowhere in sight.

"She's back in her actual body," Barry said.

Then he heard air hissing from somewhere and shifted his gaze to Donaldson, who had taken his pocketknife out and slashed each tire on the Charger's driver's side. Barry let go of the blinds and ran to the back door. Aidy was waiting there for him, looking horror-struck.

"We're going to be okay, all right?" he said, looking Aidy in the eyes. "Stay close."

They heard a knock on the door, followed by, "Barry, it's Donaldson. I need a word with you. Sorry I didn't call, but this has to do with Nancy McIntyre."

"He cut the tires on my car," Barry told Aidy.

"What are we going to do? How are we—"

"Hold this," Barry said, handing her the OC spray. "I have another car. It's parked on the side of the house. It's our only option. When I open this door, we have to be as quiet as possible."

Another knock came from the front door. "Come on, Barry. I know where Nancy is! I need your help!" Donaldson shouted.

Barry grabbed Aidy's shoulder. "Are you ready?"

Aidy bit her lip and nodded.

Barry yelled to Donaldson. "Be there in second, Sarg! Just hold on!" Then he opened the back door. The cool night air blew softly in his face. He felt Aidy take hold of his hand, squeezing it tight. He guided her around the side of the house where his Celica was parked. He thought back to the other day and realized he forgot to get that new battery.

"Shit," Barry said softly.

Aidy's eyes went wide. "What is it?

"I just remembered the Celica's battery is dead."

Her face fell. She gripped his hand tighter. "Now what?"

Barry thought for a second. His eyes widened when the idea popped in his head. "Manual transmission."

"Huh?"

"I know how I can start the car. Come on."

Before rounding the corner of the house, he peeked around to check for Elaine, hoping she didn't decide to flank while Donaldson stayed up front. He didn't see her, so he sidled up to the driver-side door, the key in his free hand. Aidy let go of Barry and went to the passenger side. He unlocked the door and slid in the front seat, leaning over to unlock the passenger door from the inside.

"Close the door quietly," he told her.

"What are you going to do?"

"Something your dad taught me years ago," he said as he put the car in neutral and released the parking brake.

Barry's house was built on a small hill. The front yard had a gradual decline, nothing major, but enough that the car would roll down it.

Barry left the driver's door open with the key in the ignition. Aidy watched him go to the rear of the car, still having no clue what he was going to do. After a second or two went by, the car started to move. She looked back and saw Barry pushing it with all his strength.

She thought for just a moment that he was using her as bait to get away, but then Barry jumped in the driver's seat and pushed the clutch pedal in. He put the shifter in first gear and lifted his foot off the clutch pedal. As the pedal rose, the Celica's engine came to life.

Barry mashed the gas pedal and the car lurched forward. He knew the concrete driveway wasn't an option, so he turned the car to the left and drove through the front yard.

From the front of the house, Donaldson and Elaine heard the car fire up. They immediately ran toward the sound and saw the Celica as it sped across the front yard to the main road. Donaldson lifted his nine-millimeter from his holster and aimed it at Barry's car. By the time he brought the gun up, though, Barry had already shifted to the next gear. Donaldson fired off four rounds as the car sped away. Every shot missed.

Donaldson looked back at Elaine. Her eyes were glowing with rage. If looks could kill, Donaldson would have died just then. "How could you have let them get away!" she shouted, then thought that potion might be wearing off already. That maybe his mind was trying to fight it off. That he missed the shots deliberately.

"You," she said, raising her hand. "You missed on purpose, didn't you?"

"What?" Donaldson said. "No, I swear."

"Give me the gun," she said.

Donaldson's brow furrowed. "What for?"

Now she knew the spell was wearing off. She didn't ask again. Her arm shot out, fingers curled as if she was digging her nails into an invisible apple. The next word out of her mouth incapacitated Donaldson. His eyes closed as he was falling backward. When he hit the grass, the gun fell out of his hand.

Elaine looked at the large man splayed out in Barry's front yard. She thought it such a waste that she couldn't use him to trick Barry. Then she had another thought; this one made her eyes bulge from her sockets.

How did Barry know about Donaldson being under her control?

A second or two passed before she remembered the cell phone on the booth's table. And next to it, a gun. What she couldn't understand was how he made the call. She knew he couldn't get out of the chair—it just wasn't possible with her taking away his ability to cast spells temporarily. She knew he communicated with Barry somehow, though. She never thought she could be so infuriated with one of her boys, but here she was seething with rage.

William and Thomas were behind her now. William's voice made her jump when he said, "What happened, Mama?"

Still glaring down at Donaldson, she said, "Do you still have the piece of paper I gave you earlier?"

"Yes, Mama."

"Hand it to me."

William dug in his pocket and pulled out the paper. It was folded into a square.

"Thank you, William. Now take Thomas back to the truck with you. We need to leave now."

Elaine tucked the note in Donaldson's front pocket, then she lifted his nine-millimeter from the ground. While the boys were running back to the truck, she aimed the gun at Donaldson's chest and squeezed the trigger.

Donaldson's eyes flew open as soon as the bullet put a hole through his blue oxford. His mouth formed a painful O shape as he tried to suck in air. His hands went to the hole the bullet had made, then he began to cough while trying to breathe.

Elaine didn't stick around to watch him bleed out or take his last and final breath; she had to get back to Hole in the Woods. If Eddie was able to inform Barry of Donaldson, he was apt to have informed him of where he was trapped too.

Elaine ran back to the truck, Donaldson's nine-millimeter still in her hand. She wasn't a fan of guns, but she was starting to come around. And if a gun was what it took to finally end Barry once and for all, then so be it.

As Elaine started the truck and put it in gear, Thomas said, "Is that man not coming with us now?"

"No," she said, keeping her eyes on the road as she exceeded the speed limit.

"Where are we going now, Mama?" William asked.

"Back where we came from," she said through gritted teeth. "Edward has ruined our plan."

"Can we help fix what he ruined?"

Her lips trembled as she gave him a strange smile before focusing on the road again. "Tonight, you boys help me kill Barry and the girl that is helping him. Your brother has to stay alive, though. If he dies, I die. Is that understood?"

"Yes, Mama," William and Thomas said simultaneously.

"Good," she said, then mashed the accelerator down harder.

Chapter 17

It had been thirteen years since Barry had driven his Celica to Hole in the Woods. When he reached the apex of the curve, he slammed on the brakes and turned off the hard road. Barry gripped the wheel tight and drove down the dirt path as fast as he thought he could in the dark. The oddly nostalgic view of this path from the inside of the Celica gave him the feeling of being sixteen again. If he hadn't been speeding through, it would have felt as if he were going out there to meet Holly at their spot. Something was missing, though. The thin branches weren't screeching along the side of the car as usual. Barry's eyes found where they had been snapped from something. It only took him a second to figure it out.

The camper, he thought. *She widened the path nearly two feet when she plowed through here.*

"You sure you know where you're going?" Aidy asked.

"Yeah," Barry said, looking ahead. "See that gate up there?"

"Yeah, why?"

"It's been locked up for years."

They were perhaps twenty feet from the gate now.

"It looks like it's been ripped off."

"I guess she didn't have a spell to unlock it," he said as he passed the gate posts.

"There isn't one that I know of anyway," Aidy said, turning in her seat to look behind them.

"Any headlights?" Barry asked.

"Not at the moment."

"Good," Barry said, slowing the car and rolling down the windows. "Let me know if you see a camper."

"Why a camper?"

"Eddie said he's inside a camper, tied to a chair."

"Why is he—"

"She knows he's been helping us."

"What the hell?" she said, turning back around. "How?"

"I don't know. I didn't have time to ask."

"So much for plenty of time to plan."

"Yeah, I know," Barry said. "Do you see anything yet?"

"Just trees," she said, leaning forward in her seat, hands on the dash. Then her eyes found something in the yellow glow of the car's headlights. It was sitting behind an old oak tree that had a heart carved in it. "Wait—I think I see something."

"I should have known."

Aidy glanced at him. "Known what?"

"Where she would have run off to."

"How's that?"

"She knew I wouldn't want to come out here."

"Ahh," Aidy said.

They were just fifty feet or so from the camper now. "Let's get Eddie and get the hell out of here."

Barry brought the Celica to a stop, the headlights pointed directly on the camper. He pulled the handbrake and left the car running before he hurried out of it. Aidy was right behind him, the OC spray in her hand.

"Shit," Barry said, as he got to the camper's door.

"What?" Aidy said, looking around.

"I forgot the flash bang."

"So?"

"I was going to use it to help us get out of here if she shows up."

"Come up with another plan after we get Eddie."

Barry nodded and gripped the door handle. When he pulled it open, he saw Eddie on the floor still tied to the chair.

"Took you long enough," Eddie said.

"How'd you know it was us and not them?" Barry said.

"I know the sound of your car. Now untie me, would you? There are knives on the counter above me."

Barry and Aidy each grabbed a kitchen knife and began cutting through the rope. Twenty seconds later Eddie was free, but he still couldn't move. The rope was tied so tight that it cut off the circulation to his extremities. Blood was flowing back into his hands and feet but, with the prospect of Elaine pulling in any second, it felt as if the blood was moving as slow as a grocery store checkout line.

Barry tried to help Eddie to his feet. His feet were still too numb, though.

"Going to have to give me a minute," Eddie said.

"We don't have a minute," Barry said. "Elaine will be here soon."

Eddie nodded. Then Barry picked him up and tossed him over his shoulder.

"Where are we going?" Aidy said.

"Away from here," Barry said, heading toward the door.

"There's only one way out of here, though, isn't there?" Eddie asked.

"Yeah," Barry said. "As far as I know."

"We better hurry then," Aidy said.

Aidy ran ahead of Barry, opened the passenger-side door, and buckled up in the backseat. Barry buckled Eddie in the front seat, closed the door, and slid across the hood to the driver's side. As he sat behind the wheel, Eddie said, "Nice slide, Starsky."

Aidy gave him a bold look. "Seriously making jokes when we're in imminent danger?"

Eddie shifted his gaze to the rearview and smiled at his daughter. "Laughter is the best medicine."

Barry clicked his seatbelt and looked over his shoulder at Aidy. "I thought you said honesty was?"

Aidy's brow furrowed. "Drive, would you!"

Barry put the car in gear, turned the wheel, and spun the Celica around back to the road they had just come down. A few seconds later, they saw headlights.

The truck was speeding toward them. "That's her," Eddie said. "We need to turn around."

"And go where?" Barry asked.

"I don't know, but a head-on collision isn't ideal."

Barry turned off the dirt path and headed back toward the camper.

"Do you have a spell in mind to incapacitate her?" Aidy asked.

"About that," Eddie said. "She did something to me while I was out. I'm not sure if she gave me a potion or used a spell, but she temporarily took away my ability to cast spells."

"How are we supposed to fight her then?"

"Still have that OC spray?" Barry asked.

"Yeah," Aidy said. "But—"

Elaine slammed into the Celica's rear-end. Barry fought for control, working the steering wheel to the best of his ability. He tried to turn without losing it, but Elaine rammed the Celica again.

They were headed straight for the oak tree with Barry's and Holly's initials in it. In the darkness, it seemed to appear out of nowhere.

Barry checked the speedometer. Elaine was pushing them at thirty-five miles per hour.

He dropped it to first gear and stood on the brake pedal. The car slowed some, but Elaine had the truck's throttle wide open. It was heavier and it had nearly three times the horsepower.

Barry glanced at the rearview mirror; Aidy's face was horror-stricken as she braced herself for the impact. Behind her, Barry could just make out Elaine's eerie smile. He was still looking in the rearview mirror when the car hit the oak tree head on.

Chapter 18

Smoke billowed out from underneath the hoods of both vehicles. One of the Celica's headlights hadn't been crushed. The truck's headlights were buried into the back of the car. After the engines shut off, it was quiet except for Aidy's moans coming from the backseat. Pain ran through her chest and shoulder area where the seatbelt held her back. It hurt for her to turn her head. It hurt her even more to see Barry and Eddie not moving in the front seats.

The airbags had deployed, but they also knocked Barry and Eddie unconscious. She unbuckled her seatbelt and looked behind her. The rear glass was shattered. Small pieces of glass were in her hair and all over the backseat. She looked for Elaine but couldn't see anything with the smoke everywhere. She needed to get out, but every movement she made sent a shooting pain through her body. She began to mumble incantations. Healing spells were Aidy's province, her one thing she excelled at as a witch.

Healing spells took time, though. She was a witch, not a miracle worker. She wouldn't be completely healed, but she didn't need to be. She just needed to be able to move.

After a minute went by, she was able to move with tolerable pain. She climbed out through the back window. Smoke was still concealing the truck. She looked around for Elaine or the boys, but she seemed to be the only one moving at that moment. Aidy made her way up to the driver-side door and pulled on the door handle. At first, it wouldn't open. The impact had pushed the body of the car into the door. She pulled harder. The door began to open. Once she had a gap large enough for her to fit between, she braced herself against the car, placed her feet against the door panel and used her legs to open it the rest of the way.

Barry's nose was bleeding. His head was lolled to the side. Her eyes filled with tears when she saw him, but she blinked them away. She shook him softly, lightly tapping his cheek to get him to wake up.

"Come on, Barry," she said. "Please, wake up."

Eddie stirred in the passenger seat. His eyes opened and saw his daughter trying to wake Barry.

"Where is she?" Eddie asked with wide eyes.

"I don't know," she said. "I can't see in the truck."

Eddie could feel his hands and feet again. The blood had finally returned. His face hurt from the airbag, but other than that he was feeling better. He removed his seatbelt and went to open his door, but it was stuck like the driver's side. While pulling on the handle, he began to thrust his shoulder into the door panel. It opened on the second try. Eddie moved quickly, running around the tree the car had hit. By the time Eddie made it to the driver's side, Aidy had removed Barry's seatbelt and was trying to reposition him.

"Grab his legs," Eddie told her. "I'll carry his upper body."

"No need," she said.

Eddie gave her a look. "What are you—"

She ran a hand over Barry's forearm and quietly recited a healing spell. A few seconds later, Barry's eyes slowly began to open.

Eddie turned his attention to Barry. "Can you walk?"

Barry looked down at his legs. "Let's hope so."

He stepped out of the car. His legs worked fine. His nose wasn't even sore; although, it could've been the adrenaline coursing through his veins helping with that. Either way, it wasn't what was on his mind.

"Where's Elaine?" Barry asked.

Aidy and Eddie looked toward the truck. Smoke was still floating all around them.

"Now or never, I guess," Barry said.

"Wait," Aidy said, digging in the back seat's floorboard. "Here."

Barry saw that she hadn't forgotten about the OC spray. "Thanks," he said, putting a hand on his belt to check for his handcuffs. "Dammit."

"What?" Eddie asked.

"I forgot to grab my cuffs when I left the house."

"I can grab the rope out of the camper they tied me up with," Eddie said.

"Take Aidy with you in case Elaine's still in the truck."

"What are you going to do if she's in there?" Eddie asked.

"Spray the hell out of her," Barry said, lifting up the canister of OC spray. "Then I'll keep her pinned down until you bring me that rope."

"Are you sure about this?" Aidy asked, moving closer to Barry.

"Don't have much of a choice."

Aidy hesitated as if there were more she wanted to tell him, but instead she nodded and went with Eddie to the camper.

Barry faced the truck, his hand squeezing the canister tight. Smoke continued to flow from under the hood. He hurried through the smoke, trying not to breathe it in. When he managed to find the driver's side door handle, he steeled himself for what would happen next.

Barry held the OC spray up as he opened the door, spraying inside the truck before he even saw Elaine.

Then he stopped when he realized the truck was empty.

"What the—"

A high-pitched scream pierced the air. It came from behind him, inside the camper. Barry felt his stomach sink to his knees.

"Aidy!" Barry yelled.

A second later, the camper Eddie and Aidy were in went up in flames and the screaming became louder.

For a moment, the image of Holly being taken into the lake flashed in Barry's mind. He squeezed his eyes shut and shook the thought away.

Barry ran to the camper, dropping the OC spray halfway there. When he reached the camper's door, he caught something out of the corner of his eye: Eddie was being dragged by Elaine and her boys. He knew she couldn't kill Eddie without also killing herself. All of Barry's focus was on finding Aidy.

It didn't take long.

The flames were all around her. Her hands were tied around the leg of the booth. She lay on the floor, tears coursing down her cheeks, eyes as round as golf balls. Barry ran in without even considering that she could be using Aidy as bait to get him too.

He grabbed the knife from the counter, and slid under the table next to her, working on the rope with the serrated edge of the blade. The rope was tight, but that only helped him cut through it. The flames were closing in, just as they did when he was in the house. When he got Aidy's hands free, he grabbed her around her torso and ran out.

Barry looked around for Eddie. He was gone. Other than the camper burning behind them, it was quiet.

Before Barry could ask Aidy what happened, she said, "They must have been hiding around the side of the camper. They came in right after we did. She incapacitated Eddie with some spell I've never even heard of before. Then the boys threw me down and tied me up."

"Did she say anything about where she was taking Eddie?"

Aidy shook her head and rested it on Barry's chest. She held him tight. Barry looked over her shoulder. Two circular lights were getting closer and closer through the smoke. The camper had burned itself halfway down and was just far away enough that the trees didn't catch. Barry discerned that the lights belonged to a car when he heard the engine revving in the distance.

"What now?" Aidy asked.

"Stay here," he said.

"No," Aidy said, and gripped his arm. "That didn't go well last time."

Barry didn't argue. There wasn't time to, anyway. The person in the car pulled up next to the truck. Barry unholstered his Glock and aimed it at whomever was driving. A man opened the driver-side door and stepped out. Barry saw a gun in the man's hand and put pressure on the trigger.

"Don't move," the man shouted.

Barry knew the voice. As the man stepped closer, Barry was able to verify whom the voice belong to.

"Donaldson," Barry said. "Don't shoot. She put you under a spell and—"

"I know what she did," he said, lowering the gun. "Calm down, I'm not going to shoot you. I'm here to help this time."

Barry holstered his Glock and moved closer to his sergeant. His eyes found the hole in Donaldson's shirt. "Did she—"

"Shoot me?" Donaldson said. "Yeah, right on your front lawn with my own gun. Good thing I always wear my vest."

"If she has your gun, where'd you—"

"I always keep another one on me," he said, raising his pant leg to reveal his ankle holster.

Barry shifted his gaze to the car Donaldson pulled up in. "And the car?"

"I commandeered one. First time I've ever had to. Now where is she?"

"She took off in the woods with Eddie and the boys."

"Eddie? Your friend?"

"It's a long story."

"We have to find her before she kills him. Come on," Donaldson said as he started toward the woods.

"She won't kill him," Barry said.

"How do you know? That witch is as crazy as a sprayed roach."

"Because," Aidy cut in, "he's her son."

Donaldson gave Barry a look.

"Like I said before, it's a long story," Barry told him.

"If Eddie dies, so does she. It's part of the spell that brought her back," Aidy said.

"And if she dies, so does Eddie," Barry added. "She didn't tell you any of this when you were uh—"

"Under her control? No, she didn't. The last few hours have been one hell of a blur, Barry. From the little I vaguely remember, she mostly wanted you dead. That was her—" Donaldson spun around. "Did you hear that?"

Barry and Aidy stood still, listening.

Donaldson's gun was out in front of him again.

"You can't shoot them, Sarge. If you shoot her, it'll kill Eddie. And those kids—"

William ran past Barry and Aidy with preternatural speed to tackle Donaldson to the ground. Donaldson fumbled the gun as he fell and lost it in the darkness. Barry instinctively pulled out his Glock and hurried over to get the kid off his sergeant. Before he could restrain William, Thomas jumped on his back, choking him from behind with the grip of a full-grown man. Barry had to drop his gun to use both of his hands.

Aidy ran up to help Barry, but then she felt a blow to the back of her head. As she fell forward, it felt as if everything around her was spinning. Everything became nebulous. Then came the thud as she hit the ground.

Behind her, Elaine stood by the lake, her hand still raised toward Aidy.

Barry spun around to find Aidy on the ground. Then he saw why Aidy had fallen. Elaine sported that strange smile, the one that said, *I've been waiting a long time for this moment.*

When she started to walk toward him, he had finally managed to break Thomas's grip and throw him down. The boy hit the ground hard, but bounced right back up as if he had fallen on a trampoline.

"Help your brother, Thomas," Elaine said. "Leave this one to me."

Barry knelt next to Aidy and put a hand on her back. He could feel her lungs working. She was still alive, but he didn't know how badly she had been hurt. Behind him, he heard Donaldson grunting and yelling for help. Barry risked a glance at Donaldson. William was on top of him, trying to sink his teeth into the flesh of Donaldson's throat. And now Thomas was rushing to help William. Barry didn't think Donaldson could handle both of them. He didn't know if Aidy would be okay. Then he wondered what happened to Eddie.

Barry looked past Elaine. He spotted a body by the edge of the lake. The headlight that still functioned on Barry's car illuminated Eddie just enough for Barry to see that his best friend was covered in blood, and that he had been bitten all over his arms and chest.

Barry stood up, coming to the realization that he was standing in almost the same exact spot that Holly had read Elaine's book thirteen years ago.

"Barry!" Donaldson said. "Do something!"

When Barry spun around to help, Thomas pushed him hard. Barry stumbled back, his foot caught something, and he tumbled over. While on his back, he looked over to see Eddie trying to get up. Then all he saw was Elaine hovering over him, staring down with that insane smile. Barry couldn't look away. She was doing something to him. He could feel his body becoming numb. He had no idea how he hadn't seen the gun in her hand, but there it was, pointed right at him.

"I've been waiting so long for this very moment, you know?" Elaine said, her finger wrapped around the trigger.

Barry tried to get up, but whatever she was doing to him was only worsening.

"No!" Barry heard Aidy shout. He broke eye contact with Elaine and found Aidy. She had an arm extended out toward him; he felt Aidy pulling the numbness away. Then he saw what he had tripped over when Thomas pushed him: his gun. It lay there by his foot, and while he felt Aidy trying to combat whatever Elaine was doing to him, he still couldn't reach it.

Barry watched as Elaine walked toward Aidy, the gun she had taken from Donaldson gripped tightly in her hand. He had forgotten completely about Donaldson now. Barry tried to kick the gun up to his hand. It slid, but not far enough so that he could grip it. Then he saw Elaine hovering over Aidy.

"I should have known you would spoil my oldest son," Elaine said as she applied pressure on Aidy's stomach with her foot. "Now he's ruined. I'll never get him back, and it's all your fault."

Barry's entire body shook as he fought to reach the gun, but he wasn't able to. All he could do was look at Aidy as she stared up at the gun in Elaine's hand. Before Elaine pulled the trigger, Aidy met Barry's gaze one more time. Then, as the gun went off, Barry squeezed his eyes shut.

Chapter 19

B arry didn't want to open his eyes. He was too afraid to look. The smell of gun smoke entered his nostrils, and the sound of the gunshot rang in his ears. He heard a voice, but his ears were still ringing. It was as if the gun had been fired right next to his head. Then he heard the voice again and realized something: it was Aidy's.

Barry's eyes opened and found Aidy. She was on her hands and knees. Tears were still in her eyes. Elaine's body lay motionless next to her. There was a dark red hole in the back of her head.

Barry noticed the gun he had been trying to reach was gone. When he looked to his right, he found it in Eddie's right hand. He was lying on his stomach, his face turned toward Barry.

"Told you I remember how to shoot," Eddie said, his voice quiet.

Barry realized he could move again. He pushed off the ground and got on his knees next to Eddie, helping him to a sitting position.

"Why'd you do it?" Barry asked, barely able to get the words out.

Aidy crawled over and kneeled next to Barry. Eddie smiled up at the two of them. "Didn't have much of a choice."

Even as Barry shook his head, trying to hold back tears, he knew his best friend was right.

"I've lived a long life," Eddie went on, his voice becoming hoarse. "I've had plenty of regrets." He was looking at Aidy now. "Things I wish I could go back and change."

Aidy nodded as the tears in her eyes began to slowly roll down her cheeks.

"It's going to be okay. You know?"

Barry nodded and kept the tears back. He didn't want the last thing for Eddie to see was his best friend falling apart. "Yeah," Barry said, sucking in a shaky breath. "We know."

Suddenly, Elaine's body disappeared. All that remained was the dress she was wearing. Smoke was coming from the dress as if it were on fire, but the smoke didn't float up; it was being sucked into the ground.

Eddie watched Elaine disappear, knowing he would be next. Then his gaze shifted back to Barry and Aidy. "I'm going to miss you guys," he said, his voice barely audible. He fixed his best friend and his daughter with one last smile. "See you when I see you."

Eddie's body turned to smoke, but it wasn't being sucked into the ground. It slowly floated up into the night sky like smoke from a campfire. Barry watched it until he could no longer see it anymore.

Then he fell apart.

* * *

He stayed on his knees, holding Eddie's clothes in his hands, and let the tears fall. Aidy consoled him the best she could, but the truth was she had been struggling with losing the father she hardly knew. Then, they heard someone walking up behind them. Barry and Aidy spun around.

"You guys all right?" Donaldson asked. His shirt had been ripped in several places and his body had scratches here and there, but he hadn't been bitten.

The boys, Barry thought. "Are the boys—"

"Alive," Donaldson said. "Yeah, they're breathing. As soon as Elaine was shot, they fell off me and went to sleep."

Barry nodded, wiping the tears off his face. "We need to get them to a hospital."

"We need to figure out what we're going to tell everyone too," Donaldson said. "They'll think we're all crazy if we tell them the truth."

"Yeah," Barry said. "I know from experience."

"I'm sorry about that," Donaldson said, putting his hand on Barry's shoulder. "I won't ever doubt you again."

Barry nodded and glanced down, noticing something in Donaldson's front pocket. "What's in your shirt pocket?"

Donaldson looked down at his shirt and lifted out the note. "This woman and her damn notes." He opened it up and used the flashlight on his cell phone to read it. By the time he finished reading, a look of disgust crossed his face. "It's a suicide note. She was going to kill both of you with my gun and try to pin it on me."

"Surprised?" Barry asked.

"Somewhat, yeah," he said, crumbling up the note. "Anyway, we need to get our story straight."

"What are we going to tell them?" Aidy asked.

Donaldson scratched his head for a minute. "We'll have to tell them you found the truck driving into Hole in the Woods. That you were in your personal vehicle. That you pulled up to the tree to search for the truck—when you discovered the camper. Then you heard your car being crushed against the tree. By the time you got out of the camper, Nancy McIntyre was gone and left the boys in the truck. Then you called me."

"What about the camper burning down?"

Donaldson scratched his head again. "I'll tell them it happened after we put the boys in the ambulance. We'll meet the paramedics by the road. Tell them Nancy probably burned it down to get rid of evidence."

Barry nodded.

"You call the medics," Donaldson said. "It'll sound better coming from you as if you just found them."

"What about me?" Aidy asked, holding Eddie's clothes.

"You can drive the car I drove here to Barry's house. We'll call Ernie tomorrow morning to return it to its owner."

"What are you going to drive, then?" Barry asked.

"I spotted my car over there," he said, pointing near the lake. "You know, I don't even remember driving it here in the first place. Must've been before I left with her to go to your house."

Barry nodded. "Probably so."

"Anyway, before I come back here, I need to tell Nancy McIntyre to get the hell out of town. Change her name, start a new life. No one will believe she was under the control of a witch when she kidnapped those kids."

"How do you know where she is?" Barry asked.

"I'm having a hard time remembering. It's like the next morning when you're trying to remember the dream you just had, but it keeps fading away. I think before we got to your place, she dumped Nancy's body off at her own house. I remember being in the truck and seeing her go inside."

"How do you know she's even alive?" Aidy asked.

"I don't," Donaldson said. "But the boys are, so maybe she is too."

Barry dug his cell phone out of his front pocket. The screen was cracked—probably from the car crash—but it still functioned. "Before I call for the medics, there's one last bit of evidence to get rid of."

Aidy and Donaldson watched Barry walk to the truck. Smoke had finally stopped coming from under the hood. He opened the driver's side door and reached in, lifting something off the floorboard.

When Barry stepped back into the light, Aidy saw Elaine's book of incantations immediately. Donaldson on the other hand was somewhat confused.

"What's that, Barry?" Donaldson asked, stepping forward to get a better look.

"This is what started this mess," Barry said. "This is how she came back all those years ago."

"The book Holly Chandler read, if I remember the statement the police got from you back then."

"Yeah," Barry said as he looked down at the book. "The one they couldn't find that day."

"What are you going to do with it?" Aidy asked.

Barry lifted his eyes from the book and met hers for a second before he faced the lake. Eddie's words filled his head: *Drown it*. Barry started walking toward the water.

As he reached the edge of the lake, he fought the urge to open the book. The longer he held it, the more he wanted to. It wasn't that the book still held any power to it—at least Barry didn't think so—but his curiosity was having a hard time keeping it closed.

He didn't hear Aidy walk up behind him. "Are you going to throw it in the lake?" she asked.

Still staring out at the lake water, he said, "That's what Eddie said to do with it."

Aidy wrapped her fingers around his forearm and looked down at the hand that held the book. Even with the lack of light, Barry saw her disgust and hatred for Elaine's book. It was clear to him that she didn't want to touch it.

When Aidy found his eyes again, she said, "Throw it as far as you can."

Barry gripped the book tight, wrenched it back, and threw it as hard as he could. The book spun in the air the way a boomerang spins when it's thrown properly. Unlike a boomerang, the book didn't come back. It plopped in the water, slowly sinking into the lake that had haunted Barry's dreams for the last thirteen years.

Chapter 20

Nothing prepares you for losing a friend. Especially your closest one. Everyone deals with death in their own way. For Barry, it had always been booze. When Holly died, he turned to the bottle. Plenty of people do. Although a person—or one's liver—can only take so much after a while.

When Barry rode in the ambulance to the hospital with Denny Molasky and Phillip Carter, he thought about Eddie. How could he not? He thought about all of the times Eddie had tried to tell Barry that he needed to slow down on the alcohol. All of the times Eddie had called to check on him. Then tears formed in his eyes. He shook them away, telling himself that Eddie wouldn't want him to feel so horrible. Eddie would want him to be happy. Elaine was gone, and life could go back to normal, right? Except normal in Barry's world was having Eddie around to joke with and make each other laugh.

Barry looked at the kids, the ones he helped save, and took a deep breath.

A minute later, they pulled into the hospital.

When the medics took the kids inside, Barry followed closely behind until a nurse stopped him.

"We'll take it from here, Detective," Nurse Sarah said, looking Barry over. "Are you okay?"

"Never been better."

"You look like you could use some rest."

"I need to make sure those kids are okay."

"What you need is to rest."

Barry shook his head in dissent.

Sarah sighed and put a hand on his shoulder. "Okay, fine. If you'll take a seat in the waiting room, I promise to let you know something as soon as I can."

Barry let her lead him to the waiting room, where he took a seat in the corner and waited. After a half hour had passed, Barry's cell started vibrating in his pocket. It was Donaldson.

"You at the hospital?"

"Yeah, in the waiting room," Barry said.

"Are the kids all right? They remember anything?"

"I don't know. I'm still waiting for someone to come out and tell me something."

"Well, I'll be up there soon."

"What about Nancy?"

"She's gone, Barry."

Barry's eyes went wide. "What do you mean?"

"I mean she isn't at her house. I checked every room in the place. She must have woken up and remembered enough to know that her only option was to flee. My guess is that she's already out of town and headed to God knows where."

"Probably right," Barry said. He heard the automatic doors open and flicked his eyes over to the waiting room's front entrance. A man and woman were rushing in. "I'll see you in a few. Gerald and Clair Carter just walked in."

Barry stood up when Gerald saw him. The man walked over with his arm stretched out.

Barry gripped his hand and shook it. He noticed that sleep deprived look in their bloodshot eyes.

"Please tell me that Phillip is okay," Clair said.

"Thank you so much for finding him," Gerald said before Barry could respond.

"I—"

The door opened and Nurse Sarah walked out. Her eyes found Barry first, then she saw Gerald and Clair standing next to him. Of course, Sarah knew of them. The whole town knew the Carters.

Sarah took a few steps and faced the Carters. "Other than a few scratches and bruises, both boys are fine," she said, then shifted her gaze over to Barry. "It's strange, though."

"What is?" Barry asked.

"Neither one can remember much of what happened to them. They can't even remember what the lady looked like."

Clair placed the palm of her hand on her forehead, and said, "They weren't drugged, were they?"

"No," Sarah said, seeing the relief flow through Clair. "They couldn't find a single drug in their systems." Sarah shifted her gaze to Barry again. "Do you happen to know how the Molasky boy lost his two front teeth?"

Barry shook his head. "I'm afraid not."

"When can we see Phillip?" Clair asked.

"Right this way," Sarah said, motioning them along with her hand.

Gerald's eyes met Barry's again before he followed the nurse. "You ever need anything—"

Barry put a hand up. "Don't worry about it. Just go make sure your son is all right."

Gerald shook his head. To his left, Clair was wiping tears from her eyes. Barry watched them walk through the door leading back to the room. The last thing he heard was the nurse telling them that they wanted to keep Phillip for observation.

After hearing that the boys were going to be okay, Barry made his way out of the hospital. Just outside of the door, he found a bench and took a seat. He started to dig in his pocket for his cell but stopped when he saw Donaldson pull into the parking lot. Donaldson shut the car off in the ambulance bay near the ER's entrance. Barry stood up and noticed that his sergeant had changed his shirt to one that didn't have a bullet hole in it.

"Any word on the boys yet?" Donaldson asked.

"They're okay. We can head back to Hole in the Woods to cordon the crime scene off."

"Did they remember anything?"

"Not much," Barry said, opening the passenger-side door. "According to the nurse. She said they don't even remember what she looked like."

"That's probably best. As the night goes on, my memory while under her spell seems to be getting fuzzier." Donaldson started the car. He was looking through the windshield when he said, "The whole time, it just felt like a dream. Like it didn't really happen."

"That's sort of how it felt all those years ago when Holly read that spell. I knew it happened, though. Even as the years went on, a part of me knew I hadn't imagined it."

Donaldson put the car in gear and eased on the throttle. "When we get to the scene, we need to go over our story again."

"You worried?"

"About others questioning our story?"

"Yeah."

"Being that you're the lead detective on the Nancy McIntyre case," Donaldson's lips spread into a grin as he looked at the road ahead of him, "I think we'll be okay."

* * *

Donaldson drove the back way to Hole in the Woods. Neither Barry nor Donaldson talked much after pulling out of the hospital entrance. Each of them seemed to be lost in their own thoughts about everything that had happened. Donaldson kept his eyes on the road while Barry looked out of his window, watching everything as it went by, thinking about Eddie.

As they neared the apex of the curve leading to Hole in the Woods, Barry saw something he hadn't noticed before in the back of the ambulance with the boys.

"Stop the car for a second," Barry said.

"Why?" Donaldson asked, glancing over.

"I saw something back there."

"What'd you see?"

"It's too dark out to know for sure, but it looked like a car hidden behind those trees."

Donaldson rolled down the windows and turned the car around, driving slowly the other way.

"Stop," Barry said.

Donaldson narrowed his eyes on what Barry had found. "Whose car is that?"

Barry knew instantly. It was parked across the street, in a small lot. An old chain-link fence served as a border between the lot and a defunct concrete plant, one that went under when Barry was still in high school. The trees on either side of the lot needed trimmed up years ago. One of the tree's low-hanging branches had curled over so far that it touched the ground; that's where Barry spotted the car.

Donaldson positioned the car he was driving so that the headlights illuminated the lot. Barry got out, letting out a deep breath as he neared the vehicle. He walked around the tree, now able to see how the car had made it back there. The branch touching the ground had been cut enough so that it would swing back and forth like a hinge. It was bungee corded to another branch, which allowed it to go back in its original position to conceal the car.

A myriad of memories rushed into his mind as he placed a hand on the trunk lid.

"Isn't that your friend's car?" Donaldson asked.

Barry almost jumped at the sound of his voice. "Yeah, it's Eddie's."

"He must've parked here so he wouldn't be implicated in the kidnapping."

"That's probably part of it," Barry said, a hint of smile on his face. "But I think he just didn't want to drive down the path to Hole in the Woods because he knew the branches would scratch the sides of his car."

"Elaine widened that path with the camper, though."

"He probably didn't know that at the time."

"I guess not," Donaldson said, looking around. "We should probably have Ernie bring his tow truck to get this out of here ASAP."

"No need," Barry said, lying down on his side. "I know where Eddie hides his key."

Barry reached underneath the rear bumper. A few seconds later, he brought out a little black magnetic box. When he slid the cover up, the key to the car appeared.

Barry unlocked Eddie's Nissan and slid in the front seat. He left the door cracked open so the interior lights would stay on. The car was nearly spotless on the inside except for the driver-side floormat where Eddie's shoes had tracked in a modicum of dirt. Barry looked around inside, seeing nothing on the floorboards or seats. Then he opened the center console; nothing in there either. Only one more compartment to check. He just hoped there would be something other than insurance papers in it.

Barry thumbed the glove box open, reached in, and pulled out a few different things. He laid it all on his lap and looked at the picture first. It was the same photograph that was in Aidy's locket, except this one had a crease that ran through the middle of it as if it had been folded once or twice. Barry flipped it over and checked the back. The date was written on the back of it next to a few words in Eddie's handwriting: *Aidy and Melinda. My girls.*

Barry went to the next one. It was, in fact, Eddie's insurance papers; he tossed those back into the glove box.

There were two more papers, and Barry realized Eddie's intentions immediately even before he read the notes attached to them. He stuffed it all back into the glove box, wanting Aidy to be present for those last two papers. He knew he needed to hurry up and get the car out of there anyway.

While Donaldson held the branch back for him, making just enough room for the width of the car, Barry started the engine, rolled the window down, and shifted to first.

Barry drove the car back to his house, listening to the sound the engine made under acceleration. He listened to the wind as it passed by the open window, trying to keep his mind elsewhere. He tried, but the fact that Eddie was gone was still in his head.

When he pulled into his driveway, Aidy came outside of the house. Her red-tinged eyes went wide when she saw the car.

Barry killed the engine.

Through the rolled-down window, Barry said, "Hop in."

Aidy slid into the passenger seat, her eyes wandering around the car. After a few seconds, she looked at Barry. "How—"

"Eddie parked it near the woods. Hid it behind some trees."

"You brought it here so the department wouldn't ask questions?"

"That's one reason."

"What's the other?"

"Open the glove box."

Aidy furrowed her brow, confusion crossing her face for a moment. When she opened the glove box, she found the photograph first. The confusion was replaced by a soft smile. She ran her fingertips along the picture of her and her parents. When she flipped it over to read the back, Barry saw her face change. He saw her eyes filling with tears. She was biting her lip, doing her best to hold back. To say she was struggling would be an understatement.

Barry reached over and pulled out the papers that remained in the glove box, finding the insurance papers first again. While he was putting those away, he realized his hands were shaking. They didn't usually, but his nerves were fried. He was trying to hide the emotional stress he had endured, but it was revealing itself in ways he had little to no control over.

When Barry found the papers he was looking for, he noticed something he hadn't seen earlier; there was a paperclip with a folded-up piece of paper attached to them. Barry handed the papers to Aidy and held on to the note.

Aidy read them over and looked at Barry. "These are titles."

"I know," Barry said with a nod. He skimmed over the folded-up note and handed it over to Aidy. "I think this will help explain things."

Aidy gripped the paper in both hands. Underneath the car's dome light, Aidy began to read what was written on the paper aloud.

"To Aidy or Barry. Hopefully both of you."

Aidy glanced at Barry. He saw her lips trembling.

"It's okay," he said. "Let's just read it silently."

They shifted closer together, each of them holding one side of the paper.

If you're reading this, it's probably because I had to kill my mother. And if I killed her, which no son should ever have to do, then I suppose I'm probably dead too. And if that's the case, don't waste your tears on me. I lived a long, long life. I wasn't haunted by Elaine's incessant exhortations the entire time. I had some time to enjoy myself over the years. And what I've learned in that time is that life isn't easy, but the good people you find and keep around sure make it easier.

Anyway, let's get down to business. I'm sure you've seen what this note was attached to, and I've already signed in the proper spots. My semitruck you can sell to help Aidy get a leg-up in this crazy world we live in. It's in good shape and up on maintenance by yours truly. I think it'll bring in a pretty penny. As for my Nissan, it's yours, Aidy. Now, of course, Barry will have to teach you to drive a manual, but it's nothing you can't figure out.

I wish I had more time to write, but I don't. As soon as I left you two, I grabbed the titles, a piece of scrap paper, and a pen. I'm sitting in my car, which you must've found if you're reading this, wishing I'd have come clean to you both sooner. I can only hope you both understand the situation I was in and what the spell I was a part of was doing to me.

I have to go now. Elaine is waiting on me. I feel like something is different. Like she knows somehow. It's probably nothing, but just in case, I figured it would be best to write this note.

See you when I see you,
Eddie

At some point while they were reading, Aidy had grabbed Barry's arm and leaned her head on his shoulder. Her warmth felt nice. He thought how it could feel so right to have feelings like this for someone he met just a day or two ago. It was as if he had known her for much longer. It sure did feel that way.

Around the time they finished reading the note, Barry saw headlights shine in the Nissan's rearview mirror.

"Who's that?" Aidy asked, not recognizing the car.

"It's Donaldson," Barry said. "I have to go back to Hole in the Woods to cordon off the crime scene and get the story straight with the department."

Aidy nodded wearily. "When will you be back?"

"Probably a few hours, if I'm lucky."

"I'll wait up."

"You look like you could pass out at any minute," Barry said with a gentle smile, then handed her the titles. "Take these and go get some rest. Just lock the doors before you go to sleep, okay?"

Aidy took the titles and grabbed the Nissan's door handle. She went to pull it but hesitated.

"Aidy," Barry said when she stopped moving. "What's wrong?"

Aidy pushed the hair back from her face as she turned to meet his eyes.

"Aidy," Barry said when he saw her moving closer to him.

He felt the warmth of her hand as she wrapped her fingers around the nape of his neck. She leaned in, underneath the dome light of the car, and kissed him lightly on the mouth.

Chapter 21

A month after Eddie killed Elaine in Hole in the Woods, Barry was working on a new case. Thankfully, this one didn't involve witches, wizards, or witchcraft at all; although, he really didn't believe he'd ever have a case like the Nancy McIntyre one again. In this new case, a man was reported missing about a week ago. No leads, no witnesses, just a welfare check on a man that wasn't at his residence. No one had heard from him in a week or so, but today they would find him in the parking lot at a grocery store on the east side of Abbott. Several shoppers had walked in to inform the store manager that a foul odor was coming from a Buick in the parking lot. After the third or fourth complaint, the store manager called to have it towed away.

Ernie arrived in his tow truck half an hour later. As soon as he got out, he smelled the putrid odor emitting from the trunk. He clamped his nostrils shut with his thumb and forefinger, closed his door, and drove to the other side of the lot. Ernie didn't have Barry's cell phone number, but he did have Donaldson's.

"Hey, Ernie," Donaldson said, answering the call.

"I was called to tow this Buick away in the grocery store parkin' lot. There's a nasty smell comin' from the trunk."

"Okay. And?"

"I don't think it's rott'n ground beef."

Donaldson understood now. "Which grocery store, Ernie?"

"The one on the east side of town."

"I'll call Barry and be there in a few minutes. Stay put."

Not long after the call, Ernie saw Barry pulling into the parking lot. He stopped his Charger next to Ernie's tow truck.

"That the car, Ernie?" Barry asked as he walked up to the tow truck.

Ernie stayed seated in the truck. "Yeah, that's the one. I hope you have some Vick's to shove up your nose. It's bad, Barry."

"Not my first rodeo," Barry said, dropping Ernie a wink.

Ernie smirked. "Wise man must've told you that before."

Barry chuckled and went over to the Buick. The smell was horrible, of course. As soon as Barry caught a whiff, he was sure of what he'd find inside the trunk; he knew the acrid smell of a dead body when it entered his nostrils.

Barry tried to lift the trunk lid, but it wouldn't budge. He checked all four doors, and they were all locked too. He walked back to the Charger and dug around in its trunk for a minute. As he headed back to the Buick with the lockout tool in his hand, Donaldson pulled in the lot.

Barry waited for him to drive over. Donaldson rolled the window down and said, "Should I park over by Ernie's truck?"

"Yeah," Barry said, sliding on a pair of disposable gloves. "I think we're going to have to cordon the area off real soon."

"I'll call a few squad cars and the crime scene unit in as soon as we're sure there's a body."

Barry nodded and walked over to the Buick's driver-side door. He slid the thin piece of metal down between the glass window and rubber window seal, fishing for the correct rod that would unlock the car. When he felt the lookout tool hook around something promising, he raised the tool up and grabbed the door handle. The smell worsened when he opened the door. He quickly found the trunk-release handle and pulled it. He heard the trunk's locking mechanism release and walked around to the back of the car. Donaldson had just made it over when Barry began to lift the trunk.

"That's the guy that went missing," Barry said. "Isn't it?"

"Yeah, that's him," Donaldson said, squeezing his nostrils shut with his thumb and forefinger. "Go ahead and close it. I have to make a few calls."

Barry took his gloves off and went into the grocery store to apprise the store manager of the situation in the parking lot. With that taken care of, he made his way back to the parking lot. Before he reached the car, his cell phone started to vibrate in his pocket.

He quickly read the name on the screen before putting the phone up to his ear. "Dad?"

"Hey, Barry, are you busy?"

Barry looked around at the squad cars pulling in the lot. "Somewhat. What's going on?"

"It's your mother."

Barry stopped walking. Suddenly it became hard to breathe.

"Is she okay?"

"It's important that you get here soon. She wants to tell you herself."

"Tell me what?" Barry said, trying to keep his voice steady.

"She made me promise not to tell you. She said she wanted to tell you in person."

"Are you at the house?"

"Yeah, we're here."

"I'll be there as soon as I can."

"Drive safe. Don't go rushing—"

Barry had already hung up and hurried over to Donaldson. His sergeant was on the phone still, but when he saw Barry's face, he told the person on the other line to hold on for a second.

"What's wrong, Barry? You haven't looked like that since, well, you know." He was referring to when Eddie died in Hole in the Woods.

"Family emergency," Barry said. "I have—"

"Go, Barry. Don't worry about this right now. I have it under control."

Barry nodded and jogged over to his car. Despite being told not to rush, Barry did just that. He pulled in his parents' driveway maybe five minutes later. There was another car already there: Eddie's Nissan. Aidy opened the Nissan's door and stepped out when she heard Barry shut his car off next to her.

"Do you know what's going on?" he asked Aidy.

"Your dad wouldn't tell me."

"How'd you get here before I did?"

"He called me first."

"Why would he do that?"

"He said he knew you would rush over," Aidy told him. Then she took Barry by the hand. "Come on."

Barry had rushed over, but now he was hesitant to go inside. He feared bad news, of course, but waiting around wouldn't change anything. As soon as he realized that, he let her lead him to the front door.

Barry's dad answered the door just seconds after Aidy pushed the door-bell. He met Aidy's eyes first. "I told you he'd rush over, didn't I?"

Aidy smiled softly and nodded.

Then Carl Kendall's eyes shifted over to his son. "Come on in."

As Barry stepped inside, he looked around at the familiar walls of his childhood home.

They'd been painted since he had lived there, but they were the same walls nonetheless. While he was walking to the dining room, he thought about his mother; how she went from a lively woman to one that had to fight every single day to keep herself from giving up. He thought about how unfair the world really was, how sometimes we're just simply dealt the hand given to us.

When they reached the dinner table, Barry's mom wasn't there.

"She's in the bathroom," Carl said. "She'll be out in a minute."

They all took a seat. Barry's eyes wandered around the room and found a new framed photograph on the wall next to the one of Barry and Holly at the homecoming dance; it was the photo Barry showed Aidy the night Elaine came to his house. The one of Barry's first day at Gene's Tire, where Eddie had his arm slung over Barry's shoulder with an ear-to-ear grin. What Barry hadn't told Aidy that night was that his mom had been the one who took that picture.

Aidy saw that faraway look in Barry's eyes. She could tell he was lost in a memory, probably one from that very day. Out the corner of her eye, she saw Barry's mom standing in the hallway, looking at her son.

"That was always my favorite picture of you two, you know?" Martha said.

Barry shifted in his seat and smiled when their eyes met. "I know."

Martha's eyes swept the room. She sighed and said, "I sure do miss Edward."

Barry nodded. "Me too."

Barry never told his parents the truth about Eddie being the son of a witch that was over a hundred years old. He knew he'd come off sounding crazy. They'd say he was traumatized, that's all. Just like when Holly died. He'd thought about telling them, but in the end, he decided it best to let them think he died a hero, which really isn't that far from the truth.

Martha walked over and sat down at the table next to Carl. She was sitting directly in front of Barry, her hands folded primly in her lap.

"You look good together," Martha said, her eyes flicking back and forth between Barry and Aidy.

Barry's face reddened. "Thanks, Mom."

The room was silent for a few moments. Then Carl said, "You should probably go ahead and tell them, Martha. Barry rushed over to hear the news."

Martha nodded and found Barry's eyes. "The doctors told me something interesting this morning," she said. "Something that surprised them."

Barry lowered his head, steeling himself for the blow. "It's not getting worse," Barry said, raising his head back up. "Is it?"

Martha's brow furrowed for a second or two. "Oh, honey, no. I'm in remission," she said with a soft smile. "Complete remission."

* * *

Before Eddie died, Barry would have gone right back to work after being told the good news, but now he lived life a little differently. The case would be there tomorrow. The man in the trunk was dead; therefore, the man wouldn't be calling him with why-haven't-you-found-my-killer questions any time soon. Barry still immersed himself in his work, as almost all detectives do, but not like he used to. He made more time for his family, and he even booked a cabin in Gatlinburg, Tennessee. Barry had a plethora of vacation time saved up, and it wasn't difficult for Aidy to convince him to go. Soon after he agreed, he wondered if she'd used some sort of spell to get him to go and decided that it was fine if she did.

After eating a late lunch with Aidy and his parents, followed by several embarrassing stories courtesy of Martha, Barry looked out of the window and realized how much time had passed. The sun was starting to set, and Barry suddenly had an urge to go. It wasn't only because of the embarrassing stories, either; there was something else telling him to go. He wrapped his mother in a tight hug before walking out of the house.

In the driveway, before Barry and Aidy got in their vehicles, he said, "I need to go to Hole in the Woods real quick."

Aidy didn't question him about why he needed to. She only asked, "Would you like some company?"

Barry smiled slightly and gave her a nod. "Let's get there before it gets dark."

They stopped by Barry's house first. He parked his Charger in the driveway and slipped into the passenger seat of the Nissan Aidy's dad left her. He watched her shift through the gears, something she had learned just a few weeks ago, but she looked as if she had been driving a manual for years.

They were coming to the curve. When they reached the apex, Aidy slowed down and pulled the car off the road. The path was still wide enough from the truck and camper that the Nissan wouldn't have branches scratching down the side of it. Barry hadn't been back since the investigation, which lasted about a week. Nancy was never found, and the department ended up putting the case on the back burner since the kids were returned home safe and sound.

There was a new gate at the entrance of Hole in the Woods. This one was heavy duty with corner poles concreted deep in the ground. Barry climbed over the gate first so he could assist Aidy when she climbed over. Once Barry helped her get her feet on the ground, he looked at the path leading up to the lake. Then he looked back at the Nissan; in a strange way, it almost felt like Eddie was there with them still. Maybe it was the car. Maybe it was being at Hole in the Woods. Either way, it was a nice feeling.

Barry felt Aidy take him by the hand. There was a good distance between them and the lake, but the walk up to it seemed to fly right by.

They reached the lake just as the sun was setting. A cool breeze blew softly around them as they looked out at the tea-colored water. Barry wrapped an arm around Aidy. She rested her head against his upper arm.

"What're you thinking about?" she asked.

Barry glanced over, seeing that Aidy was still looking out at the water, and shifted his gaze out at the lake again. "Almost everything."

"What're you leaving out?"

"Just the bad memories," he said. "Those aren't nearly as much fun to think about."

"So, why did you really come out here?"

"I don't know. Sometimes it just doesn't feel like it's over. Like she's really gone."

"So, closure then?"

"Maybe. Maybe I was hoping to find something."

She turned to look at him. "What exactly did you expect to—"

Something behind Barry snagged her gaze.

"Aidy?"

"What is that?" She pointed to the tree behind him.

Barry followed the tip of her finger. It was pointed at the tree with his and Holly's aged initials. On the ground, around the same spot Barry had found the note from Elaine, was a folded-up piece of paper. His eyes never left the piece of paper as he walked over to the tree. He felt his throat getting tight as he bent over to pick it up off the ground.

"Open it," Aidy said from behind him. "This must be the something you were supposed to find."

Barry opened the note. There was only one word written on it: *happiness.*

Barry turned around to see a tight-lipped smile across Aidy's face. He thought it an awfully good smile. One you couldn't help but return with a smile of your own.

"Doesn't take being a detective to know that this is your handywork," Barry said, lifting up the note. "What is with your family and notes?"

Aidy chuckled and moved closer to him. Her hands slid behind him, resting just under the nape of his neck. "Nothing gets past you, does it, Mr. Holmes?"

"That's right," Barry said, leaning closer to her. "But you can call me Sherlock."

"Doesn't get much smoother than that, does it, Sherlock?" she said with a grin and a roll of the eyes. "Would you just kiss me already?"

Barry leaned in, pressed his lips against hers, and felt a refreshing wave of exactly what was written on the note by the tree.

Happiness.

Acknowledgments

Thanks are due to Janie, Savannah, Tara, and everyone else at Jan-Carol Publishing for all their hard work. I'm grateful JCP took a chance on a new writer by publishing my first novel, *The White Room*, and even more appreciative that we were able to work together on a second novel.

Thanks to Susan Harmon and Sarah Cottrell, who both read the manuscript and provided me with excellent feedback.

Lastly, thanks to everyone that purchased my first novel, everyone that purchased this one, and those that continue to support me. It truly means a lot.

www.ingramcontent.com/pod-product-compliance
Lightning Source LLC
Chambersburg PA
CBHW030319020726
47493CB00004B/1079